"How am I supposed to stay on the saddle?" Nerissa demanded crossly.

"You hook an unmentionable part of your anatomy . . ."

"Don't be a nodcock, Miles! Which part?"

"Your knee." He grinned openly. "Sorry, I didn't think to explain. You hook your right knee around the horn, see, here, at the front of the saddle, and put your other foot in the stirrup. I'll guide it in for you. Let's try again. Balance yourself with a hand on my shoulder. That's it."

This time, as a still more unmentionable part of her anatomy hit the saddle again, Nerissa jerked her right knee up and forward. From the waist down she was immovably swaddled. Falling forward, she grabbed Vinnie's mane in both hands. The saddle horn jabbed her in the ribs.

Miles fumbled at her left leg. "I c-can't find your f-foot," he stuttered. "You're all tangled up in your t-train." Helpless with laughter, he staggered backward.

"Miles!" she wailed.

"Let go and slide down, as you did before. I'll catch you, I promise."

Cautiously she transferred one hand to the horn, clung with the other to the saddlebow, then decided to trust him and let go. As she slithered down, Miles caught her to his chest and held her.

For a few seconds his eyes were close to hers, his mouth inches from her own, his heart beating against her breast. Breathless—with annoyance, naturally— she snapped, "Put me down!"

He obeyed, setting her gently on her feet and at once removing his hands from her waist. "I'm sorry." His voice still quivered with amusement. "I didn't realize a sidesaddle makes for such complications."

ZEBRA REGENCIES
ARE
THE TALK OF THE TON!

A REFORMED RAKE   (4499, $3.99)
by Jeanne Savery

After governess Harriet Cole helped her young charge flee to France—and the designs of a despicable suitor, more trouble soon arrived in the person of a London rake. Sir Frederick Carrington insisted on providing safe escort back to England. Harriet deemed Carrington more dangerous than any band of brigands, but secretly relished matching wits with him. But after being taken in his arms for a tender kiss, she found herself wondering—*could* a lady find love with an irresistible rogue?

A SCANDALOUS PROPOSAL   (4504, $4.99)
by Teresa DesJardien

After only two weeks into the London season, Lady Pamela Premington has already received her first offer of marriage. If only it hadn't come from the *ton's* most notorious rake, Lord Marchmont. Pamela had already set her sights on the distinguished Lieutenant Penford, who had the heroism and honor that made him the ideal match. Now she had to keep from falling under the spell of the seductive Lord so she could pursue the man more worthy of her love. Or was he?

A LADY'S CHAMPION   (4535, $3.99)
by Janice Bennett

Miss Daphne, art mistress of the Selwood Academy for Young Ladies, greeted the notion of ghosts haunting the academy with skepticism. However, to avoid rumors frightening off students, she found herself turning to Mr. Adrian Carstairs, sent by her uncle to be her "protector" against the "ghosts." Although, Daphne would accept no interference in her life, she *would* accept aid in exposing any spectral spirits. What she never expected was for Adrian to expose the secret wishes of her hidden heart . . .

CHARITY'S GAMBIT   (4537, $3.99)
by Marcy Stewart

Charity Abercrombie reluctantly embarks on a London season in hopes of making a suitable match. However she cannot forget the mysterious Dominic Castille—and the kiss they shared—when he fell from a tree as she strolled through the woods. Charity does not know that the dark and dashing captain harbors a dangerous secret that will ensnare them both in its web—leaving Charity to risk certain ruin and losing the man she so passionately loves . . .

Carola Dunn

The Lady and the Rake

ZEBRA BOOKS
KENSINGTON PUBLISHING CORP.

ZEBRA BOOKS are published by

Kensington Publishing Corp.
850 Third Avenue
New York, NY 10022

First Printing: April, 1995

Printed in the United States of America

Chapter One

"Me bloody tights is split again, dearie."

Bess Rigby bounced into the dingy wardrobe room where Nerissa's sewing table was squeezed in between racks and shelves of clothes. A gust of cheap violet scent joined the mingled odors of greasepaint and sweat—many of the costumes were too flimsy to be washed, and the best Nerissa could do was to air them well after each wearing.

"Split again!" she groaned.

" 'Fraid so. Good job I didn't turn me back on the audience last night." Scarlet hose dangled limply from her plump hand. In her present role as Rosalind, Bess—or, rather, her legs—still drew whistles from the gallery, but her hips were gradually succumbing to a liking for sweetmeats. Her present protector, a wealthy York grocer, was more generous with his wares than with the rubies Bess craved.

"I'll see what I can do," said Nerissa with a sigh as she took the tights, "but there is not much left to darn."

Lucian Gossett's handsome face and carefully arranged blond curls appeared over Bess's shoulder. "Finished my kilt yet, darling?"

"Not quite." Nerissa twined an errant strand of straight, mouse-brown hair, which had escaped from her braids, around her finger. If only he meant it when he called her darling, she mourned, she'd stay up all night stitching and ironing those endless pleats for him. "I'll have it ready for opening night, I promise."

"But, darling, I simply must have it for the dress rehearsal."

"Afraid you'll get your sword tangled up in your skirts?" Bess jeered. "That'd be a laugh, Macduff losing the fight for a change."

"One does need to practice, darling," Lucian snapped.

"Mr. Wingate don't need practice," she needled him. "Borrow his kilt."

"Papa has played Macbeth a dozen times," Nerissa pointed out pacifically. "One way or another he always manages to lose the fight as Shakespeare intended. I'll see what I can do, Lucian."

The actor went off looking sulky.

"I'll be damned if he don't snitch to Mr. Fothergill," said Bess.

"He wouldn't! I didn't mean I shan't have it done in time, at least if I don't have to darn your tights. They'll only split again tonight. Mr. Fothergill is simply going to have to lay out a few shillings for a new pair. After all, we've had good houses all week."

"*As You Like It* always goes down well, and Rosalind's a treat to play, specially with your dad as Orlando. It's a good thing for me your ma don't do breeches parts. Still, she's got Lady MacB next week to make up. But let's face it, love, the York Playhouse just ain't got the Theatre Royal's prestige."

"Our company is quite as good as theirs. If only we could scrape together enough money for new seats and some gilt paint!"

"Witches onstage!" Young Jem, perennial page, third murderer, apprentice, messenger, et cetera, scurried along the narrow, drafty corridor summoning the cast for the beginning of the rehearsal. He popped his head around Bess's ample form. "Nerissa, Mr. Fothergill wants to know is Macduff's kilt going to be ready for the dress rehearsal?"

"Tell Mr. Fothergill yes, if he'll buy new tights for Rosalind so I don't have to darn the old ones again."

"Better get a bigger size next time." Grinning, Jem pinched Bess's rear end. She squealed and slapped his hand. "Hey, I nearly forgot. This came for you." He delved into his pocket, produced a crumpled, grubby piece of paper, and handed it to Nerissa.

"If it's another invitation from Sir George Clemence, Mama will be on her high ropes. She told him in no uncertain terms that I don't dine alone with gentlemen."

His grin broadened. "I heard her. Shouldn't think it's Ol' Clammy-Hands, though. It wasn't delivered by a groom; the postman brought it. Come on, Bess, the blasted heath awaits."

"That's Miss Rigby to you, brat."

As the actress left, Nerissa stopped the boy. "Jem, I've let out your court breeches. Can you try them on now? You're not on for a while, are you?"

"No, but I want to watch your ma do the weird-sister bit. Mrs. Wingate's a hell of a good witch. I reckon our Bess is getting too broad in the beam to play a withered crone." He eyed Nerissa's figure judiciously. "You'd make a good 'un if you could act worth a damn."

"But I can't," said Nerissa as he ran off. She was rarely asked to play even a speechless court lady or shepherdess, for stage fright froze her so completely, she might be a pillar or a tree rather than a living, breathing human being.

If only she could play Juliet to Lucian's Romeo, perhaps he'd see her in a different light.

Sighing, she turned over the letter in her hand and smoothed it flat. The bright September sunlight pouring in at the small window sparkled on tinsel and spangles and cheap paste gems as she peered at the direction. The neat, precise hand, half obscured by a fluffy smear of toffee from Jem's pocket, was quite unlike Sir George's scrawl.

She couldn't remember ever receiving a real letter before, only billets doux from gentlemen who assumed that any female associated with the theater must be lightskirt. Those she was herself unable to dissuade, Mama generally dealt with quite satisfactorily. Anthea Wingate was, after all, accustomed to regal roles. The more persistent pursuers were confronted by Papa in one of his sword-bearing costumes. He had only to loosen the sword in its scabbard to establish his daughter's respectability beyond a doubt.

With her sewing scissors Nerissa pried open the seal. Her first reading of the letter left her so incredulous, she had to go back and read it again from the beginning. Then, blue-striped dimity skirts gathered in one hand, the letter waving wildly in the other, she dashed along the corridor toward the stage, crying, "Mama! Mama!"

A lifetime of training slowed and hushed her as she reached the wings. On the stage, her father and

Banquo approached the three witches. Of the three, only Mrs. Wingate managed without rags and makeup to give the impression of a "secret, black and midnight hag" as they danced widdershins about an imaginary fire. Tall and slender like her daughter, her dark hair untouched by gray, she seemed to have shrunk into decrepit, tottery, malevolent old age.

"Stop swinging your hips, Miss Rigby," called Mr. Fothergill from the auditorium. "That's not the sort of lure you're casting for Macbeth."

Bess gave Mr. Wingate a saucy wink. Everyone laughed, and Nerissa took advantage of the interruption to step onto the stage. She was too impatient to wait. Besides, her news might affect everyone there, and it wasn't as if her mother made any secret of her birth, though nor did she flaunt it.

"Mama, Papa, I have a letter from my grandfather's lawyer!"

"From Sir Barnabas?" her father exclaimed.

"From his lawyer," she reiterated as the entire company flocked around her.

"We don't want anything to do with the old dastard," said Mr. Wingate adamantly. "He cast off your mother without a groat when she married me, and it's too late for him to repent now."

Mrs. Wingate, restored miraculously to grace and dignity, laid her hand on her husband's arm. "Wait, Frederick. Let's hear what Father wants. We may reject his interfering with ourselves, but if he means to do something for Nerissa . . ."

"It seems he's dead, Mama."

"Well, I for one cannot pretend to be sorry," Mr. Wingate said. "I beg your pardon, Anthea, but your father never had any claim on my regard."

His wife sighed. "I am only sorry for his own

sake that he did not attempt a reconciliation sooner. Nerissa, my love, what has the lawyer to say?"

"Mr. Harwood writes that if I attend the reading of Sir Barnabas's last will and testament, I shall hear something very much to my advantage."

"Very much!" said Bess. Jem whistled and Lucian regarded Nerissa with a new interest.

"Mr. Harwood says you must attend the reading?" asked Mrs. Wingate sharply. "Where is it to be?"

"At Addlescombe, Mama."

"He expects you to travel all the way to Dorset?" her father demanded, incredulous.

"The will demands it, and prohibits his giving further details until then. If I do not go, I shall hear nothing more. Surely Sir Barnabas would not insist if I am to inherit only a few guineas, or a small keepsake?"

"Oh, yes, he would, the old curmudgeon!" said Mr. Wingate. "I don't trust him an inch, live or dead."

"But I must go, Papa! Suppose the bequest is enough to buy new seats and repaint the playhouse? I cannot bear to lose the chance."

"Suppose it's a miniature of Sir Barnabas to remember him by," her father retorted. "I daresay it would cost all of twenty pounds to send you, even with an outside seat on the stage, what with a night at a London inn and a little extra for emergencies."

"Emergencies!" Mrs. Wingate exclaimed in dismay.

"Yes, emergencies, Anthea. I cannot allow my daughter to travel so far alone."

Quite apart from the possible inheritance, Nerissa saw her chance of adventure escaping her, her chance of a few days' respite from the dreary round of stitching and pressing. "Let me go, Papa," she cried. "I shan't speak to strangers, or ... or do anything else foolish. I shall be quite safe. Mama, surely you don't wish to reject Grandfather's peace offering?"

Her mother's regretful look showed her opposition was weakening.

"I might as well throw twenty pounds in the fire as trust to Sir Barnabas's nonexistent benevolence," Mr. Wingate grumbled, running his hand through his dark hair in a theatrical gesture intended to portray harassment without disarranging a single lock.

"We'll all dub up," Bess suggested eagerly, fumbling in her pocket. "It'll be like risking a bit on the prancers. Here, dearie, here's half a yellow boy to start with. You deserve a bit of a holiday anyway, even if there ain't no more comes of it."

"I'll put in five guineas," said the tightfisted Mr. Fothergill, to Nerissa's astonishment, adding with a reckless air, "Nothing ventured, nothing gained!"

Following their example, the rest of the company produced half crowns and sixpences. Even Jem donated a sticky penny, carefully picking off the fluff before he added it to the hoard. Their generosity brought Nerissa near tears.

"Th-thank you all," she stammered. "Even if I don't inherit a fortune, I shall pay you all back somehow."

Lucian scowled as he handed over two silver shillings with obvious reluctance. "What about my kilt, dammit?" he complained.

"The will is not to be read till the first of October," said Nerissa, wistfully wishing his ill humor stemmed from the prospect of losing her company, not her skills. "I'll finish your kilt before I leave."

"No good will come of this," said her father gloomily.

"I'm the witch, Frederick," Mrs. Wingate admonished him. "Leave the prophesying to me. Nerissa is a sensible girl, and if nothing else, thanks to the generosity of our friends, she will see a little of the world."

"Then that's settled," said Mr. Fothergill, and clapped his hands. "Back to work, if you please, ladies and gentlemen. We'll start from the beginning of Scene Three, and please try, Miss Rigby, to remember that you are tempting Macbeth to a kingdom, not to your bed."

"You can't just kick me out of your bed like a slut you picked up in the street!" screeched Dorabel. "I'm an actress, I am, not a common harlot." Her eyes glittered with rage between heavily blackened lashes.

Half the crowd in the Covent Garden Greenroom turned to stare, but Miles said coolly enough, "I'm sorry, Dolly, it can't be helped. I had reverses at the Cocoa Tree last night and I can't afford to keep both of you in the style you deserve."

"So 'e's chose me," Charmaine crowed, flaunting her splendid half-clad bosom at her rival and tossing her improbably red curls. " 'E don't fancy you no more. You can go 'ang yerself, yer old bag."

"I'll be damned if I don't see you hanged first, bitch!"

"Bitch yerself!" Charmaine flung herself with clawed fingers at Dorabel, ripping her exiguous lime-green-satin bodice.

Dorabel retaliated, fingernails aimed at Charmaine's rouged cheeks. Miles grabbed her around the waist from behind.

"Ouch!" he yelped as a flailing elbow caught him in the ribs. "Ladies, please!"

To his relief, Lord Thorpe had Charmaine firmly by the wrists. "I must say, Courtenay," the viscount drawled, "life in your vicinity has never a dull moment."

"My aim must ever be to entertain my friends," said Miles ironically. "Dolly, I told you from the first that I live by my wits and my pockets are often to let. Be a good girl, let's agree to part amicably."

"What's that thieving whore got that I don't?" Dorabel whined.

"Lemme kill 'er!" shrilled Charmaine.

"Oh, to the devil with both of you!" Disgusted, Miles released his hold and turned away. "Go ahead and kill each other, for all I care. There are other fish in the sea."

He sauntered off, relaxed, yet instantly ready to swing around to intervene if the slightest sound suggested the two actresses were really tearing each other limb from limb.

Thorpe joined him. "Damned if I can make out how you always have the ladybirds squabbling over you," he said admiringly, "when you never have a feather to fly with, let alone to feather their nests."

"It's my natural charm and manly beauty, Gerald. There's something about black hair, blue eyes, and a broken nose to which females naturally gravitate."

"Ha! M'sister Lottie says you'd be the very image of a pirate if you were bearded and a trifle taller."

Laughing, Miles glanced back, to see his whilom mistresses with their arms about each other, temporarily united in their temporary hatred of men.

Doubtless each would find a new lover tonight, he thought cynically. Already Levison and young Grant were bearing down upon them.

A pretty redhead in a canary-and-rose-striped sarcenet gown glided up beside him. "Looking for company, Mr. Courtenay?" she inquired coyly.

Miles ran his eyes slowly up and down her lush figure and smiled. "I'm not looking for creampot love," he warned. "It's low tide with me."

Shamelessly matching his deliberate scrutiny, she took his arm. "From what I've 'eard, you've other things to offer a girl. Let's give it a try for tonight, eh? I'm Roxanna, and dee-lighted to make your acquaintance, I'm sure."

With a gallant bow, Miles raised her hand to his lips. "The pleasure is all mine, madam," he murmured.

Lord Thorpe sighed and shook his head. "What I wouldn't give for your reputation!"

"Deserved, I assure you."

"Braggart! Will you and Miss Roxanna join Suzette and me at the Piazza for supper? I'll pick her up at Drury Lane and we'll meet you there."

Some hours later, after an energetic and satisfactory night, Miles strolled homeward through the bustling early-morning streets. Always an abstemious drinker whatever his other sins, he was in excellent spirits. He exchanged cheerful greetings with maids scrubbing front steps, bought from an itinerant vendor a hot meat pie which he shared with a stray dog, dropped a shilling in a blind beggar's palm, and arrived at his lodgings whistling "Cherry Ripe" out of tune.

His landlord, a retired gentleman's gentleman, accosted him when he was halfway up the first flight of stairs. "There's a letter for you, Mr. Courtenay, sir." He held up the folded sheet just out of Miles's reach as he leaned over the banisters. "And this month's rent's not been paid and next month's is due tomorrow, not to mention laundry and such."

"Tempus fugit, Burkle, which in the vernacular is *how time flies!* Let me have it, there's a good fellow. I'll give you something on account today, I swear it."

"Paid in full, sir, or no letter."

"You're a hard man, Burkle. Still, I expect the letter can wait. Lady Luck's bound to smile on me soon."

"It's been redirected three times, Mr. Courtenay," said Burkle sourly.

Miles was unsurprised. He removed from lodging to lodging often, with the rise and fall in his fortunes, though he'd never yet done a moonlight flit. Perhaps it was time to seek out cheaper rooms, which meant Burkle must be paid. Besides, a real letter sent by the post was a rarity. Most of the communications he received were brief notes from friends, appointing a meeting place; scented love letters from the more literate of his *chères amies;* or invitations from those ladies of the ton who had not yet consigned him to outer darkness.

"All right, Burkle," he said with a sigh, "come up and I'll settle the score. This month's, at least. As you pointed out yourself, October's rent is not due until tomorrow." He continued up the stairs, the landlord lumbering after him.

His purse lighter by eleven guineas, his conscience by a debt paid, he slit open the seal of the letter. Holding it in one hand and tugging off his neckcloth with the other, he moved to the window to read it.

"Confound it!" He raced out to the landing and shouted down the stairs, "Burkle, is today really the thirtieth?"

The landlord's injured face turned up to him. "Have I ever lied to you, Mr. Courtenay?"

"Hot water! At once, if not sooner!"

Washed, shaved, and dressed for driving in a brown coat, buckskin breeches, and top boots, Miles hurried toward St. James's. The caped greatcoat over one arm and portmanteau in the opposite hand were scarcely suitable burdens for a gentleman, but few if any of the Polite World were yet about. He ran up the steps of Lord Haverford's mansion and beat a tattoo on the door.

As the porter opened the door, the butler was crossing the marble-floored hall with a steaming coffeepot.

"Bristow!" Miles cried, entering without ceremony. "Is Lord Thorpe at home?"

"I shall inquire in a moment, sir," replied the butler, unmoved, and he proceeded on his stately way toward the breakfast parlor.

"It's urgent. Wake him if necessary." Miles set down his portmanteau on the floor, tossed his overcoat on a chair, handed hat and gloves to the porter, and ran his hand through his hair.

From the breakfast parlor came Lady Haverford's stentorian tones. "Tell Mr. Courtenay to come here," she commanded.

Bristow reappeared sans coffeepot. "Her ladyship requests the pleasure of your company, sir."

With a groan, Miles complied, saying over his shoulder, "For heaven's sake, tell Thorpe I need him."

The Marchioness of Haverford, who happened to be his godmother, possessed a figure as imposing as her voice. Dressed in eau de Nil figured silk, she sat at breakfast with her youngest daughter, a pretty young lady in pink jaconet muslin who blushed as she caught Miles's eye. She it was who had likened him to a pirate.

He made his bows. "I beg your pardon for intruding, ma'am. I did not expect any of the family to be down."

"Lottie has fittings this morning. Well, Miles, what brings you bellowing for Gerald at this unlikely hour? Have you breakfasted?"

"As a matter of fact, no." He was ravenous, he realized, and it would be crack-brained to set off for Dorset on an empty stomach.

"Sit down, dear boy, and Bristow shall bring you a beefsteak. Lottie, pour coffee for Mr. Courtenay."

"Yes, Mama." Lady Charlotte blushed again as she handed him the cup. Miles wondered what tales she had been told about him. Though the marchioness had a kindness for her girlhood friend's orphaned son, she'd have left her daughter in no doubt of the ineligibility of a penniless rake.

Not that Miles had the slightest intention of losing his freedom in wedlock, even for the sake of repairing his fortunes.

Either her ladyship had forgotten that she wanted to know what brought him there so early, or she feared his business with Thorpe was not proper for a young lady's ears. She chatted about the coming entertainments of the Little Season while he attacked a large beefsteak with fried potatoes.

He was halfway through it when Bristow reappeared and said discreetly in his ear, "Lord Thorpe's man says his lordship did not retire until daybreak, sir, and he won't take it upon himself to wake him."

Miles nodded. "Never mind, I'll do my own dirty work," he said, and rapidly finishing his breakfast, he made his excuses and ran upstairs to his friend's chamber.

It took a wet sponge to rouse Thorpe and a pint of strong coffee to bring him to something approaching coherence. "Wanna borrow my curricle?" he asked incredulously. "At dawn?"

"It's not dawn, Gerald, and I have a hundred and thirty miles to go by nine tomorrow morning."

"Hunnerd thirty! Wha' the devil?"

"My godfather is dead . . ."

"Didn' know y'ad one."

"Sir Barnabas Philpott, Baronet, of Addlescombe, in Dorset. If I'm not there at the reading of the will, I'll inherit nothing."

That caught Thorpe's attention. "Will, eh? Plump in the pocket, this Philpott fellow?"

"Plump enough."

"My dear chap, of course you can borrow the curricle. Tell you what, I'll drive my grays the first couple of stages, see you well on your way." He swung his legs out of bed and bellowed for his valet. "Or shall I come all the way with you?"

"Lord, no. I wouldn't for the world subject you to the swarm of spongers the old man kept hanging on his sleeve. He deplored my behavior, you know, and probably summoned me down posthumously in order to cut me off with a shilling. I wouldn't be surprised if he regarded his last will and testament as a final opportunity to read me a sermon."

"I can't believe he'd have demanded your presence if he hasn't left you something worth having."

"You didn't know my godfather," Miles pointed

THE LADY AND THE RAKE 19

out dryly. "Dyspeptic, straitlaced, mean-spirited, and utterly determined to be proved right. He said I'd go to the dogs and nothing is less likely than that he'd lift a finger to prevent it. All the same, I'll have to gamble on his relenting at the last and leaving me a fortune. I'm going to get there in time even if hiring post-horses takes my last penny."

Chapter Two

"But I can't ride. There must be some other way to get there!" said Nerissa in desperation.

"Shank's mare, miss," said the tapster indifferently, returning to polishing a pewter tankard, "leastways till Thad comes back wi' the gig, which'll be around noon."

"I have to be at Addlescombe by *nine.*"

She had clambered down from the roof of the stagecoach in Riddlebourne, in a dank gray dawn with rain threatening. After a night squeezed between the iron rail and a stout farmer, in constant fear of falling into the road, she was stiff and chilled through. The bread and butter she had snatched at the brief supper stop the previous night seemed an age ago. All she wanted was a hot meal and a warm bed.

The Stickleback Inn, a small hostelry of gray Portland stone, could doubtless supply both. What it could not supply, having no pretensions to being a posting house, was a vehicle to carry Nerissa on to her grandfather's house.

Shank's mare? Nerissa was a townswoman accustomed to walking no farther than from one side of the city of York to the other, with an occasional stroll along the river or the city walls on a Sunday. Her cheap jean half boots were far from adequate for a lengthy tramp. Still, she was not quite ready to give in.

"How far is Addlescombe?" she asked.

"A matter o' six or eight mile, miss. Ye c'n leave your box an' send f'rit later."

Eight miles! It might as well have been as far off as the moon. But perhaps the reading of the will would be delayed for some reason. Perhaps if she arrived before the end, Mr. Harwood would make an allowance for her difficulties. Having come so far, she *must* try.

She picked up the brown paper parcel with clean linen and her toothbrush. "If you please, will you direct me?"

The tapster stepped out of the inn with her and pointed along the street. "Turn right, 'n' follow the road along the stream, miss. That's the Riddle, see. First fork in the road, go left across the bridge, second go right 'cross that bridge, then on through Riddle Abbas 'n' Kingstonriddle. Jus' past the village, by the big oak, the Addle joins the Riddle. There's a lane'll take ye along the Addle to Addlescombe. Can't miss it." He scratched his head ruminatively. "Leastways, if ye finds yoursel' in Upriddle, ye has missed it."

Thanking him, Nerissa hugged her gray duffel cloak close around her and plodded off. "First bridge left, second bridge right," she repeated to herself. She'd worry about the rest later. Surely someone in the villages would point out her way.

By the time she reached the second bridge, she knew she wasn't going to make it on foot. In a daze of fatigue, she sank down onto the low parapet and hid her face in her hands.

And then she heard the sound of hooves and wheels. A dusty curricle turned the corner behind her and started across the bridge. In a final access of hope, Nerissa jumped up and waved her arms.

As the curricle stopped beside her, she cried out, "Sir, please, are you going to Riddle . . ." A flood of heat rose in her cheeks as she realized the name of the next village had utterly vanished from her mind.

The driver's red-rimmed blue eyes brightened with amusement and a grin transformed his tired, unshaven, rather cynical face. "No, ma'am, I fear I prefer cards to charades," he informed her, tipping his hat to reveal ruffled coal-black hair. His broken nose gave him a slightly sinister air—an Iago, or a Cassius. "However, I can offer you a lift as far as Kingstonriddle, if that will be of assistance to you. I am bound for Addlescombe."

"For Addlescombe?" Nerissa forgot her embarrassment and the stranger's disreputable appearance. "How excessively fortunate, so am I."

Miles gazed down at the young woman. Her face pale with dark circles beneath the wide-set, dark-lashed gray eyes, she looked as exhausted as he felt. She could be a governess in her plain, travel-stained gray cloak, a wisp of brown hair escaping the hood, but as far as he knew, Addlescombe had no need of governesses. More likely, she was a rival for Sir Barnabas's fortune.

If he left her behind, she'd miss the reading of the will, which might be to his benefit. What a pity he had not yet sunk to such depths of iniquity! He leaned down to give her a hand up.

As she settled beside him, he urged the horses onward. A prim and proper miss to all appearances, he thought, though as a last resort she had let a stranger take her up in his carriage. He wouldn't put it past his godfather to hold her up to him as an example of the rewards of virtue.

"Thank you, sir." Her voice was soft, but with a curious clarity of enunciation. She sat erect despite her weariness, her clasped hands resting composedly upon the parcel in her lap. "It is of the utmost importance to me that I reach Addlescombe by nine o'clock. I hope you are familiar with the way, for the directions I received thoroughly muddled me."

"Addled you, as one might say?"

Glancing down, he received a smile of singular sweetness. Her gray irises had an irregular circle of green around the pupils, he noted.

"My wits are addled indeed," she agreed. "The roof of a stagecoach is not a restful place to spend the night. Perhaps I had best introduce myself, sir. I am Nerissa Wingate, the late Sir Barnabas's granddaughter."

"His granddaughter? I wasn't aware that he had any children, though I have a distant memory of a wife long since deceased." A sudden notion crossed his mind: Could Miss Wingate be a descendant on the wrong side of the blanket? Had the baronet in youth indulged in the profligacy for which he later condemned his godson? After all, popular mythology claimed that reformed rakes made the strictest puritans.

He put away the intriguing possibility for the moment. He didn't want to embarrass the young woman at his side by inquiring into her parent's legitimacy. "I beg your pardon, Miss Wingate, I don't mean to pry. I'm Miles Courtenay; Sir Barnabas was my godfather. I imagine we are in Dorset on the same errand."

"In hopes of an inheritance," she said candidly. "I ought to have arrived yesterday, but when I reached

London, the waybill for the stagecoach was already full."

"And I received the lawyer's letter only yesterday. I've driven day and night."

"Then you must be as tired as I. Let us hope the will is not too long, or I shall fall asleep in the middle."

They fell silent as he negotiated the twists and turns of the narrow lane between high hedges. Occasional gates gave glimpses of green meadows, with the course of the Riddle marked by willows and poplars, yellowing already. Just before Kingstonriddle they were held up by a herd of cows crossing from one field to another in a leisurely manner. Miles saw Miss Wingate's hands clenched tight in an agony of impatience.

"Don't worry," he reassured her. "We'll be there in time. It's less than a mile to the turning."

"You must have come this way often."

Her tone was questioning, and he guessed she was eager to discover on what terms he had stood with the baronet. Two could play at that game.

"Often enough, though not of recent years. And you?"

"Never, but of course Mama grew up at Addlescombe."

So Miss Wingate's mama was the straying sheep, it seemed, not Sir Barnabas. Miles was too tired to work out whether that increased or decreased his chances of a substantial legacy. He drove through the village and turned off along the Addle, a narrow, crystal-clear brook slipping smoothly along over its flinty bed.

They passed through a belt of woodland and emerged into a valley surrounded by high green hills.

"I do believe the sun is coming out," Miss Wingate exclaimed. "Perhaps it is a good omen."

"Perhaps," Miles grunted.

"How the stream sparkles! The countryside is very pretty, is it not? I have never lived in the country."

He roused himself to regard the familiar scene. Here the Addle meandered between beds of watercress. On either side, rusty-red cattle grazed the lush pastures while winter wheat already striped the pale, chalky arable fields with green. A team of hedgers and ditchers with scythes, billhooks, and spades stood aside to let the curricle pass. Miles noted repairs to a five-barred gate, the new wood yellow in contrast to the weathered gray of the old. No fallen, rotting timber marred the autumn-hued copses, and a multitude of sheep dotted the encircling hillsides.

Sir Barnabas had always been an exacting though fair landlord, and apparently he had not loosed the reins in his latter years. Addlescombe was still a rich, productive estate.

The sight pleased Miles, though it was a long while since such matters had had any relevance to his life. That was not likely to change. The manor and the farms would presumably go to his godfather's younger brother, heir to the baronetcy. Unlike Miles, Neville Philpott had been willing to put up with Sir Barnabas's misanthropic autocracy in exchange for a life of ease.

Or was Neville the heir? Miles had always assumed so, but if a daughter unknown to him suddenly turned up, an unknown son seemed equally possible.

And how would that change his chances?

"Has your mother any brothers, Miss Wingate?"

"No, she is an only child, which makes it all the

sadder that my grandfather should have cast her off so thoroughly. He cannot have been a happy man, I think."

That the shabby female at his side should pity the wealthy baronet struck Miles as exquisitely humorous. A chuckle escaped him.

She looked up at him, frowning. "Why do you laugh, sir? Was my grandfather in fact perfectly contented despite the estrangement?"

"No, happy and contented are not words I'd ever associate with Sir Barnabas. I beg your pardon for laughing, ma'am. Truth to tell, I'm too fagged to know what I'm about."

"Then let us hope you will not upset us in the ditch," she said tartly.

He grinned and shook his head. "Never fear. I can manage the last half-mile."

The lane branched. To the left the square church tower and part of the village were visible, straggling along the lower slopes on the west side of the valley. Taking the right fork, over a flat stone bridge, Miles pointed ahead with his whip.

"There's the house."

Addlescombe Manor, starting as a thatched brick-and-flint farmhouse, had sprawled in all directions at the whim of succeeding owners. Here two stories, there three, with dormer windows scattered at random. Parts were built of gray Portland stone, parts of local yellow stone, giving it a patchwork appearance. Walled kitchen gardens at one end, together with the stables at the other, added to the apparent length of the house.

"It's very large," murmured Miss Wingate, her fine eyes widening.

"I'll set you down at the front door and drive around to the stables."

"Oh, no, pray take me with you!"

"As you wish, but you need not fear them, you know."

"It's just that I'm sure there must be a butler, and I should not know what to say to him. *Them?*" she added in a tone of deep foreboding. "You mean a number of people live here? Who are they?"

"A choice assortment of purse-pinched relatives, living at the old man's rack and manger, and at his beck and call. I shan't describe them. You'll meet them soon enough."

"Mama did mention that her uncle and his family lived here when she was growing up, but that was more than twenty years ago. So they are still here?"

"They were six years ago."

As he drove into the stableyard, Miss Wingate was silent. No doubt she was contemplating the existence of considerably more competition than she had expected for Sir Barnabas's fortune.

A groom hurried to the horses' heads and Miles stepped down, every muscle protesting the long drive. Following him without waiting for assistance, Miss Wingate stumbled a little. He quickly put out his hand to steady her, alarmed by her pallor.

"Are you all right?"

She gave him a tremulous smile. "A trifle dizzy. I shall be quite all right when I have had something to eat. Do you think we are too late for breakfast?"

"My dear girl, why did you not tell me you're hungry? I have an apple in my pocket." He produced it.

"My savior!" She pulled off her glove, serviceable York tan, worn but well kept, and took the apple. "Thank you, sir, I am simply ravenous."

"Eat as much as you can before we meet anyone," he advised.

"Oh, dear, I suppose it is not good manners to march munching into a strange house," she said in dismay as they entered by a back door.

"Fustian! I was merely thinking that it would be a pity to waste any of it."

At this attempt to put her at her ease, her lips curved upward, and Miles was struck again by the enchanting quality of her smile. Apart from that and her eyes, she was no beauty. Her chin was too pointed, her nose undistinguished, her hair—what he could see of it under the hood—of a commonplace brown. As she walked beside him, crunching the apple, he realized that she was taller than he'd thought, the top of her head on a level with his eyes. Himself of middling height, he was generally attracted to shorter females, with a preference for a voluptuous Pocket Venus. Miss Wingate's figure was disguised by her cloak, but he rather thought she was on the skinny side.

Of course, whatever the cause of her mother's exile, Miss Wingate appeared to be respectable, whereas the creatures he assiduously pursued were invariably quite the reverse. On the other hand, she had accepted a lift from a stranger. She had more or less requested it, in fact, with no signs of bashful modesty. . . .

"What shall I do with the core?" she whispered urgently.

He whipped out his handkerchief, received the remains in it, and stuffed it back in his greatcoat pocket as they reached the small front hall. Not much wider than the passage by which they had entered, it had two more corridors leading off it and two doors besides the front door. A carpeted staircase rose to a square landing before continuing to the first floor. Against one wall stood a long-case clock, an umbrella stand, a couple of straight rush-bottomed chairs, and a half-moon table, on which Miles dropped hat, gloves, and whip.

The butler appeared. Almost as starchy as his late master, Snodgrass inclined his head in a minimal bow. "Mr. Courtenay," he said, sounding as censorious as Miles remembered him, "and . . . ?"

"Miss Wingate," Miles informed him.

"If you will please to come this way, the family is gathered in the drawing room." He opened the door to the left of the front door and announced, "Miss Wingate. Mr. Courtenay."

Snodgrass stood aside and Miss Wingate stepped into the room. Close behind her, Miles saw seven pairs of eyes turn to stare. Miss Wingate froze.

"Courtenay? What the deuce?" barked Neville Philpott.

Mrs. Chidwell raised her lorgnette and regarded the pair in the doorway with cold eyes. "Mr. Courtenay, how dare you bring your doxy to Addlescombe!" she snapped.

The clock in the hallway struck nine.

Perched on the inkstand, Sir Barnabas watched as his household filed into the library. He would have preferred a more dignified seat. However, in the weeks since his death he'd discovered that being read through was uncomfortable and being sat upon definitely painful—as well as still less dignified than the inkstand.

The rest of the kneehole desk was covered with Harwood's papers, and every chair was needed for the vultures gathering in hope of profit from his demise. He could have sat on the long table, pushed out of the way against the far wall, but he wanted to see their faces.

Despite their eagerness, they were late, he noted irritably. Nine o'clock was the hour he had specified for the reading, not for them to begin to straggle toward the library. Lawyer Harwood was an ineffectual fool.

The tubby little man stood behind the desk, nervously consulting his silver turnip watch and casting uneasy glances at his insubstantial friend and client. He was the only one to whom Sir Barnabas had so far succeeded in revealing himself, albeit indistinctly. It was to be hoped he was competent to see the terms of the will carried out to the last letter, even those he had fervently argued against.

The hopeful heirs were in for a shock, thought the late baronet, rubbing his spectral hands together in something approaching glee.

Inevitably Cousin Euphemia Chidwell waddled in first. Massive and determined in her perpetual purple, the widow always managed to push ahead of the milksop who was now Lady Philpott. Even before his death, Effie had usurped his wishy-washy sister-in-law's position as manager of his household. Much he cared, as long as it was ordered to his liking. Of course, if there was any actual labor involved, poor Sophie was the one who did it.

Jane, Lady Philpott, trailed in limply, her shawl slipping off one shoulder as usual. Sir Barnabas felt the usual surge of irritation. In other circumstances he'd have growled at her to straighten her clothes.

She leaned on the arm of her daughter, Matilda, a small, spare, loud-voiced spinster of six-and-thirty, smelling of horses and dogs. Her uncle had long since given up hope of matrimony removing her from his house. She threw back the two gentlemen

who had risen to the bait of the large dowry he offered, on the grounds that neither could keep up
with her in the hunting field.

Sophronia pattered in, last of the ladies, always a
little breathless, pink-cheeked, and softly plump.
Somehow her crooked cap and the hairpins constantly scattering from her white hair never annoyed
Sir Barnabas as did Jane's shawl. He had been
tempted to bequeath a little extra to Sophie. She'd
not reap the benefit of it, though, having been
firmly under her sister Euphemia's thumb since
childhood.

Neville was next, *Sir* Neville now, strutting like a
pouter pigeon in the glory of his new title. He had
never taken the least interest in the Addlescombe
estate and was utterly unfit to run it.

So was his son, Aubrey. Once a beautiful youth,
Aubrey at forty expended all his energy in fighting
the encroachment of the years. He had never married because a plain wife was unthinkable and a
pretty one too much competition. Sir Barnabas
snorted as the creak of his nephew's corset reached
his ears. Man-milliner!

His other nephew, his sister's son, entered with
the grave mien proper to a clergyman. The Reverend Raymond Reece was a sanctimonious sapskull
with the most deplorable Romish tendencies, but no
one else had offered him a living and after all, he
was family.

And that was the lot, except for the servants,
unless . . .

Sir Barnabas's breath caught in his throat, or
would have had he been breathing. The girl was
Anthea's image. She must be about the age Anthea
had been when she faced him with defiance in her

eyes and announced that she'd marry Frederick Wingate or no one.

His daughter marry a strolling player! Out of the question, not even worthy of discussion.

So she had run off with the fellow. He had managed to hush it up, giving out that she had gone to stay with relatives, and later that she had accepted a suitor and was living in a distant part of the country. None of the neighbors had ever been so impertinent as to ask him for further news of her.

Anthea had written to her father announcing her marriage. He had not replied. A second letter notified him of the birth of her child. Again he had not responded, but he had kept the letter. Nerissa was the chit's name, a constant reminder of the theatrical world with its notorious immorality, in the midst of which his granddaughter had been brought up.

No one could have guessed it by looking at her. In her simple olive-green dress, long-sleeved and high-necked, her hair pinned up in braids, her face innocent of paint, butter wouldn't melt in her mouth.

But after all, that was the nature of the beast. The most infamous Cyprians were capable of appearing on the stage as the innocent Miranda, the maligned Desdemona. What the hussy hoped to gain by this show of modesty now that her grandfather was dead, he failed to guess. Perhaps she hoped to influence Harwood in her favor.

Too late. The will was written. She'd have her chance to reform her wanton ways, but Sir Barnabas was certain she would fail.

The same went for his unshaven godson. Miles was a good-for-nothing, care-for-nobody libertine and gamester beyond redemption. Sir Barnabas owned he'd be astonished if the wastrel accepted his challenge, let alone met it, even for the sake of a fortune.

All any of them cared for was his fortune, the late baronet muttered silently, sweeping the assembled company with an invisibly scornful gaze.

The last of the upper servants filed in and closed the door. Euphemia shifted weightily in her seat, taking it upon herself to glance around the room through her lorgnette as if it were her business to ensure everyone's presence. Her complacent air turned to an indignant glare as she noticed Nerissa beside a lounging Miles in the back row of chairs.

"Mr. Harwood, pray have that . . . that *person* ejected," Euphemia demanded with an imperious gesture.

Nerissa raised her chin in defiance—so like her stubbornly disobedient mother! She opened her mouth to protest, but the inimical stares turned on her apparently stopped the words in her throat. No doubt she was used to a more appreciative audience.

Snodgrass stepped forward. To the butler's habitual supercilious tone was added a hint of relish: He was glad of a chance to thwart Effie, who constantly interfered in his duties. "Mr. Harwood, sir, the young lady is Miss Wingate. I admitted her according to your instructions."

The lawyer stood up, beaming. "To be sure, Snodgrass. Miss Wingate, I am William Harwood, your late grandfather's attorney. Allow me to welcome you to Addlescombe and to hope that your stay here will be a happy one."

Sir Barnabas glowered at him. A happy stay was not at all what he had in mind for the jade.

However, Harwood's words had magically changed the attitude of the rest of his family. Raymond Reece was the quickest off the mark.

"My dear Miss Wingate—cousin, if I may make so bold," he said in his oily way, "may I be the first to welcome you to the family. 'For this thy brother was lost and is found.' " He proceeded to introduce himself, and then the rest as though she were his protégée.

"Your grandfather!" grumbled Euphemia. "Well, I am sure I don't know how I could have guessed, though now I see you do bear some resemblance to Anthea. We have been forbidden to mention your mama's name these twenty years and more, and one cannot be expected to recall . . ."

"I remember her very well," squeaked Sophie. "We used to visit Addlescombe quite often before she left home. I was prodigious fond of dear Anthea."

Her sister gave her a reproving frown. "So were we all, Sophronia, and naturally we have not forgotten her, but we were unaware she had a daughter. I am delighted that your grandfather saw fit to relent at the last, my dear child," she added unconvincingly.

Nerissa seemed overwhelmed by her sudden popularity—an accomplished actress indeed. Sir Barnabas looked on with cynical amusement as they fawned over her. Doubtless they were all afraid that as his closest relative present, his only direct descendant, she'd get the lot. Ha!

With increasingly exaggerated throat-clearings, Harwood called the meeting to order. An expectant silence fell.

"Ahem." He settled gold-rimmed spectacles upon his nose, picked up the three closely written sheets of parchment, and began to read. " 'I, Barnabas Elijah Philpott, Baronet, of Addlescombe in the county of Dorset, being of sound mind, do declare this to be my last will and—' "

"Cut the twaddle," Sir Neville advised impatiently.

Harwood frowned over his spectacles. "Sir Barnabas gave particular instructions that every word was to be read. To continue."

Amid much fidgeting, he completed the preliminaries. "As you have all already been instructed," he continued, "Sir Barnabas forbade any observance of mourning, either in clothes or in conduct. He here gives his reason, which I regret the necessity of pronouncing. 'Any such observance can be only the rankest hypocrisy, too extravagant for even me to stomach though I have lived surrounded by fawning hypocrites. Anyone disregarding this requirement will forfeit his or her bequest.' "

"No mourning!" Jane moaned. "What will people think?"

"Everyone knows Barnabas was eccentric," snapped her husband. "Go on, Harwood."

His will was going to confirm everyone's opinion of his eccentricity, Sir Barnabas thought with relish.

The lawyer went on to list minor bequests to butler, housekeeper, valet, cook, bailiff, coachman, head groom, and head gardener. All appeared satisfied. Though no warmth had entered into their relationship, Sir Barnabas had always paid them well, and they had served him well, for he tolerated no less.

Dismissing the servants, Harwood moved on to the last item on the first page. "Er-hem." He turned pink. " 'To my friend and counsellor, William Harwood'—hmm-hmm—'the sum of five hundred guineas,'—er, yes, most generous—'provided he shall at once take up residence at Addlescombe

Manor and there reside as long as may prove necessary to superintend the implementation of the further terms of this, my will and testament, in no case to exceed a period of six months.' Er-hem, yes."

"What the deuce?" Neville blustered. Since his brother's demise, the new baronet behaved as if Addlescombe belonged to him. To have an uninvited guest forced upon him added to the unease caused by the unexpected arrival of his unknown niece.

"Terms?" Euphemia shrilled. "What terms?"

"Sir Barnabas set certain conditions to be fulfilled before the remaining legacies are executed."

"Conditions!"

The lawyer cast a reproachful glance toward the inkstand as his dead friend and client cackled.

Poor Sophie was confused, as usual, Sir Barnabas noted. Miles had adopted an unconvincing pose of boredom, while Nerissa was trying to look as if her head were in the clouds, her mind elsewhere. However, the pair would soon give him their full attention, and the rest already wore altogether satisfactory expressions of surprise and alarm.

The late baronet hadn't enjoyed himself so much for years.

Chapter Three

Nerissa struggled to keep her eyes open. She wished she had consumed the core of Mr. Courtenay's apple, for the rumbling of her stomach must surely be audible to him, if not to everyone in the room.

She peeped sideways at him. If he heard the gurgles and groans, he was politely ignoring them. In fact, he was gazing at the picture over the mantelpiece with an air of utter boredom.

It was a boring picture, she decided, a still life of peaches, wine bottles, and a dead fish. If she went on looking at it any longer, she was certain to fall asleep. She scanned the room. Apart from the fireplace, the door, and two windows with red brocade curtains, all four walls were lined with ceiling-high bookshelves.

A treasure house of calf-bound, gold-tooled books, and most of them not plays! She had learned her letters from plays. At home in York the small house was full of books of plays, scripts and manuscripts, and parts of plays. She'd like to sample these shelves if she were permitted to stay long enough. If she could only keep her eyes open.

Blinking, she returned to contemplating the gentleman seated beside her.

He wasn't at all handsome, not to compare to Lucian Gossett. His nose was a trifle crooked, his dark brows too heavy, his bristly jaw too square. Nor was he as tall as Lucian. She had to admit, however, that there was something rather dashing about the combination of black hair and blue eyes, even with the addition of a day's growth of beard.

His clothes, though plain and travel-stained, were of good quality cloth and well made, a cut above the showy but shoddy garb favored by theatrical people. She recalled that the vehicle he had taken her up in was no shabby gig, but an elegant curricle. The very fact that he had rescued her suggested that he did not regard her as a rival. Mr. Courtenay had no desperate need of his godfather's fortune, she concluded. He must have dashed down from London just to show his respect for the deceased.

She, to the contrary, needed every penny of whatever small sum might have been left her. The proceedings so far gave her the impression that she had been invited as much to tease the residents of the manor as for any serious purpose. However, if Sir Barnabas was capable of such malice, he had probably directed it equally at his granddaughter. She dared not let her hopes rise too high.

All the same, she really must try to concentrate upon the endless reading of the will.

" 'The following bequests subject to the conditions hereinafter set down,' " droned the lawyer.

" 'To my nephew the Reverend Raymond Reece, confirmation in the living of the church of St. Botulph in Addlescombe village, and a supplement of twenty pounds per annum to the stipend thereof.' "

"Twenty pounds," exclaimed the parson in disgust, "and upon conditions!" He brightened—momentarily—as Mr. Harwood continued.

" 'In addition, to be expended in furnishing the vicarage, the sum of ten pounds. As my nephew Reece has eaten well at my expense for fifteen years, he has no doubt saved sufficient funds to adequately supplement this amount.' "

The dome of Mr. Reece's head turned crimson beneath the carefully arranged strands of hair. " 'Lay not up for yourselves treasures upon earth, where moth and rust doth corrupt,' " he squawked. " 'Consider the lilies of the field.' "

Mr. Harwood regarded him sternly over his spectacles. "If you mean to indicate that you have not saved your stipend, sir, I fear there is nothing to be done. Pray permit me to continue. 'To my cousin Euphemia Chidwell, two hundred pounds per annum, that she may rent a cottage and hire a servant of her own to harass, to the relief of mine.' "

A wordless choking sound emanated from the stout lady in purple. Cousin Euphemia Chidwell, Nerissa repeated to herself, attempting to sort out her new relatives. The Reverend Mr. Reece's introductions had served only to confuse her. Cousin Euphemia, harasser of servants, was the one who had taken her for Mr. Courtenay's convenient and demanded her expulsion. She rather thought she did not care for Cousin Euphemia.

" 'I consider this adequate, since she is certain to browbeat her sister, Sophronia Datchett, to whom I hereby leave a like income, into sharing her household.' "

Cousin Sophronia was the plump little lady in lavender, now bleating in mingled gratitude and dismay. "How very kind of dear Cousin Barnabas. Indeed, Effie, you know I shall do whatever you think right."

"I should hope so, Sophie," snorted her sister. "A proper mull you always make of things if left to yourself. But really, a cottage! Impossible."

Nerissa only wished she could be sure of so much as two hundred pounds a year.

" 'To my niece, Matilda, the choice of any horse in my stables, one hundred pounds per annum, and upon her marriage . . .' "

A neigh of protest rose from the front row.

Nerissa's attention wandered again. Her late grandfather clearly delighted in oversetting his heirs, and her expectations were at a low ebb. He had probably left his fortune to an orphanage.

Would Mr. Courtenay take her back to Riddle-bourne? After the unplanned extra night in London, had she enough in her purse for the fare to York? Would she be invited to stay for luncheon? If not, she'd find her way to the kitchens and beg some bread and cheese and a glass of milk before she left.

She looked up, startled, as Mr. Courtenay nudged her arm. He handed her a handkerchief spread open to reveal two crumbling biscuits.

"I just remembered I had them in my pocket," he whispered.

"*Thank* you, sir!" As she silently nibbled, resisting the urge to crunch them up, she noticed a darn in one corner of the handkerchief.

A swift glance at Mr. Courtenay disclosed what she had missed before. The elbows of his brown coat were threadbare and the toes of his boots were scuffed beneath the blacking. So he did need a substantial inheritance as it turned out, which made it all the kinder of him to ensure her arrival at Addlescombe on time.

She very much feared they were both to be disappointed.

She had missed some of Mr. Harwood's reading. Aubrey Philpott was now looking as disgruntled as his somehow fossilized face permitted. At first she had been surprised by his youth, but then the eye of experience had discerned the artificially brassy tint of his hair, the lines beneath the carefully applied face powder. There was something vaguely familiar about him.

" 'To my sister-in-law, Jane, my mother's topaz parure, a set of hideous objects she has long coveted although they render her still sallower than the hazard of nature.' I beg your pardon, Lady Philpott, but I am required to read every word," Mr. Harwood apologized.

Lady Philpott moaned. Her husband hushed her, leaning forward in eager anticipation.

"Yes, yes, man, go on."

"To my brother Neville, who sold his house in order to have an excuse to batten on me forever . . ."

As the lawyer read, Nerissa studied her uncle. Sir Neville was a tall, thin man in his sixties whose receding chin and forehead gave him an air of ineptitude. At present, however, he radiated confidence, suggesting he had dismissed the possibility of his brother leaving the estate to a female or outside the family.

No doubt his confidence was justified, Nerissa reflected regretfully. He was the new baronet and Addlescombe was probably entailed upon the heir to the title, though Mama hadn't been sure of that.

Again, woolgathering, she had missed Mr. Harwood's words. Their import was easy to guess from the incredulous fury that distorted Sir Neville's fishlike features. She was aware of Mr. Courtenay abruptly sitting upright beside her as the baronet's mouth opened and shut soundlessly.

"That's all?" he croaked at last. "But . . . Addlescombe! And there must be at least a hundred thousand in Consols! What the deuce?"

Nerissa and Mr. Courtenay exchanged a glance in which hope was suddenly kindled.

"Please, Sir Neville," said Mr. Harwood unhappily, "I assure you I had very little influence upon your late brother when it came to writing his will. I succeeded in reversing his original intention of completely cutting out you and your immediate family on the grounds that he has supported you. . . . But you are eager to hear the remaining provisions. Allow me." He cleared his throat.

Two hundred a year, Nerissa prayed, fingers crossed. One hundred a year. Just enough to get her back to York without starving to death on the way. Mr. Courtenay or the Foundling Hospital could have the rest with her goodwill.

" 'The remainder of my worldly goods and chattels, including the manor and demesne of Addlescombe and all money whatsoever not hitherto accounted for, is to be divided equally between the only two persons with a claim to my benevolence who have never attempted—in the vulgar phrase—to sponge off me, namely, my godson, Miles Courtenay, and my granddaughter, Nerissa Wingate, upon—' "

He was cut off by cries of outrage. Nerissa sat stunned until Mr. Courtenay's hand closed over hers.

"Don't rejoice too soon, Miss Wingate," he said

with an odd little smile. "I don't believe we are yet safe home."

"Upon!" bellowed Mr. Harwood in an unexpectedly loud voice. As the babble ceased, he went on in his normal, rather diffident tones. " 'Upon the following conditions.' " He took a deep breath, visibly steeling himself.

With a coldness in her middle, Nerissa wondered whether her grandfather was going to demand from the grave that she sever all connection with her parents. Sir Barnabas had obviously not forgiven his daughter for marrying against his wishes, or he'd have left his wealth directly to her.

Such a condition would be impossible to fulfill. Better the struggle to make ends meet with Mama and Papa than to live in luxury without them. But, oh, to be so near and yet so far!

"Miss Wingate, Mr. Courtenay," the lawyer appealed to them, "pray understand that I am not about to relate my own sentiments but to read Sir Barnabas's words as dictated to me."

"I understand," said Mr. Courtenay sardonically, "and I shall not hold you to blame for my godfather's fulminations, sir, I promise you."

Biting her lip, Nerissa nodded.

" 'I'—that is, Sir Barnabas—" The lawyer looked despairingly at the inkstand on the desk as though it might relieve him of his unpleasant task. It failed to respond. " 'I am giving Miles and Nerissa their chance, although I am convinced it is impossible that they shall succeed in observing my terms.' "

Sir Neville perked up.

" 'Miles Courtenay, having squandered his patrimony in wild living, has continued to bring disgrace upon his name by using the proceeds of his incessant gambling to indulge in the vilest debauchery, in the pursuit of actresses and other promiscuous women.' "

"Mostly actresses," murmured Mr. Courtenay, unrepentant, "and not merely pursuit, but capture."

Shocked, Nerissa reinspected him. She would never have guessed he was one of those obnoxious gentlemen like Sir George Clemence, who hung about greenrooms looking for females to pester with their attentions. She had quite liked him, but perhaps his motives in taking her up in his curricle had not been as altruistic as she supposed. He had fed her, true, but then, Sir George's attempt at seduction had involved endless boxes of bonbons and invitations to dine with him.

"Your turn," Mr. Courtenay said dryly, motioning toward the lawyer.

" 'As for my granddaughter,' " Mr. Harwood was saying, " 'I judge Nerissa less at fault than my godson in that she did not choose to be bred up in the licentious atmosphere of the theater. Yet as the twig is bent, so grows the tree. Loath though I am to apply it to my own progeny, I cannot deny that the word actress is synonymous with strumpet.' "

"B-but . . ." Nerissa stammered as every head swung around to stare at her.

With her usual helpless feeling before the onslaught of a myriad eyes, she turned in entreaty to Mr. Courtenay to defend her. The interested gleam in *his* eye incensed her, but before she could react, Mr. Harwood hurried on.

" 'However, I offer Miles and Nerissa an opportunity to reform. They shall receive the above inheritance provided that for the period of six months from the date of the reading of this, my testament, *primo,* Miles shall enter into no wager for money or other valuable consideration; *secundo,* Nerissa shall so amend her dress and behavior, eschewing theatrical vulgarity, as to prove herself an acceptable acquaintance to the gentry of this neighborhood; *tertio,* they shall both reside at Addlescombe Manor and live chaste, fornicating neither with each other nor any other.' "

Nerissa hid her burning face in her hands.

"To the devil with the old bastard," roared Mr. Courtenay, jumping to his feet. "Alive he failed to rule me, I'll not let him succeed dead."

. Giving him a commiserating glance, the lawyer plowed on. " 'If either fail to observe these conditions, the other shall receive both shares. If both fail, all moneys and property hereinbefore mentioned shall be disposed of according to the further provisions of this will, which are not to be divulged at this time.' "

Miss Sophronia waved a vinaigrette under the moaning Lady Philpott's nose, while the rest converged on Mr. Harwood in a clamor of complaints.

"All these years of taking care of him," Mrs. Chidwell berated him, her mighty bosom heaving with fury, "and you let him insult me in favor of a pair of debauched strangers."

"I'll contest the deuced thing," Sir Neville spluttered. "Clearly my brother was not of sound mind."

Feeling a hand on her shoulder, Nerissa looked up.

"Now you know why I ceased to visit my godfather long since," said Mr. Courtenay with a mirthless grin. "Being lectured on my sins is one thing; being denounced in public is another."

"Shall you really give up a fortune rather than submit to his rules?"

He subsided onto his chair, his grin becoming rueful. "The gentleman doth protest too much, methinks," he misquoted. "The truth is, I cannot afford to stand upon principle. The old devil has caught me at a low ebb."

"Then you mean to stay?" She was not sure whether to be glad or sorry. To be living in the same house with a libertine was not a comfortable prospect. On the other hand, given his helpfulness so far, she had little fear that he'd try to prevent her inheriting her half, and, more than content with half, she did not regard him as a hateful rival. In fact, she could not help liking him. With the rest of the household furiously resentful, he'd be an ally.

Always supposing Mama and Papa agreed to let her remain at Addlescombe—but she had little doubt of that. Though content herself, Mama had always regretted her daughter's exile from the life of the gentry.

"Yes, I'll stay." Sighing, Mr. Courtenay ran his hand through already disheveled hair. "I'm holding a devilish hand, though. Sir Barnabas was right in that it's true I've a singular weakness for actresses. Let me congratulate you, by the way. I'd like to see you onstage. I'll be damned if you don't play the demure damsel to perfection."

"I'm not an actress!" Nerissa declared irately. "I haven't the least jot or tittle of Thespian talent."

"You're not?" he exclaimed, startled. "Then what maggot got into the old man's head?"

"You see, my father has always been an actor. He was with a London company that came to play in Porchester one summer, and Mama met him and they fell in love. Sir Barnabas refused to countenance a marriage, so Mama ran away with Papa."

"She went on the stage?"

"Yes, but she and Papa remain devoted to each

other and live perfectly respectably. It is possible, you know!"

"Don't comb my hair," he said with a sardonic look. "Unlike your grandfather, I'm willing to believe it."

"My grandfather was not altogether wrong," she reluctantly acknowledged. "Mama did not want to bring me up in the environment of the London theater. Although they were both doing very well in town, we moved away when I was a little girl."

"Provincial actresses have much the same reputation as their town kin," said Mr. Courtenay dryly. "I take it your parents continue to tread the boards?"

"At the York Playhouse now."

"But you didn't follow them into the profession."

"No. I feel like Hero."

"A hero? Oh, *Much Ado About Nothing*. The innocent accused of lechery. I trust you don't mean to swoon away like one dead?"

"I'm far too angry."

"A cross between Beatrice and Hero, then. You see, my knowledge of the theater extends beyond its female denizens. But if your only association is through your parents, how very unfair of Sir Barnabas to tar you with the same brush."

She flushed. "Well . . ."

"Don't tell me you sing and dance? No wonder your grandfather—"

"No! As a matter of fact, I'm the playhouse's wardrobe mistress," she said defiantly.

"A seamstress!" Mr. Courtenay burst out laughing.

"And I loathe, abhor, and detest needlework. Whatever your plans," said Nerissa with dignified determination, "I intend to earn my share of Grandfather's fortune and never set another stitch in my life. So you will just have to forget your horrid designs upon my person!"

A sudden grinding noise like fingernails on a writing slate raised the hair on her arms. Mr. Courtenay winced, too, so it wasn't his doing, and no one else was near enough. Neither of them could possibly have guessed that it was Sir Barnabas gnashing his teeth.

The impertinent hussy meant to prove him wrong, did she? Wardrobe mistress, actress, dancer, or opera singer, it was all one to him. She belonged to the dissolute world of the theater. He had made known his conviction that she was incapable of observing the terms of his will, and no shameless lightskirt was going to give him the lie.

If her resistance to Miles's seductive wiles turned out to be stronger than expected, then the late baronet would be forced to lend his rakish godson a ghostly hand.

Chapter Four

"*Please*, ladies and gentlemen," said Mr. Harwood in a harassed voice, "if you will excuse me, I must explain to Miss Wingate and Mr. Courtenay the practical details of their residence at Addlescombe."

"Courtenay said he's not staying," Aubrey Philpott pointed out querulously, smoothing with a manicured hand the tresses disordered in his agitation.

"I've changed my mind," Miles announced. If he hadn't already decided to stay, the thought of that counter-coxcomb inheriting and letting the rich fields of Addlescombe go to rack and ruin would have persuaded him.

How difficult could it be to live for six months without women or the cards? He knew men who were addicted to gambling, who would wager large sums on raindrops trickling down a windowpane, or the color of the next carriage to turn a certain corner. Others, outwardly less reckless, drank while they played until their skill and judgment were destroyed. Miles himself gambled to win. Carefully calculating odds, he avoided brandy and never imbibed more than his bottle of claret during a night at the tables.

Lady Luck was notoriously fickle, yet for several years he had kept himself in reasonable comfort on the proceeds of the cards.

However, if caution prevented ruinous losses, it equally made the winning of a fortune unlikely. Sir Barnabas had offered him that chance, and all he risked was six months of virtuous tedium. In London he might have doubted his ability to resist temptation. At Addlescombe there were no actresses to lure him from the path of righteousness.

He was perfectly prepared to believe Miss Wingate's claim that she was no actress. Her beautifully articulated speech was the only hint that she might have been on the stage, and in his vast experience most Thespians dropped into the sloppiest way of talking offstage. Recalling the screeches, whines, and foul language of Charmaine and Dorabel, he grinned.

If Sir Barnabas had expected Miss Wingate to cause his fall, he had missed his mark. Not only had she turned out to be a respectable young woman, she was not at all the sort of flamboyant female who attracted Miles.

Which was not to say that he hadn't taken a liking to her. She had more spirit than he would have expected beneath that meek, drab exterior.

He bowed ironically as Sir Neville passed him on the way to the door, supporting his wife. The new baronet's scowl reminded Miles that it wasn't only his godfather's sermons that had driven him away from Addlescombe. The jealous dislike of the rest of the family had not made his visits any more pleasant.

Miss Sophie was another matter. She gave him a

timid smile and stepped toward Miss Wingate, her hand held out. Euphemia grabbed her arm.

"Come, Sophie, we must discuss what is to be done about this shocking situation." She stalked out with her sister in tow.

Mr. Harwood had moved two of the straight shield-back chairs closer to the desk and now he invited Miles and Miss Wingate to take them.

"A moment, sir," said Miles. "Could this conference possibly be postponed? I have had no breakfast, and Miss Wingate's neither breakfast nor, I suspect, dinner last night."

"Not to mention no sleep," she added with a grateful glance. "I fear, sir, I shall not understand the half of what you tell me."

"My dear Miss Wingate, how sadly remiss of me! We lawyers become so involved in our own concerns, we tend to forget the human needs of others."

"It's not your fault," she assured him. "We arrived only just in time for the reading of the will, and it didn't seem possible to ask that it be delayed while we ate."

"No, indeed." Mr. Harwood sighed. "I regret to say I am compelled to follow the late baronet's stated wishes in every respect. However," he said, brightening, "if you have no objection to a tray in here, nothing forbids your eating while I describe your situation to you in general terms. The details may wait until you have rested. Pray ring the bell, Mr. Courtenay."

Miles obliged.

"Will not Lady Philpott dislike our eating in the library?" Miss Wingate asked anxiously.

"Lady Philpott, ma'am? Her ladyship has no authority in the matter. Addlescombe belongs to you and Mr. Courtenay unless you prove yourselves unworthy—in Sir Barnabas's view. For the next six months the house and estate are yours to order as you will, though within certain strict limits, naturally."

"Limits?" Miles asked. "How strict? If our only freedom is to choose whether to eat in the library—"

Snodgrass came in. "You rang, sir?" he said to Mr. Harwood.

"Mr. Courtenay rang. He and Miss Wingate are now your employers."

"Very good, sir." The butler bowed impassively, but Miles had caught a glimpse of both curiosity and relief in his face. No doubt the man had expected Sir Neville to be his new master—and had feared to find Mrs. Euphemia Chidwell as his mistress. "I shall endeavor to give satisfaction," he continued, and awaited orders.

"I'm sure you will, Snodgrass," said Miles. "We'll have breakfast for two, in here, if you please. Miss Courtenay, what would you like?"

Drooping in her seat, she looked at him blankly. The poor girl was too weary to make even so simple a decision.

"Bacon and eggs?" he suggested. "Toast? Tea?"

She nodded. "Yes, please."

"I'll have cold meat, any kind but plenty of it, muffins if you have them, and ale. Will you join us, sir?" he asked the lawyer.

"Most kind." Mr. Harwood's eyes twinkled behind his spectacles. "A cup of coffee would not come amiss, and perhaps a muffin. Though I have already broken my fast, I must confess I am particularly partial to a toasted muffin with marmalade." He patted his round belly lovingly.

"I daresay you need to recruit your strength after

this morning's exertions," Miles commiserated. "That will be all for now, thank you, Snodgrass."

"Very good, sir." The butler turned to depart.

"Wait," said Miss Wingate. "Snodgrass, have chambers been prepared for myself and Mr. Courtenay?"

"I believe not, miss, no instructions having been received." He hesitated. "Mr. Neville—Sir Neville, I should say—and her ladyship have moved into the best bedchamber, miss. And Mrs. Chidwell into the second best and——"

"And so on down the line, I take it," said Miles impatiently. "As Sir Barnabas's granddaughter, Miss Wingate is entitled to the best room."

"Oh, no, I would not put anyone out. In truth, I care not where I sleep so long as there is a bed."

Miles eyed her with exasperation. Evidently it was not going to be easy to teach the chit to stand up for her rights, though she had at least overcome her qualms about addressing the butler.

However, for the moment he gave in. "Fit us in where you can," he told Snodgrass, and dismissed him with a wave. As the door closed, he turned back to Mr. Harwood. "Two questions, sir. First, as we are joint heirs, when Miss Wingate and I come to cuffs, who prevails?"

"I never come to cuffs with anyone!"

He grinned at her indignation. "Poorly phrased. I beg your pardon. Shall we say, on the doubtless rare occasions when we disagree."

"Er-hem." The lawyer cleared his throat diffidently. "In cases where you are unable to reach a compromise, I am appointed adjudicator. I shall endeavor to be impartial."

"I'm sure you will, sir. Secondly, am I correct in supposing that one of the limits on our authority is that we cannot eject our unwanted guests from the manor?"

"You are, Mr. Courtenay. I regret to say, you are. For six months, or until the matter is otherwise finally settled, the Philpotts, Mrs. Chidwell and her sister, and Mr. Reece are entitled to remain here. They will not receive their bequests until then."

Miles groaned. "I was afraid of that."

"And I am obligated to stay," Mr. Harwood apologized.

"We don't mind that a bit," said Miss Wingate at once, "do we, Mr. Courtenay?"

"Not a bit. But will it not disrupt your business, sir?"

"My son does most of the business these days. What little I still handle—old clients, you know—I can carry on here, if I may use this room occasionally."

"Of course," Miles assured him. "We shall be glad to have you in the house. We count on you to see fair play."

Mr. Harwood flushed with pleasure. "I shall do my best," he promised. "I must approve every expenditure, you know, but I shall not quibble overmuch."

"I take it Sir Barnabas expected us to try to feather our nests and then ignore his dictates. Are you also to judge whether we meet or fail his requirements?"

The lawyer's cheeks turned still pinker, and he fussed with his papers. "I am, but I assure you I shall demand absolute proof of ... er-hem ... of misbehavior. Mere report will not suffice."

"You'll have to catch us in flagrante delicto, in fact," said Miles dryly.

"Us!" exclaimed Miss Wingate with a baleful

look. "You may speak for yourself, sir. I have not the slightest intention of misbehaving, with or without witnesses."

The door opened and two footmen came in with laden trays, which they set on the long table. Unseen, Sir Barnabas slipped in behind them. Not that he needed an open door, but creeping through keyholes was undignified and uncomfortable, and wafting through walls hard work and as painful as being sat upon. Ghosthood presented its own special difficulties.

He had left the library with the others, eager to hear how they planned to deal with what Effie described as the "shocking situation."

They had gathered in the breakfast room, where the usual princely spread was laid out on the sideboard. During his lifetime, breakfast had been served at eight, and latecomers went hungry. Since his death, only Sophie and Matilda had risen so early, Aubrey sometimes not leaving his chamber till noon. The reading of the will had rousted the counter-coxcomb out—and much good it had done him.

He sat now with his usual breakfast of dry toast and weak China tea. "It will scarce keep me in coats," he moaned. "How can I maintain a decent appearance on—"

"Coats!" said Matilda. "You have enough coats to last a lifetime. How am I to hunt with only one mount?"

"My poor children," wailed their mother, dabbing her eyes with a lace-trimmed handkerchief. "I shall sell the topazes and divide the money between you. I'm sure I shall never wear them after your uncle was so monstrous insulting."

Sir Barnabas grinned.

His brother scowled. "Better worry about estates, not insults. What the deuce was he about, leaving Addlescombe away from the baronetcy? There have been Philpotts at Addlescombe for two hundred years."

"At least you have the use of the house in Bath, rent free and fully furnished," Raymond Reece observed sourly. "How am I supposed to refurbish the vicarage decently on ten pounds?"

"Bath?" The awful truth dawned on Matilda, who had been too wrapped up in her own woes to take in her family's exile from Dorset. "I can't live in Bath. It's much too far to hunt with the Blackmoor Vale!"

"Fiddlesticks!" snapped Euphemia, driven to postpone the consumption of the second half of her plateful of devilled kidneys, ham, eggs, and buttered rolls. "If you will all cease your useless laments for a moment, we can decide how to contrive that these intruders fail to inherit, as Cousin Barnabas clearly intended."

"Oh, no," Sophie protested, her round face pink with agitation at her daring in contradicting her sister. "Surely Cousin Barnabas *expected* the poor dears to fail, not *intended.*"

"It's all one," said Euphemia, exasperated. "Barnabas could never abide having his opinions refuted, so it is our duty to ensure that they shall not be. Don't meddle where you don't understand, Sophie."

"I beg your pardon, Effie," murmured the crestfallen little lady.

A pang shot through the spot where Sir Barnabas's heart had once resided. He ignored it. In life he had allowed the memory of his long-ago grievance to stop him intervening in Sophronia's be-half. It was too late now.

"For a start," Euphemia continued, "we cannot permit Miles Courtenay and that cozening actress to indulge their lecherous natures undetected. One of us must be with them every minute of every day."

"And night," put in Neville. "We shall have to set a watch on their chamber doors."

Fools! stormed Sir Barnabas, unheard. Nothing could be better calculated to keep Miles and Nerissa out of each other's arms and beds than knowing themselves observed.

Perhaps Raymond somehow picked up his thoughts, for he objected. "They will not get up to any mischief if someone is always with them. We need to keep them under surveillance without their knowledge."

"Whenever possible," Neville agreed dubiously.

"Only when they are together," his wife ventured to suggest.

"Don't be a ninny, Jane," said Euphemia. "Young Courtenay may prefer actresses, but I daresay he will not turn up his nose at dairymaids and village wenches."

"And actresses prefer wealthy protectors," Raymond informed them—to Sir Barnabas's dis-gust: a country parson should know nothing of such matters—"but we cannot risk Miss Wingate taking a fancy to some handsome yokel without our knowl-edge. We must keep as constant a watch as possi-ble."

"Well, I can't spare much time for spying," said Matilda. "We're in the middle of cubbing, and it's only a month till the Blackmoor Vale's first meet of the season."

"Don't be so selfish, Mattie," whined Aubrey.

"It's not only your future at stake. If I'm not to inherit Addlescombe one day, we'll both go home by
beggar's bush."

"One of you had best marry a fortune,"
Euphemia advised contemptuously, then paused
with an arrested air. "Good gracious, why did I not
think of it sooner? Aubrey, you must marry
Nerissa!"

"I don't wish to marry anyone, let alone a fallen
woman. Besides, I'm her uncle or something."

"Fiddlesticks—merely a first cousin once removed, a perfectly proper match."

"Proper!" wailed Jane. "How can you speak of
that doxy as a proper match for my son?"

Euphemia waved her podgy hand airily. "A little
sacrifice may be necessary in order to recoup our
fortunes. Raymond, you are equally eligible. A clergyman ought to have a wife."

"An unchaste wife will scarce enhance the dignity of the clergy," Raymond pointed out, "and
besides, you know my views on celibacy."

"Fiddlesticks!" Euphemia repeated. "You pretend
to all this High-Church, incense-and-surplices nonsense because you believed Barnabas would put up
with papist rubbish but not with supporting your
wife and family if you wed."

Sophronia forestalled a squabble. "I think it
would be very nice if dear Matilda married Mr.
Courtenay and made him part of the family."

Everyone gaped at her, including Sir Barnabas.

Euphemia shook her head in disbelief. "Of all the
muddle-headed widgeons! Matilda is years older
than Courtenay, and he is accustomed to the most
beautiful Paphians in London."

"Only eight years older," Jane protested. "What

does that signify? Such scapegraces are the better for an older wife to keep them in order."

Sir Barnabas noted that even she hesitated to claim beauty for her leather-complexioned daughter.

Matilda had her own notions. "I'll be damned if I'll marry a town beau," she roared in a voice extraordinarily loud and deep for her meager form. "Don't suppose the damned fellow's even capable of keeping his seat over a rasper."

"Mind your tongue," Euphemia reproved her. "Barnabas may be gone, but stable language still does not belong in decent company. Well, we need not consider marriage unless matters become desperate. Obviously it will be better to cut out Courtenay and Nerissa entirely. Let us plan our campaign."

Sir Barnabas frowned. He was pleased that they were all convinced that by thwarting Miles and Nerissa they'd ensure their own wealth. The dissolute pair would be caught the moment they strayed from the straight and narrow. On the other hand, they seemed to have forgotten the other stipulations of his will.

Admittedly, making Miles give up gambling and Nerissa behave like a lady had been afterthoughts, though he had listed them first. His aim had not been solely to make their lives more difficult. In the unlikely event of their passing the third test, giving his fortune to a gamester and a vulgar upstart would be as bad as giving it to the parasites who had battened on him all these years.

But, of course, the two extra conditions simply made it all the more certain that Miles and Nerissa were going to fail.

When Snodgrass brought in fresh tea, coffee, and

chocolate, Sir Barnabas slipped out of the room and repaired to the library. The door was closed.

As he contemplated irritably the prospect of squeezing through the keyhole, his two footmen arrived. Though they unknowingly opened the door for him, he was affronted by the trays of food they bore. Eating in his library! In his day, no one had ventured into the room unless summoned, let alone treated it as a dining parlor.

His temper was not improved when he heard Nerissa announce that she had no intention of misbehaving. Defying him again? Hah! He'd see about that.

In a burst of childish petulance, he jogged her elbow as she poured herself a cup of tea. It was his first attempt since his demise to affect anything in the physical world, and it took more effort than he had expected. Drained of energy, he slumped back onto the nearest vacant chair as hot tea sloshed into the saucer and splattered over the glossy, well-polished surface of his walnut library table.

That would teach him to act in a passion, he thought gloomily.

"I'm sorry," said Nerissa miserably, setting down the teapot with excessive care. Her elbow felt peculiar, sort of cold and tingly. She clasped it in her other hand.

"Not at all, not at all." Mr. Harwood mopped up the splashes with a large pocket handkerchief. "The wood is so well waxed, it won't show a thing, I assure you, my dear young lady."

"You *are* tired," Mr. Courtenay observed as he emptied the saucer into the slop basin. "Here, I'll pour. Eat, and you'll soon feel better."

Their kindness was already making her feel better. A few mouthfuls of crisp bacon and buttered eggs restored her further, until she was even able to lend more than half an ear to Mr. Harwood's continued explanations.

"You mean I may buy new clothes?" she exclaimed, thrilled. "And I shan't have to make them myself? Anything I want?"

"Within reason, Miss Wingate. I cannot give my approval to extravagant ball gowns, since you are unable to spend a night away from Addlescombe. But within reason."

"I may choose my own?" A sudden dismaying thought struck her. "Oh, but I don't really know what is proper for a lady to wear in the country."

"Perhaps your relatives will advise you," said the lawyer doubtfully. "Lady Philpott, or . . . well, not Miss Matilda, I suppose."

"I wouldn't trust any of them," declared Mr. Courtenay. "They'd deliberately lead you astray to ruin your chances with the neighboring gentry. I'll help you choose."

"But you are accustomed to consorting with actresses," Nerissa pointed out, grateful but skeptical. "I am already thoroughly familiar with their notions of appropriate dress."

"My dear Miss Wingate, I don't spend all my time *consorting* with actresses. I not only consort with the Polite World in town, I am not infrequently invited to house parties, so I believe myself qualified to advise you."

"I beg your pardon, I didn't know. Pray don't be offended, sir. Will you really help me?"

"Of course. It will be my pleasure. We'll steal a march on those tabbies."

Sir Barnabas noted the effect on Miles of the dazzling smile Nerissa turned on him. Maybe I won't need to intervene after all, he decided smugly.

Chapter Five

"Miss? Miss! You said to wake you at four." The soft, slow voice had vowels as broad as Yorkshire's, yet quite different.

Nerissa drifted gently out of sleep. Who . . . ? Where . . . ? This wasn't her narrow bed in the tiny back chamber in York. She sat up, bewildered, and rubbed her eyes.

"I brung you tea, miss, and a good bit o' lardy cake, still warm fro' the oven it is, seeing as you missed your luncheon."

"Thank you." She blinked at the chubby maid in her gray dress and white apron and cap. "You're Maud."

"That's right, miss. Mrs. Hibbert said I'm to wait on you, long as I give satisfaction, miss." Maud gave her an anxious look as she set her tray on the bedside table and poured tea.

"Mrs.—? Oh, yes, the housekeeper. I'm at Addlescombe!" The morning's events flooded back into her mind.

"Please, miss." The maid's fingers twisted a corner of her apron. "If I does summat wrong, will you tell me how to do it right? I'd like fine to be your abigail."

"Heavens, Maud, I've never had an abigail in my life. I shan't know if you do something wrong. We shall just have to work it out together."

"Oh, yes, miss!" said the girl with a joyful smile on her rosy face. "And I 'spect her ladyship's abigail'll tell me how to go on. I'll just unpack now, shall I, miss?"

"But I left my box at the inn in Riddlebourne."

"Mr. Harwood sent a groom for it, miss. 'Tis just outside the door."

She bustled around, opening curtains to admit a flood of pale gold afternoon sunshine, and fetching in Nerissa's battered box from the passage. Nerissa lounged luxuriously. As she sipped the tea and nibbled on the lardy cake, a rich concoction studded with currants and glazed with sugar, she examined her chamber.

Some twelve feet square, the room was light and airy with white walls and ceiling and two large sash windows on adjacent walls. The curtains were of pale green calico patterned with ox-eye daisies, matching the coverlet of the tester bed. Above the plain white-painted wood mantelpiece hung a water-color of a meadow where a rust-red cow munched on still more daisies. Nerissa smiled at the contented beast.

Maud put away Nerissa's few garments in the clothes press and set her brush and comb on the small dressing table. Polished wood gleamed in the slanting sunshine. Everything was simple but spotless, unpretentious but in excellent condition.

As Maud shook out and hung the last of three dresses, Nerissa became aware of a low rumble of voices coming through the wall behind her bed. A clank and a swoosh followed.

"What on earth is that noise?"

"Mr. Courtenay ordered a bath, miss."

"He has the next chamber?" she asked, suppressing an idiotic urge to turn and look at the wall. Naturally the presence of an unclad gentlemen on the other side of it had nothing to do with the strange sensation in her middle. She put the twinge down to the excessively large slice of fresh-baked lardy cake she had just consumed to the last crumb.

"Yes, miss. These two rooms on the side passage were the only chambers left in this wing," Maud informed her. " 'Tother bedroom wing's all shut up like, all under holland covers."

There was no sense in opening an entire wing just for Mr. Courtenay, she had to agree. Besides, it was nothing to her if he had the next room, nor if he chose to take a bath. In fact, that sounded like an excellent notion after three days on the road.

"I don't suppose I could have a bath, too, Maud?"

"O' course, miss. I'll go see to it this minute."

As she hurried out, the strains of "Cherry Ripe," slightly off key, echoed through the wall.

Nerissa had heard the song often enough and knew perfectly well that the cherries referred to were not fruit, but a woman's lips. The double entendre had never disturbed her before. If she now couldn't help wondering what it would be like to be kissed by Mr. Courtenay, it was entirely Sir Barnabas's fault for putting such notions into her head.

Glancing once more around the room in search of distraction, she noticed for the first time a door in the wall behind her bed—a connecting door, to Mr. Courtenay's chamber. Painted white, it was almost invisible.

She slipped out of bed, glad of the green and

brown rag rug on the chilly floorboards, and made quite sure the bolts at top and bottom were firmly shot on her side.

Miles was dressing when he heard the unmistakable sounds of a bath being prepared next door. Miss Wingate was following his example. How fortunate that she was too tall and slender—and far too respectable—to attract him, otherwise he might have been tempted to weave a fantasy about those sounds.

His gaze wandered involuntarily to the connecting door. He tore it away sternly and concentrated on his neckcloth.

"Admirable, sir, if I may be so bold." The cadaverous face of his godfather's valet brightened until it was merely mournful instead of lugubrious. "It must be confessed that the late Sir Barnabas took little interest in his attire and continued to wear the styles of the past century until the end. I anticipate with pleasure serving a gentlemen conversant with the London fashions."

"I don't aspire to àlamodality, Simpkins, merely to making a presentable figure in society. I trust you're not expecting a dandy for a master."

"Oh, no, sir," said Simpkins, shocked. "We already have one dandy in the house. False calves, sir," he whispered, "dyed hair, and no doubt you heard his Cumberland corset?"

"Ah, Simpkins, but Mr. Aubrey was a beautiful young man. You and I cannot know what pressures are felt by an aging beauty." Miles ran a brush over his thick black hair and stood up to allow the valet to help him into his coat.

"Very true, sir, though I venture to say, sir, that you will never need false calves nor padded shoulders." He bestowed twin pats of approval on Miles's robust shoulders. "We shall aim for a neat propriety of dress."

"The neatest and most proper Porchester can supply," Miles promised him, amused by the man's assumption of their common goal.

He noticed that Simpkins did not blink at the mention of Porchester rather than London as the source of his clothes. No doubt the servants were acquainted with every detail of the will by now. He wondered how many would side with himself and Miss Wingate, how many with the family they knew. Sir Barnabas had suggested that Mrs. Chidwell, at least, was less than popular with his staff.

On the other hand, while servants resented the sort of Turkish treatment they received from Euphemia Chidwell, equally they despised a weak master—or mistress. Miss Wingate, with no experience of ruling a large household, had actually dreaded meeting the butler.

She also suffered the handicap of the shocking reputation given her by her grandfather. A young man might sow his wild oats and be looked upon with indulgence; a young woman received none of the same tolerance.

With a last glance at the mirror, Miles went down to the housekeeper's room.

When he visited Addlescombe as a child, Mrs. Hibbert had been an unfailing source of barley sugar. A brisk, imperturbable woman in her fifties, dressed in black as befit her station, she greeted him with delight.

" 'Tis that good to see you again, Master Miles, or Mr. Courtenay, I should say."

"Master Miles will do very well, if I may still call you Hibby."

"That you may, sir. Now sit you down and take a dish of tea, for you missed drawing-room tea, if I'm not mistaken. Or will a glass of wine be more to your liking?"

"A glass of the home brewed, if that's a jug of it I spy on your table."

"Nay, 'tis new cider."

"Excellent." He poured himself a glass of the crystal-clear pale-gold liquid from the earthenware jug. "If there's anything as good as Addlescombe ale, it's Addlescombe cider."

"Sir Barnabas had his standards, Master Miles, as well you know."

"None better," he said ruefully. "I'm astounded that he considered me fit to take over the estate."

"Fitter nor some. 'Tis a pity you've to share with another," said Mrs. Hibbert with severe disapproval.

"Miss Wingate has more right to be here than I," Miles pointed out. "She's the old man's own granddaughter."

"That's as may be. Fond as I was of Miss Anthea, I never thought the day'd come I'd be taking orders from an actress."

"What makes you think she's an actress?"

"There's precious little Lady Philpott don't tell her abigail."

"I suspected the servants knew all."

"Only the upper servants," she said with a sniff. "The under servants are better off unaware of such scandalous doings."

"But it's your Miss Anthea who's the actress, Hibby. By the way, you'll be glad to hear she's happy in her marriage."

Looking as much surprised as glad, the housekeeper said skeptically, "And how would you be knowing that, Master Miles?"

"Miss Wingate told me her parents are devoted to each other. They live most respectably together despite the notoriety of the theatrical world, from which they have shielded Miss Wingate. She is *not* upon the stage." He hesitated. *Wardrobe mistress* sounded too closely connected with the theater. "She's been employed as a seamstress."

"Then why did she turn up bold as brass in your carriage, sir, without never a chaperon, and you known to have a soft spot for the acting profession?"

"She came by the public coach, and I met her walking from Riddlebourne. You must know she left her box there. You'd not have had me leave her to struggle on afoot and arrive late?"

"You had ever a kind heart, Master Miles."

"And she had no chaperon because her mama works for her living and they could not afford a maid to accompany her. Come, Hibby, I know you, too, have a kind heart. Give the poor girl the benefit of the doubt."

"Sewing's a respectable trade," Mrs. Hibbert allowed dubiously. "All the same, it don't fit a female to take charge of a place like the manor."

"So she'll need your help until she learns how to go about it."

The housekeeper sighed. "You've not lost a mite of your cozening ways. Well, we'll see."

"The alternative is for Mrs. Chidwell to remain in charge for the next six months, unless you believe Lady Philpott will summon up the courage to defy her."

Her response was an eloquent snort.

Satisfied that he had done his best to smooth Miss Wingate's path, Miles finished up his cider and was about to leave, when there came a timid tapping at the door.

"Come in," called Mrs. Hibbert.

Miss Wingate came in. Her anxious gaze fixed on the housekeeper, she did not notice Miles. "Mrs. Hibbert?" she said. "Maud said you wished to speak to me?"

"No, no, no!" Miles seized her by the arm and bustled her out. "All wrong. Mrs. Hibbert," he said over his shoulder, "Miss Wingate will see you in the library in five minutes."

As he closed the door behind them, he saw the housekeeper shake her head, but she was smiling.

"What do you mean, all wrong?" Miss Wingate wrested her arm from his grip and came to a standstill. "The footman said that was Mrs. Hibbert's room, and my maid said she wanted to see me."

"My dear girl, you are Miss Wingate of Addlescombe. If your housekeeper requests a word with you, you send for her at your convenience. You don't rush to her room."

"You were there."

"I've known Mrs. Hibbert since I was a child. When you are equally familiar with her, you may drop in now and then for a friendly chat."

"Oh." Her lips trembling, Miss Wingate started back along the passage. "I've made a bad start, haven't I? She'll guess I've never dealt with servants before."

"I have a feeling she already suspected as much. Have you no servants at all in York?"

"Just Tessa, who's been with Mama since before she was married. Otherwise only a cleaning woman who comes in to do the heavy work."

"That's more than I have had as often as not. But now I seem to have inherited my godfather's valet."

"And I have an abigail all to myself," she said in awe. "At least, she's really a housemaid, but she means to learn to be a proper lady's maid."

"I'm sure she's delighted to have the chance." He pushed open the door from the servants' wing. In the brighter light of the front hall, he saw that she had changed into a droopy brown silk gown with modest strips of narrow lace at neck and cuffs. "Your Sunday best?"

"Yes, it's the dress I wear for church. I thought I'd put it on for dinner, though I know it's not nearly grand enough."

"Fustian! For a family dinner in the country it's— Good gad, girl, your hair is soaking wet!"

She put a self-conscious hand to her head. Her hair was neatly coiled and pinned up but far too dark and sleek. "I washed it before Maud told me about Mrs. Hibbert," she said defensively.

"Mrs. Hibbert can wait. You'll take a galloping consumption, drop dead, and leave me to face your relatives on my own. Go up at once and dry it by the fire."

"No." She raised her chin in defiance. "I'm perfectly warm."

"But, my dear girl—"

"I wish you would stop calling me your dear girl! If you cannot recall my surname, Nerissa will do, since we are almost related and must reside in the same house for several months."

"My dear Nerissa . . ."

She frowned at him, but she was biting back a laugh.

"I insist upon your drying your hair."

"Unless you prefer to summon Mr. Harwood to adjudicate our disagreement," she said with a green glint in her gray eyes, "pray tell me which way is the library."

"Devil take it, woman, you try my patience. This way."

He accompanied her, poked up the dying fire and added a log, and made her sit in one of the wing chairs close to the hearth. She complied without demur, but adamantly refused his offer to stay while she spoke to the housekeeper.

"Mrs. Hibbert will never have any respect for me if I use you as a shield," she pointed out, then spoiled the effect by calling after him, "Mr. Courtenay! Should I invite her to sit down?"

"Miles."

"Miles, then. Please! She'll be here in a moment."

He wasn't going to tell her he'd never been present when a housekeeper was interviewed by the lady of the house. "If her business seems likely to take more than a minute or two," he compromised. "After all, she's been with the family for decades, and you're a baronet's granddaughter, not a duchess."

Nerissa nodded, her extraordinary eyes wide as she sat tensely straight in her chair, looking very slight and vulnerable. Miles felt an unaccustomed surge of protectiveness.

He quickly suppressed the unsettling sensation. All the same, when he met Mrs. Hibbert just outside the door, he commanded in a low voice, "Be kind!"

As he reached the hall, Miss Sophie was retreating into the drawing room. Glancing back, she caught sight of him. An expression of alarm crossed her round pink face, and she scuttled out of sight. Miles frowned. Of all Sir Barnabas's relatives, he had the fondest memories of the vague, timid old lady. Also, she had been the only one at the reading of the will to make a gesture of friendship toward himself and Nerissa.

An aborted gesture, he recalled, as Mrs. Chidwell had promptly removed her. What could Euphemia have told Sophie to make her afraid of him?

He was about to follow her to try to find out, but he heard a murmur of voices in the drawing room and changed his mind. Instead, he headed for the stables to see what sort of horseflesh he had inherited.

On the way, his thoughts reverted to Nerissa. Defenseless as she seemed, she showed occasional flashes of an indomitable spirit. It took courage and determination for a young lady to travel on her own by the stage from York to Dorset. She was no milk-and-water miss who would turn tail at the first difficulty.

And she faced difficulties aplenty. Miles's compliance with his godfather's terms was entirely within his own control. Nerissa, on the other hand, had to win the favor of the neighboring gentry. Learning to run a houseful of servants would be child's play in comparison. Not that her manners were in any respect vulgar, as Sir Barnabas had expected, but there was a great deal more to being a lady than a lack of overt vulgarity.

Miles had noticed that when he swore in her presence—"Devil take it!" he had said—she had not so much as blinked. A well-bred lady would have appeared shocked and reproachful. No doubt her theatrical life had accustomed Nerissa to blasphemous and obscene language. Even Shakespeare was full of it!

She'd have to become unaccustomed, and learn how to show it. She had a great deal to learn, and there was no one but Miles to teach her.

Chapter Six

"But really, Effie, in the *library?*" said poor Cousin Sophie. "It seems so very unlikely."

Sir Barnabas, comfortable in his favorite chair at last—everyone still automatically avoided it—shook his invisible head at Sophie's innocence. Effie voiced his thoughts.

"That sort of person," she said magisterially, "will seize the slightest opportunity to misbehave."

"Anyone might have gone in at any moment," Sophie answered continuing her brave protest. "Indeed, Mrs. Hibbert did, and dear Miles left, which is why I stopped lurking in the hall. So very mortifying to be caught lurking."

Mrs. Hibbert had gone to see Nerissa in the library? Sir Barnabas sat up straight. So the impudent chit was already taking over the reins! Cousin Effie would be in high dudgeon.

Indeed, her face was rapidly attaining a hue to rival her purple gown. She opened her mouth, but before her wrath exploded, Neville spoke.

"Sophie has a point," he said. He quailed before Euphemia's glare but continued. "If they were always together, we might manage to watch them every moment of the twenty-four hours, but there are simply not enough of us when they go off in different directions. Where did Courtenay go, Sophie?"

"I fear I don't know, cousin."

"You should have followed him," Effie chided.

"Oh, I could not! He *saw* me!"

"Bungler!"

Sir Barnabas knew better than to expect Sophie to defend herself with the obvious truth that there was nowhere to hide in the passage outside the library. Effie would never accept so feeble an excuse anyway. He was rather surprised when his brother came once again to the rescue.

"There are places where it is impossible to remain hidden," he said pompously, "and times and places where it is indeed unlikely that debauchery will occur. We must strive to know at all times where Courtenay and Nerissa are, but to concentrate our full efforts on the most likely moments."

With a snort of disgust, Sir Barnabas floated from the room. Miles and Nerissa had been in the house only a few hours and already his allies' resolve was weakening. He always knew they were a bunch of incompetent loobies.

Mrs. Hibbert, on the other hand, was both competent and strong-minded. He'd like to see how a hussy bred up in the theater was dealing with his fastidious housekeeper. However, he could keep his eye on only one at a time, and Nerissa was under observation. He sniffed the air, found a faint trace of Miles—not so much a scent as a hint of his passage—and followed it toward the stables.

He was perfectly capable of drawing Harwood's attention to any breach of the rules, even if he hadn't quite worked out how to manifest himself to anyone else.

While Sir Barnabas endured a tedious conversation between Miles and his head groom, in the library Nerissa breathed a sigh of relief. A fortuitous question had started the stiffly polite Mrs. Hibbert reminiscing about Mama's childhood. After that, the housekeeper had remained cordial, advising her new mistress rather than challenging her. Though Nerissa was still muddled about the duties and responsibilities of the lady of the manor, she hoped for Mrs. Hibbert's continuing help.

However, she dared not count on such forbearance. Mrs. Hibbert probably didn't know her grandfather's will had described her as an actress and a whore. The servants had left by the time that part was read, she recalled. The housekeeper's attitude was bound to change when she found out, but Nerissa didn't quite dare broach the subject in order to deny it.

When Mrs. Hibbert left, Nerissa sat by the fire, considering her best course of action. She didn't think a respectable servant would ever confront her face-to-face about so scandalous a rumor, so how was she to deal with it?

Perhaps Miles would explain for her. He had known the woman since childhood and was on friendly terms with her, and he seemed to believe Nerissa's claim of innocence.

She already owed him so much, though. She had definite qualms about putting herself under further obligation. After all, he had not quibbled with Sir Barnabas's opinion of him as a debauched gamester. Perhaps he expected her gratitude to take tangible form sometime in the future, if not at once. Nerissa shivered as her imagination suggested what tangible form a libertine might demand.

Yet he had been very kind, and he must have realized from the first that she was a rival for the baronet's fortune. Now that he had shaved, his eyes no longer red-rimmed with fatigue, he didn't look dissolute anymore. At least she'd ask his advice.

A footman came in to light candles, and Nerissa realized that the autumn afternoon had faded to dusk outside the windows.

Carrying a candelabrum from the mantelpiece, she moved to the desk to write to her parents. Despite the manifest difficulties ahead of her, she wanted to stay. She wanted to prove to herself that she was capable of more than turning a length of shoddy plaid cotton into a kilt.

In a desk drawer she found paper, pens and penknife, and sealing wafers. The brass inkstand was half full of ink. There was nothing to hinder her but uncertainty as to how to persuade Mama and Papa to let her stay at Addlescombe. If she told them she had been outrageously insulted by Sir Barnabas's will, her presence was bitterly resented by her relatives, and her only ally was a wastrel with a penchant for actresses, they'd order her home at once.

As she dipped a quill in the ink, a white-capped head peeked around the door. Cousin Sophronia scurried in, then stopped in dismay, her hand clapped to her mouth.

"Oh, dear, you are busy," she squeaked. "I do beg your pardon for interrupting."

"Not at all, Miss . . ." Nerissa cast her mind back to long-ago introductions. "Miss Datchett."

"Oh, please, everyone calls me Miss Sophie. Though you are some sort of very distant cousin, are you not? Effie explained, but I fear I did not follow her. I seldom do," she confided with a nervous glance over her shoulder, "but I'm sure you ought to call me Cousin Sophie."

"If you will call me Nerissa, ma'am."

"I will when Effie is not about. Are you writing to your mama? Do please send dear Anthea my fond remembrances."

"I will, Cousin Sophie. Won't you sit down?"

"I cannot stay more than a minute. Effie doesn't know I have come. I just want to tell you that I don't mind a bit if you inherit Addlescombe, and two hundred pounds a year is excessively generous, and I would so like to be friends, but you must promise to keep it secret from my sister," she finished breathlessly.

"Why, yes, of course," said Nerissa, surprised. "I'll be delighted to be friends, and I promise not to tell Mrs. Chidwell."

Cousin Sophie's round face crinkled in a happy smile. "Good, then, that's settled. Oh, dear, I must run." She darted around the desk and dropped a soft kiss on Nerissa's cheek, then trotted off toward the door. Reaching it, she stopped, turned, and exclaimed, "Dear Miles, such a nice little boy."

The next moment she was gone. Nerissa couldn't help smiling as she looked after Sophie. What a dear little lady, and what a joy to have at least one of her relatives accept her with goodwill!

Something glinted on the red Axminster carpet. Going to investigate, Nerissa found a hairpin. There was another by the desk and a third on the polished floorboards by the door. She didn't think they were hers—though her hair often escaped its pins, the pins rarely escaped her hair—so they must be Miss Sophie's.

Quickly she collected them and hid the evidence of her elderly cousin's presence at the back of a drawer. The tyrannical Mrs. Chidwell should not learn of her sister's timid rebellion from her, she vowed.

She returned to her letter, glad to be able to put in a cheerful reference to Cousin Sophie's amiability.

For some time she pondered what to write about Miles. She could not leave him out altogether, for she was sure to want to mention him in future letters. In the end she simply wrote that she'd have missed the reading of the will had not Sir Barnabas's godson, bound upon the same errand, taken her up in his curricle. That would predispose her parents in his favor. Mama might even remember his childhood visits. Fortunately, Cousin Sophie said he had been a nice little boy.

And a mischievous one, Nerissa was prepared to wager.

She signed the letter, folded it, wrote the direction, and sealed it with a wafer. By writing very small, she had fitted all her news on one sheet without even crossing her lines, so her parents would not have to pay for a second sheet. The postage from Dorset to York was surely shockingly high. She hoped Mr. Harwood would approve paying for their reply, for she must save the few coins left in her purse in case she failed and had to return home with no inheritance.

At home one simply left a letter at the post office, but Addlescombe certainly had no such convenience. What was she to do with hers, now that it was written? There was such a dreadful lot she didn't know, she thought, sighing.

She'd ask Miles. With a rueful smile, she decided she had best start keeping a list of all the things she needed to ask Miles.

As she reached the hall, letter in hand, Snodgrass was crossing it.

"Snodgrass!" About to ask him if he knew where

Mr. Courtenay was, she told herself not to be such a poltroon. Notwithstanding his haughty air, the butler was her servant, however temporarily. "Snodgrass, I have a letter for the post," she informed him in her most dignified manner.

"If you put it on the table here, miss, it will go out tomorrow. One of the grooms rides down to Riddlebourne every day to the receiving house."

"Thank you, Snodgrass. That will be all."

He inclined his head and went on his way. Nerissa was glad she had summoned up the courage to request his advice. He had not seemed to see anything out of the way in her ignorance. She only wished she had thought to ask him Miles's whereabouts, too.

She started as the long-case clock struck the half-hour at her elbow. Half past six. Mrs. Hibbert had told her Sir Barnabas always dined at seven. She was used to an earlier dinner because of the demands of the theater, but she saw no reason to upset a long-standing arrangement. Besides, her mealtimes for several days had borne no relationship to the usual.

Everyone must be above stairs, changing for dinner, she guessed. Having already put on her best dress, she turned to the door that a vague memory from that morning told her led to the drawing room.

Earlier, skewered by inimical stares, she had not taken in the appearance of the room she now entered. It seemed to have been formed by throwing together two smaller rooms, for an arch of heavy beams divided it in half, each part having its own fireplace. The furniture was just as she would have expected from what little she had seen of the rest of the house: plain, but comfortable and exceedingly well kept. Though the predominant colors were a cool willow-green and white, window curtains of the same red as in the library added a touch of warmth. Generous fires burned on both hearths.

A gentleman rose from a chair by the farther fire. To her relief, Nerissa saw it was Miles. In a black coat, cream waistcoat, and buff pantaloons, his cravat tied in an elaborate knot, he looked alarmingly elegant. She rather thought she preferred him in buckskins, boots, and a driving coat.

His smile made her momentary shyness vanish. "I expected you to be here sooner, since you dressed for dinner earlier," he said.

"I was writing to my parents. This is a very pleasant room, is it not?"

"Comfortable enough. Is your hair dry yet? Come and sit down by the fire. I've been wanting to ask you how you got on with Hibby."

"Amazingly well. Too well, in fact. She cannot be aware that my grandfather believed me an actress and . . . and not respectable. When she discovers—"

"Don't vex yourself, she knows already. One thing you will learn about a large staff of servants is that they always know everything."

"You are sure? But she was so affable in the end."

"I told her it was all Sir Barnabas's fancy and a load of twaddle," he said smugly.

Nerissa was taken aback. "Oh, I see. Thank you."

"You don't object? I'd not have opened the subject, I promise you, but since it came up, it seemed a good idea to clear up any little misunderstanding."

"Yes, I do thank you. I was going to ask your advice," she confided, "and I hoped you might offer to speak to her for me."

"I thought it would be dashed difficult for you to do it. Oh, by the way, that's another thing I wanted to mention to you." He hesitated, looking a trifle embarrassed.

"What?"

"Well, there's no harm in 'dashed,' but earlier I ... hmm ... called upon Old Nick, shall we say, and you didn't bat an eyelid. A lady of refinement would have frozen me with her disapproval, and I'd have humbly apologized for not minding my tongue in her presence."

Nerissa raised her hands to her hot cheeks. "Oh, dear! Mama taught me never to use such expressions, but to show one's displeasure at every improper word used in the theater would be impossible, and dreadfully unpopular. I suppose I have grown so used to it, I simply don't notice."

"So I guessed." He grinned. "However, let me here and now proffer my apologies for my slip and promise you I shall endeavor in the future not to say anything that *ought* to shock you."

"I shall endeavor, in the future, to *be* shocked if you do," she said primly.

At that he laughed, but he quickly sobered and asked, "You don't mind my mentioning it? It was disgracefully impertinent of me."

"Oh, no. I have a great deal to learn, and if you don't help me, who will? Besides, I am persuaded your intentions were good, for Cousin Sophie assured me that you were 'such a nice little boy.' "

"How sadly lowering! There I was, trying to impress you as a fine fellow, a man of the world, an out-and-outer, and Miss Sophie has destroyed my pretensions with a phrase. Might I inquire when this devastating blow was delivered?"

Nerissa told him about her very distant cousin's fleeting visit to the library. "You may imagine I am delighted to find at least one of my relatives well disposed toward me. She's a dear, but she seems to be completely under Mrs. Chidwell's thumb."

"She always was, as long as I can remember. I have a vague recollection of hearing that she served as companion to her sister before Chidwell died and they moved to Addlescombe."

"That was after Mama was married, I think. Do you happen to know . . ." She fell silent as Sir Neville and his wife entered the room.

Miles rose in deference to Lady Philpott. Nerissa wondered whether she should follow suit. As if he read her mind, Miles laid his hand briefly but firmly on her shoulder. His warm touch through the thin silk sent a rippling thrill through her.

Blame her grandfather for making her so much aware of Miles's vigorous masculinity, she thought angrily.

But no, she was letting Sir Barnabas's meddling make her oversensitive. A certain perturbation was entirely natural in the circumstances, for she was about to come face-to-face with her great-uncle, and the new baronet had by far the best excuse for resentment. He had had every reason to expect to inherit Addlescombe along with the title.

She raised her chin. The will was not her fault, and she refused to apologize for it. She echoed Miles's unconcerned "Good evening."

Sir Neville looked disconcerted. For a moment Nerissa was sure he would not respond. Then Lady

Philpott mumbled "Good evening," and her husband sheepishly did likewise.

However, Lady Philpott took a seat by the other fireplace. From a box on a stand beside her chair she extracted some needlework, and bent her head over it. Sir Neville stood with his hands clasped behind his back, apparently studying with extraordinary diligence a portrait of a rather scrawny bag-wigged gentleman carrying a shotgun.

"Your grandfather," Miles informed Nerissa. " 'An unforgiving eye and damned disinheriting countenance.' Scarcely worthy of such concentrated attention."

"This is ridiculous," she said. "We cannot live six months with the house divided between Montagues and Capulets refusing to speak to each other."

"Cheer up, m'dear—Nerissa, I mean. I wager it won't last long."

"Really?"

"Sooner or later one of them will realize they had best turn us up sweet lest we win," he said with a look of cynical amusement. "I'd put a monkey on its being the parson who first comes to his senses."

"Why?"

"Because he cannot remove from the vicinity without losing his living. The clergyman who cold-shoulders his patron hasn't been born yet. He'd quickly learn which side his bread is buttered. Yes, a monkey on your cousin Raymond to be first past the post, but the others will complete the course in the end."

Nerissa sighed. "I suppose that will be better than being sent to Coventry, though I had rather have their honest friendship."

"Little hope of that, I fear, except from Miss Sophie. But don't despair. Anything is possible."

"If they will not be friends, it shall not be for want of trying on my part, but tonight I'm still too weary to make the effort."

Mr. Harwood came in and, after a few words with the Philpotts, joined Miles and Nerissa. Chatting with Miles and Mr. Harwood, Nerissa scarcely noticed that the others, as they entered, all stayed at the far end of the room.

As the clock in the hall began to strike the hour, the lawyer said, "You two will take the head and foot of the table, of course. Fortunately we are close to the dining room door." He indicated a door in the wall opposite the fireplace, beside the beam dividing their half of the room from the other.

Miles grinned. "I take it you fear I shall have to battle Sir Neville for my rightful place."

"Oh, no," said Nerissa in dismay. "Surely it cannot be proper in me to come to pulling caps with Lady Philpott over who sits where."

"I doubt you'll have any trouble with her ladyship," Miles reassured her, then spoiled his reassurance by adding dryly, "It's Euphemia you'll have to watch out for."

"Mrs. Chidwell does have an inflated notion of her position in the household," Mr. Harwood acknowledged. His gaze remained fixed on the door and when, at that moment, it began to open, he quickly offered Nerissa his arm. "Come, Miss Wingate. I hope you will allow me the pleasure of taking you in."

"Please do, sir. When you said Miles—Mr. Courtenay—and I must sit at either end, I was afraid I should be isolated and left to eat my dinner in silence."

He smiled at her in a fatherly way and patted her hand.

"Dinner is served," Snodgrass announced.

Mrs. Chidwell, who had not sat down on entering the drawing room, surged forward, but Nerissa, Mr. Harwood, and Miles reached the door first. The lawyer escorted Nerissa to one end of the table, held her chair for her, and took his place beside her. To avoid the indignant eyes of Lady Philpott and Mrs. Chidwell, she surveyed the room.

White walls, the same cheerful red curtains, and over the mantel a painting of a dog with a dead duck drooping in its mouth. More appropriate than the fish in the library, but she could not care for it.

"May I change things around in the house?" she asked Mr. Harwood.

"You will have a free hand after six months, ma'am, but until then I fear I cannot authorize any major expenditures for furnishings."

"I don't wish to buy anything, just to move a few pictures about. Otherwise I like the way the house is decorated and furnished, what I have seen of it."

"Sir Barnabas believed in quality but refused to pay extra for what he described as frivolous fal-lals. You see the china is sturdy blue-and-white Spode. You will find the same with your dinner, good English food in season, well cooked but without fancy sauces, which he abominated."

Nerissa became aware that Cousin Sophie had taken the seat on her other side and was nodding vigorously. "Bad for the digestion, he said," she whispered after a swift glance to see if Euphemia was watching her.

With friends on either side, Nerissa enjoyed the meal. She was perfectly content without fancy sauces, never having tasted any, though she missed Yorkshire pudding with the roast beef. She mentioned the lack to Mr. Harwood, who advised her to consult Cook. They chatted about the city of York and its superb minster, which the lawyer had once visited and admired. Cousin Sophie ventured an occasional murmur when her sister was particularly absorbed in her food.

Only one course was served, but with several removes. Nerissa finished with a slice of apple tart. Swallowing the last morsel, she dabbed her lips with her napkin and commented to Mr. Harwood on the excellence of the pastry. Tessa, her mother's maid, had a heavy hand with pastry, she was explaining, when she realized that everyone was watching her. Even Miles seemed to be trying to convey a silent message from the other end of the table.

The dreadful, familiar paralysis struck. Nerissa was unable to think, unable even to begin to consider what she might have done wrong. Their combined gazes—curious, expectant, avid—pressed upon her like a physical mass, crushing her chest so she could not breathe, could not stir.

And then, despite Euphemia's scrutiny, Cousin Sophie risked touching Nerissa's hand. "Shall we leave the gentlemen to their port, dear?" she inquired gently.

The bonds of inertia snapped. Fiery-cheeked, Nerissa led the ladies back to the drawing room.

Nothing on earth could have persuaded her to stay, to await the gentlemen and the tea tray. Tonight Lady Philpott and Euphemia Chidwell were welcome to fight over who was to do the honors.

Nerissa didn't even want to see Miles, who had failed to warn her. No doubt he was as shocked as anyone that she, who had staked her claim to be hostess, had not known she was expected to give the signal to depart from the dining room.

Humiliated, she fled to her chamber.

Chapter Seven

If Nerissa expected to lie long awake, agonizing over the impossibility of mastering every detail of ladylike conduct, she was mistaken. She fell asleep the moment her head touched the soft, feather-filled pillow. Thus, given her nap the previous day, it was not surprising that she should have wakened early.

A pale light filtered around and through the flowery curtains. For a few minutes she enjoyed the warm comfort of her bed, then she reached for the navy serge dressing gown Maud had draped over the chair beside her. There was too much exploring to be done to entice her to lie in. Besides, she wanted to be abroad before she had to face anyone who had witnessed her stupidity last night.

The fire in the small grate—a fire in her bed-chamber!—had burnt out, but its warmth lingered, taking the chill off the early October air. Bare-footed, Nerissa pattered across to the window and parted the curtains.

She had been too tired the previous day to notice that her room had a splendid view westward over the valley. Now much of it was invisible, hidden by floating patches of autumn mist with the crowns of trees protruding here and there. Her breath on the windowpane did not help, so she raised the lower sash and leaned out, her loosely plaited hair falling forward over her shoulder. The far hills rose above the mists, their crests gilded by the rising sun. She took a deep breath of deliciously crisp air, scented not with the dank miasmas of a town but with the mysterious, enticing, unknown smells of the countryside.

Unknown except for one. Her nostrils twitched as the unmistakable aroma of new-baked bread reached her.

In the wardrobe she found the olive-green dress she had traveled in, already washed and pressed for her by her new maid. It had ribbon drawstrings at the neck and beneath her breasts, so it was easy to put on without help. She scrambled into it, grabbed her gray cloak, and sped down to the kitchens.

As she entered the high-ceilinged room with its huge hearth and walls hung with copper pots, the cook was turning a loaf out of its tin and knocking on its bottom crust to test it. A tall, brawny, red-faced woman enveloped in a vast white apron, she turned a look of suspicious disapproval on Nerissa.

She had done it wrong again. Real ladies obviously did not pop into the kitchen before breakfast.

Too bad, Nerissa thought crossly. It was her kitchen, or at least half of it soon would be. She, in some obscure, convoluted way, paid Cook's wages.

"Good morning," she said with a smile. "I'm Miss Wingate. Can you spare a slice of your bread before I go out for a walk? The smell is simply irresistible."

Slightly mollified, Cook bobbed a clumsy curtsy. "Oh, aye, miss, there's plenty. Will tha help thysen?" She gestured at a rack of cooling loaves with a breadboard and knife beside it. "Lil," she called, turning to remove another pair of golden-crusted loaves from the built-in oven beside the fire, "bring t'best bootter fro' t'larder."

"You're from Yorkshire!" Nerissa exclaimed, carving herself a crusty doorstep as a skinny little maid scurried in with an earthen pot of butter. "I've just come from York. I've lived there for years."

Cook thawed still further. " 'Twas in York I started in service, miss. T'kettle's on t'boil. Will tha take a cup o'tea? 'Twon't take but a minute to mash."

"Thank you, not just now. I want to be out and about. Have you any fresh milk?"

"Aye, miss, t'lad brought up t'can an hour since. Lil, fetch a jug o' milk for miss. Mind how tha goes, now."

The wide-eyed kitchen maid scurried off again, to return with a blue-and-white striped jug. When Nerissa thanked her, she turned crimson and curtsied. Nerissa suspected neither Lady Philpott nor Mrs. Chidwell, and certainly not Sir Barnabas, had ever so much as noticed the child's presence, let alone thanked her.

The milk was richly yellow with cream, an altogether different liquid from the thin bluish stuff purchased from street sellers in York. Between sips, Nerissa asked Cook why, as a Yorkshirewoman, she had not served Yorkshire pudding at dinner.

"T'master—t'auld master—didn't fancy it, miss, and nowt were served but what he fancied."

"Well, I fancy it. Will you make it next time we have roast beef? And parkin for tea?"

"Wi' pleasure, miss," said Cook, beaming.

Nerissa went off with a hunk of bread and butter in her hand and a satisfying feeling that she had found another ally.

Though she wanted to see the gardens among other things, she didn't care to go straight from her confrontation with Cook to another with a gardener. She followed a faint path across the park toward the upper end of the valley. As she strolled, she kept a wary eye on the grazing cows, hoping that the beasts who had so generously supplied her with milk and butter would not take it into their heads to approach too close.

With relief she reached a stile and climbed over into a lane. The hedgerows were wreathed with orange and scarlet garlands of bryony berries and silvery old-man's beard. Nerissa's mother had taught her the names of these plants on riverside walks in York, but she had never seen them growing in such profusion. Pretty as they were, she found her attention concentrated mostly on her feet as she picked her way between the muddy ruts. She was about to give up and turn back, when another stile beckoned her onward.

The sun had risen above the brow of the hill behind the house to disperse the mists and sparkle on the dew. Climbing the stile, she discovered the other side of the hedgerow to be overgrown with brambles, still bearing late blackberries. She stuffed her gloves in her pocket and stopped to taste them.

Amid the tangle of prickly stems and yellowing leaves, countless spiders lurked in their dew-spangled webs. Admittedly the webs had a delicate beauty of their own, but Nerissa did not care for the eight-legged occupants. The better to reach between both spiders and thorns in her quest for the few unshriveled berries, she took off her cloak, folded it, and set it on the stile.

She was reaching up with purple-stained fingers for a bunch dangling overhead, when she heard the sound of approaching hooves. A rider on a roan gelding cantered across the field toward her.

"Halloo, Nerissa!" he called.

Recognizing Miles, she waved. On horseback, sitting tall in the saddle, handling his spirited mount with practiced ease, he looked less than ever like a debauched wastrel.

As Miles drew rein, Sir Barnabas ventured to open his eyes. Whisked along through the air, hanging on like grim death to a single tail hair, he didn't know what would have happened had he let go in mid-flight. He didn't want to know.

His insubstantial feet drifted down to meet substantial ground, and he sighed in relief. He wasn't going to travel that way again!

"Good morning," said Nerissa. Sir Barnabas almost answered before he remembered she could not see him.

"Good morning." Miles swung down from the saddle and doffed his hat with a smile. "You are the very picture of a country lass."

"And you of a country gentleman."

Sir Barnabas snorted at this exchange of inane compliments between the Bond Street beau and the piece of Haymarket ware. Still, compliments might lead to more significant exchanges, though the season was hardly conducive to a tumble in the hay. What could he do to help? He cast about for ideas.

"I want to apologize for last night," said Miles soberly, "for not warning you. I hadn't thought about our being host and hostess, and when Harwood sprang it on us, it was too late to consider all the pitfalls."

"I cannot hold you responsible for my own stupidity."

"Ignorance, not stupidity. Quite different, and I

had offered to guide you. I'm a little surprised that you didn't guess what was needed when all the ladies turned to you at the end of the meal."

"That was the trouble!" The girl actually blushed. She really was an excellent actress, Sir Barnabas thought absently. He had spotted a spider dangling from a glistening thread just above her head, and it had given him a splendid notion.

"Everyone was staring at me," Nerissa continued. "It was like being onstage, before an audience. I suffer so dreadfully from stage fright that I cannot move or think."

"I see! That explains a good deal."

"It explains why I am not an actress," she confessed. "I daresay I would be otherwise, perfectly respectable of course, like Mama. Not that being an actress, respectable or not, could change the likelihood of my committing the most dreadful faux pas."

"Not dreadful," said Miles. "Not last night at least, though I can't speak for the future. I've been to more than one formal dinner given by a fashionable newlywed bride who has made just the same mistake. No one would have thought twice about it if you had not been surrounded by people hoping you'd do something wrong."

While they talked, Sir Barnabas was concentrating on a delicate maneuver. The spider's gossamer thread was so flimsy, he had no difficulty swinging it aside till the creature hung above Nerissa's shoulder.

Alarmed, the spider dropped the last few inches. It sat on the greenish-brown woolen cloth for a moment, planning its next move. Sir Barnabas's cold, once-bony finger poked it toward Nerissa's neck.

As its eight feet scampered onto her bare skin,

Nerissa clapped her hand to her neck. Too late. Urged on by Sir Barnabas, it had already dived for cover down the high but loose front of her bodice.

"Something went down my dress," she cried, clutching her bosom.

And that bosom now claimed all Miles's attention, just as the late baronet had intended.

"A leaf?"

"Something with *legs.*" Twitching, Nerissa pulled at the neckline of her gown and tried to peer down it. "It's scuttling about."

"I'll help you get it out," Miles offered, a gleam in his eye.

She played the outraged maiden well, too. "Certainly not," she snapped. "Please go over to the stile and make sure no one comes. And keep your back turned. And *hurry.*"

Grinning, he obeyed. Led by the reins, his mount followed, tossing its head as it passed Nerissa.

The moment Miles's back was toward her, Nerissa turned her back on him, untied the bow at her neck, and pulled down the front of her dress. Her chemise was cut lower. As she held it away from her body and squinted down it, Sir Barnabas saw the white globes of two small but softly rounded breasts.

"I can't find it," she wailed.

"Do, pray, permit me to be of assistance, ma'am," said Miles, the formality of his words belied by his laughing voice.

"No!"

"Then might I suggest that if you cannot find it from above, you try to shake it downward, to the ground."

"Oh, yes, I will," Nerissa said gratefully. She loosened the ribbon at the high waist of her gown.

Sir Barnabas watched every gyration of her slim body. There was no harm in it, for after all, he was her grandfather, and dead, besides. He just wanted to see how far his shameless granddaughter would dare to disrobe in the open air.

She twisted and jiggled and jumped up and down. Perhaps she was an opera dancer rather than an actress? The gelding caught sight of her and rolled its eyes nervously. What a pity Miles, in a most unexpectedly well-behaved manner, was observing her orders rather than her undulating quivers.

Nerissa stopped and stood still with an intent expression. "I can't feel the horrid thing moving now. I do believe it's gone."

"Congratulations. Shall I . . ."

"Keep your back turned!" She retied the ribbons, straightened her bodice, smoothed her skirts. "There, I'm decent. Oh, bother, my plait has come undone. I knew I should have pinned it up."

About her shoulders flowed a rippling cape of light brown hair touched with shimmers of pure gold by the rising sun. Miles's eyes widened in admiration.

Self-conscious, she gathered it back from her face with both hands. As she raised her arms, her breasts pressed against the fabric of her gown and Miles's admiring gaze slipped down from the cloud of sunlit hair.

On the whole, Sir Barnabas was satisfied with the effects of his spider ploy.

Nerissa let her hair drop. "I haven't anything to tie it up with," she said helplessly. "I cannot walk into the manor with it hanging loose. Everyone will be about by now."

"Your cloak will hide it." Looping the reins over

his arm, he held out the drab gray garment for her to don.

"Of course. I'd forgotten I had it with me."

An excellent disguise, thought Sir Barnabas as she pulled it around her shoulders and raised the hood. No one seeing that dingy drapery would guess it concealed a bird of paradise. He'd be interested to see what sort of indecent, vulgarly garish apparel she appeared in when Harwood gave her a free hand to purchase whatever she wished. She'd never have the strength to resist, he was sure, even for the sake of keeping up the image she wished to convey.

Miles's thoughts were also on a new wardrobe for Nerissa. He had taken an intense dislike to the shabby cloak, which seemed to eclipse her personality as well as her figure. Not that her gowns were much better. Those he had seen hung on her like sacks. Assuming she had made them herself, her sewing might be appropriate for theatrical costumes, but she'd never make a living as a modiste.

She had said she hated sewing, he recalled. He hoped she'd find life at Addlescombe more to her liking, despite her unpleasant relatives.

"Are you going on," he asked, "or has your encounter with the wildlife given you a disgust of the country?"

"Not at all." She smiled. "At least it didn't bite me, and the blackberries were some compensation. I should like to explore farther, but I'm unaccustomed to walking such a distance so I had best turn back now. I mean to walk every day until I can go all the way to the tops of the hills without difficulty. There must be marvelous views."

"There are. That's where I'm headed. But you could go much farther afield if you rode. I daresay we can find a mount in the stables to suit you—or did you not bring a riding habit with you?"

"I've never had one. I've never had a chance to learn to ride," she said wistfully.

"What a shocking deficiency in your education!" he teased. "It's time it was remedied. Your lessons will begin as soon as you can have a habit made."

"Really?" Her face glowed, her wonderful eyes bright as stars. "You will teach me? You are doing so much for me already."

"Since I am your grandfather's godson, I consider myself your god-uncle, or something of the sort. I've no idea what are the duties of a god-uncle, so I am at liberty to invent them as I go along."

Nerissa laughed. "Thus far, your invention meets with my unqualified approval," she said. "Well, I must not keep you any longer from your ride, uncle."

"*Don't* call me uncle or I'll abdicate the role," he threatened with a grin. "I'll be on my way, then. I look forward to the time when you will accompany me."

Mounting, he waved a salute and turned the roan's head toward the far side of the field.

A trot, a canter, a gallop, and they sailed over the five-barred gate. He leaned forward to pat his mount's neck. A prime bit of blood he was, one of Matilda Philpott's two hunters, though belonging to the estate, not to her personally, or he'd not have brought him out. There was a fine hack, too, which she rode, and an ambling prad used by Raymond Reece about his parish duties.

None of the others rode, and the only other saddle horse was an elderly mare put out to grass when Sir Barnabas had to give up riding. She would do admirably for Nerissa's lessons.

He was glad Nerissa wanted to ride, and that the creature falling down her gown had not made her take the countryside in aversion. How he had managed to refrain from turning his head when she was disposing of it he wasn't at all sure! He'd been rewarded, when she held back her hair, by a glimpse of a figure far more shapely than the hideous cut of her gowns had hitherto revealed. Her hair, too, had been a revelation, the sun's touch transforming the ordinary brown into sunshine.

Yet what he recalled most clearly was a slim hand stained reddish-purple with blackberry juice, and the guilty way she had hidden it behind her when she saw him. He smiled to himself.

Sir Barnabas was also glad Nerissa wanted to ride. Miles would be helping her to mount, lifting her down, picking her up when she fell. Nothing could be more conducive to intimacy, he thought, drifting homeward behind her.

Later they would ride together, though, beyond his reach, for he wasn't going to try to keep up with a horse ever again. Still, winter was coming. They'd not get up to much mischief out of doors. He congratulated himself on being clever enough to die in the autumn.

He blinked as his vision blurred. A lingering patch of mist? No, he could see quite well to either side.

He recalled his sight blurring as he died, before he reopened his eyes on his new existence. Never say he was going to leave this spectral state before he saw his last wishes carried out! He blinked again, hard.

Something dangled just before his face. Squinting, he focused on it. A spider? The ghost of a spider! The reproachful gaze of eight eyes told him as clearly as words that the unfortunate arachnid blamed him for its demise, squashed to death somewhere in Nerissa's undergarments.

Being haunted by a spider was peculiarly disconcerting, especially as he was a ghost himself. He hit out at it.

His hand went right through it. Though, with an effort, he was able to move material objects, it seemed to be impossible for a ghost to move a ghost. He turned his head to one side. The spider, its palps twitching, still hung two inches in front of his nose.

Slowly it began to swing back and forth, a handbreadth this way, a handbreadth the other, constructing an invisible web.

Sir Barnabas arrived back at the manor an hour later, dizzy, cross-eyed, and in a frightful temper.

Chapter Eight

Washed, dressed in her blue-striped dimity, and with her hair properly pinned up, Nerissa went down to the breakfast room. Despite her unwonted exercise, she was not particularly hungry after her bread and butter and blackberries, but she was ready for a cup of tea.

She was also ready to face the family. Yesterday's fatigue forgotten, invigorated by the walk, she was ashamed of the way she had let their unfriendliness intimidate her.

Nonetheless, she rather hoped to find Miles in the breakfast room before her.

No one was there but Raymond Reece. He jumped to his feet, bidding her "Good morning," and bustled around the table to seat her opposite himself. Nerissa almost laughed aloud. Had not Miles decided that the parson would be the first to see where his best interests lay?

"Tea, if you please, sir," she said in answer to his query, "and those apples look delicious."

"Permit me to peel one for you, ma'am. But come, you must call me Cousin Raymond, for that is our relation, is it not? 'Behold how good and how pleasant it is for brethren to dwell together in unity.' " He smiled as he set a cup of tea before her and picked up a fruit knife, but his eyes were coolly assessing.

She politely accepted the apple he peeled and quartered. Desperately seeking a subject of conversation that could not possibly lead to either the theater or her inheritance, she asked him about his parish.

Somewhat to her surprise, he seemed well acquainted with all his parishioners and their trials and tribulations. Indeed, he described them to her in what she considered quite unnecessary detail. Gammer Smithson had lost all her teeth and could eat only sops; Ted Carter's feckless wife was expecting her ninth though she couldn't clothe the first eight; Jos Bedford invariably drank up all his wages at the village tavern, which rejoiced in the name of the Addled Egg; Old Amos, who had lost his leg at Trafalgar, suffered from dreadful rheumaticks in wet weather. . . .

"Of course," said Cousin Raymond, regarding Nerissa with obvious pessimism and a hint of malice, "as the lady of the manor, you will wish to do what you can to alleviate their troubles and to encourage them to remedy their ways. Aunt Jane, I fear, has not been as active in this regard as one might hope."

"I—I will do my best," Nerissa stammered. How many things there were to learn! In this matter, alas, Miles was unlikely to be knowledgeable. Nonetheless, she turned to him with relief when he came into the breakfast room as she sipped the last of her tea.

"Did you enjoy your ride?"

"Splendid!" His color high from the fresh air and exercise, he looked less dissipated and debauched

than ever. "Whatever her faults, your cousin Matilda is a good judge of horseflesh, and—"

"You've been riding Samson!" Matilda burst into
the room on Miles's heels and glared at him accus-
ingly. Her skinny figure in a severely practical
brown habit quivered with fury.

"Yes." He continued calmly to the sideboard and
peered under the silver covers of the chafing dishes.
"You were out on Grandee and I don't believe
Hippolyta is quite up to my weight. Ah-ha, sau-
sages."

Matilda scowled. "Hippolyta is a superb hack."

"Without a doubt," Miles soothed her as he piled
high a plate. "But I ride at eleven stone and you
can't be more than nine."

"Eight and a half," she admitted grudgingly.
"What do you think of Samson?"

"Magnificent."

Thereafter, the dialogue deteriorated to a discussion of blood lines, well-sprung ribs, length of bone,
sloping shoulders, and let-down hocks. The Reverend Raymond departed with an expressive grimace
at Nerissa, and she soon followed. Miles raised his
hand in a negligent wave as she left.

Feeling lost and rather forlorn, she wondered
what she ought to be doing. Mrs. Hibbert had said
something about menus, but Nerissa had been too
anxious and bewildered to take her questions in
properly. Someone had to decide what the household was to eat each day, she supposed. Was she expected to prepare a menu, or merely to approve it?
Should she consult Cook or the housekeeper? She
shuddered at the thought of offending either.

Perhaps Miles knew the answers, but she didn't
want to display her ignorance before Matilda. As
she hesitated outside the breakfast room door, Miss

Sophie came trotting toward her, her dove-gray gown swinging about her ankles. She waved a piece of paper with an anxious air.

"Good morning, dear. I am so glad to have found you, for whatever Effie says, I am sure you are the one to decide upon the menu now."

"I was just wondering, Cousin Sophie. Mrs. Chidwell is accustomed to write it out?"

"Oh, no, dear. Each evening she tells me what to put down for the next day and I write it in the morning, only I fear I frequently forget precisely what she has said. And then Cousin Jane sometimes insists on having her say, and so often Effie wants something the gardens cannot supply. She says Tredgarth, the head gardener, is monstrous disobliging, but of course the poor man cannot grow what is not in season, can he?"

"I imagine not," Nerissa agreed, smiling.

"I must say he sometimes becomes quite alarmingly grumpy, but it is all right in the end. He and Cook pay Effie's scolding no mind, and I am quite used to it."

"Well, I shall take the blame in the future, if you will be so kind as to help me at first."

Miss Sophie beamed. "Certainly, dear, for Effie is still abed. We shall be quite peaceful in the morning room." She led the way into a small, sunny sitting room decorated in peach and white with flowered chintz upholstery.

Nerissa very soon decided that whatever she did could be only an improvement on Miss Sophie's muddle-headed efforts. Cook must have been struggling for years to make head or tail of menus full of crossings-out and changes and question marks. With renewed confidence she thanked her elderly cousin and went off to find Mr. Tredgarth.

It seemed reasonable to her to discover which fruits and vegetables were available before deciding what dishes to order.

As she wandered through one of the walled kitchen gardens between neat beds of onions, carrots, Brussels sprouts, and cauliflowers, Miles joined her. "You should have sent for Tredgarth," he reproved her.

"I knew you would say that. I wanted to see the gardens for myself. Miles, there are no flowers anywhere!"

"I daresay it's too late in the year."

"Nonsense. When I left York the gardens were full of Michaelmas daisies and chrysanthemums, oh, and autumn crocus and asters, too. Even a few roses. We are much farther south here. I haven't even seen any rosebushes."

"I don't know anything about flowers," he said dismissively.

"You seem to know a great deal about horses," she snapped. "You and Matilda were getting on like a house on fire."

"Her opinions on horses are well worth listening to. I trust your tête-à-tête with the parson was equally satisfactory?"

"Cousin Raymond was so obliging as to provide me with any amount of useful information."

"Did I not say he'd be the first to attempt to weasel his way into your favor? Having succeeded without the least difficulty, he'll aim at your affections next."

"How dare you, sir! You may be so desperate for . . . for female companionship as to take a fancy to Cousin Matilda, but I, I assure you, am not so easily won." Her nose in the air, her heart in her half boots, she turned away. "If you will excuse me, Mr.

Courtenay, I must speak to Mr. Tredgarth. Cook is expecting a menu."

"I came to ask if you'd like to go into Porchester today to order some clothes, but no doubt you mean to rely upon your cousin Raymond for advice. I trust you will find him an expert on the proper modes. Good day, Miss Wingate."

Nerissa swung around, but already he was stalking away, his boot heels crunching angrily on the gravel path. Pride forbade her calling after him.

She was *not* jealous of his admiration for Matilda. After all, she had met him only the day before, though it seemed like weeks ago. She simply didn't want to see him taken in and cheated out of his inheritance. And if her spirits were sorely lowered, it was because she had lost her best ally at Addlescombe.

With a sad sniff she went in search of the gardener.

Seated atop the nearest wall, Sir Barnabas chuckled. At first, hearing the sound of quarreling voices as he wearily approached the manor, he had been disgusted. Miles and Nerissa at loggerheads was the last thing he wanted. Then he had recognized the squabble for what it was—a lovers' tiff. Already they were sufficiently attracted to each other to resent attentions paid to anyone else.

Moreover, from his perch Sir Barnabas had an excellent view of Sophie skulking behind a bed of yellowing, red-berried asparagus. He caught a glimpse of Raymond peering through the misted glass of a greenhouse. His granddaughter and his godson were under close observation.

His evil temper banished, the baronet bounded down from the wall with such alacrity that he left the spider's fading ghost behind. In high good humor, he followed Miles into the house.

Miles's humor was the reverse of cheerful. However, by the time he reached the front hall, he was able to laugh—ironically—at Nerissa's claim that he was attracted to Matilda Philpott. He, who had kept as mistresses some of the most seductive actresses on the London stage!

Miles was sorry Reece had managed to worm his way into her confidence. No doubt the poor innocent trusted Reece because he was a clergyman. Next thing he'd be sneaking into her bed, and she'd not know how to defend herself. From what she had said, Miles guessed that her parents had always guarded her against the advances of scurvy knaves like . . . like himself?

All right, so he was a rake, but he had never seduced innocence. He preferred ripe women, women of experience, which only went to prove that he couldn't possibly be jealous of Nerissa's fraternization with Reece. If he was disturbed, it was just because with so much money at stake, he didn't trust the fellow an inch farther than he could see him.

It was up to him to protect her from the deceitful cur.

For a start, he couldn't let her rely upon her cousin's advice on her new wardrobe. When she came in, he'd persuade her to go into Porchester with him. In the meantime, he would follow her good example and begin to familiarize himself with the duties of his new position.

Feeling virtuous, he went off to the estate office at the back of the house, near the stables. He was studying a large-scale map of Addlescombe and its tenant farms, when Nerissa tapped on the door half an hour later.

"Snodgrass said you were here."

"The man knows everything."

"Am I interrupting you?" she asked warily.

"No, no, come in. The bailiff ain't here and I don't care to tackle the account books without him." He gave a careless wave at the shelf of heavy black tomes beneath the high, narrow window.

Nerissa's eyes widened. "You have to know what is in all those?"

"Lord, no. I'll need to wade through the past few years to see how things have been going on so that I'll know what to look for in the current accounts. To tell the truth, I'm not looking forward to it above half, but it's all too easy for a lax landowner to be cheated."

"Will I have to understand them, too?" she asked in dismay. "Mrs. Hibbert said something about accounts."

"The household accounts are your province. I'll take care of these—unless you suspect *I* shall cheat you?"

"Oh, Miles, of course I don't! I just came to tell you Tredgarth says there are no flowers because my grandfather considered growing them a waste of garden space and the gardeners' time."

"Old killjoy."

"And to say I hope you will relent and take me shopping in Porchester? I cannot ask Cousin Raymond to help me buy clothes. I don't want the sort of dowdy fashions a country parson would approve." She looked down with disfavor at her shabby blue-striped dress. "Or else he might try to persuade me to wear the sort of gaudy, improper gowns actresses favor, hoping to give the neighbors a disgust of me."

Miles grinned as he rolled up the map and tied it

with a tape. "As I warned you yesterday, though you were half asleep at the time, I believe. I'm glad you are not taken in by his sudden friendliness."

" 'One may smile, and smile, and be a villain,' " Nerissa quoted sagely. "I have been helping Mama and Papa con their lines since I was first able to read, and one cannot learn half of Shakespeare's plays by heart without learning something of human nature."

As she spoke, she led the way from the office into the corridor. Miles heard a squawk of alarm, and sprang forward.

Before he reached her side, Nerissa said, "I'm sorry if I startled you, Cousin Sophie. Were you looking for me?"

"Gracious, no, whyever should you think so?" gabbled Miss Sophie. Then she changed her mind. "That is, yes, dear, I . . . I want to ask you . . . to ask you if . . . er, um . . . if you have arranged to-day's menu with Cook," she finished in a burst of inspiration.

Nerissa answered her soothingly, but Miles frowned in puzzlement as he followed them along the corridor. Though Miss Sophie was notoriously scatterbrained, surely she could not have forgotten whether she was looking for Nerissa or not. He smelled a rat, and he was certain Euphemia Chidwell was responsible for its existence.

Raymond Reece was not the only one from whom Nerissa needed protection.

He was still frowning, trying to guess what dire plot Mrs. Chidwell had in mind, when the butler came toward them.

"Mr. Courtenay, sir, Mr. Harwood requests a word with you in the library when convenient," he said.

"Oh, no!" Nerissa exclaimed. "Not now. We shall never get away."

"While you put on your bonnet, I'll just go and tell him we are on our way out," said Miles, shepherding the ladies onward into the front hall. "Snodgrass, order the landau brought around immediately."

The butler looked unwontedly flustered. "Beg pardon, sir, but Sir Neville and my lady set off in the landau not five minutes since, with Mrs. Chidwell and Mr. Aubrey."

"Then we cannot go to Porchester?" cried Nerissa, her voice sharp with disappointment.

Miles gave her a warning look. Snodgrass might know everything, but there was no need to make him a present of the fact that Euphemia had set her sister to distract Nerissa while the rest made off with the carriage.

"Where have they gone?" he asked.

"I believe her ladyship intended to pay a few calls, sir."

"Thank you, Snodgrass, that will be all."

The moment the butler was out of sight—listening around the corner no doubt, thought Miles cynically—Nerissa said with chagrin, "I wish I might have gone with them to visit the neighbors."

"Much better to wait until you have new clothes," Miles consoled her.

"Yes, indeed," Miss Sophie agreed.

"But as I'm not there to deny it, they will tell everyone I'm an actress."

Miss Sophie patted her arm. "Oh, no, dear. Euphemia did suggest it, I confess, but Jane pointed out that to have so disreputable a relative must reflect upon us all. Effie had to admit that people will already be looking askance because we are not to wear mourning. Really, dear Barnabas did become a little peculiar in old age."

A faint snort made itself heard. Snodgrass suppressing a cough, Miles guessed. "I fear Mrs. Chidwell may not be persuaded to hold her tongue," he cautioned Nerissa. "You'll forgive me, Miss Sophie, if I venture to remark that your sister is not always entirely amenable to reason."

"Who should know better than I, dear boy," she said sadly, then added, brightening, "Why do you not take the traveling coach if you wish to go into Porchester today?"

"There is a coach, too?" Nerissa asked. "Then we can go after all."

"Ha!" This time the snort was Miles's own. "That ancient boneshaker! I asked the coachman about it yesterday. It was built before springs were invented, six horses are needed to shift it, and even then it cannot be moved at more than six miles an hour. Always supposing we had six carriage horses, which we don't, we'd be so long on the road, we'd have to turn and come back almost as soon as we arrived."

"Miles, your curricle! I nearly forgot it. We shall be there in no time."

He shook his head. "Not mine, alas. As soon as I discovered I wasn't going to be able to return it to its owner myself, I sent a groom to drive it back to town. He took a letter asking Gerald to retrieve my belongings from my rooms before my landlord decides I've abandoned them."

"No curricle," Nerissa sighed. "Well, at least the groom can bring your goods back with him."

"There's little enough worth bringing, since Sir Barnabas has—doubtless by some oversight— permitted us to acquire new wardrobes."

"If we ever manage to reach Porchester."

"The gig!" Miss Sophie exclaimed, beaming.

"No room for a maid," Miles pointed out.

"Oh." The little lady was crestfallen.

"A maid?" said Nerissa. "I don't need a maid. Do let us take the gig, Miles."

"You cannot go without your abigail to chaperon you."

"Of course I can. I never had an abigail until yesterday."

"Now you have one, and you must take her," he decreed.

"I don't see—"

"Truly, you must, Nerissa," Miss Sophie confirmed anxiously. "Since you are going into town, and particularly as you will be fitted for dresses, it would be most improper to have only a gentleman for company. If you like, dear, I shall go with you, too, whatever Effie may say."

"That is excessively kind of you, Cousin Sophie, but who knows when we shall be able to take the landau?"

"I'll make quite sure it is at our disposal tomorrow," Miles assured her. "We'll take a footman as well. Miss Wingate of Addlescombe shall shop in style."

"Miss Wingate of Addlescombe! Oh, dear, I have just thought—suppose Mama and Papa refuse to let me stay after all?"

Mr. Harwood came into the hall at that moment and heard Nerissa's words. "Is that likely, Miss Wingate?" he inquired, worried.

"It would not greatly surprise me, though I did not write to them the half of the horrid things Grandfather said in his will. They were most unwilling to let me come in the first place, especially

Papa, and besides, I am needed in the theater," she explained, and added wistfully, "I daresay you cannot let me buy clothes until you are sure, sir."

The lawyer took off his spectacles and peered around with a furtive air. "On the contrary, my dear young lady," he whispered. "I suggest you order what you wish as soon as may be and have the bills sent directly to me. If we discover at a later date that your parents withhold their permission—well, who could have guessed that they might throw away a fortune for their daughter?"

"Bless you, Mr. Harwood. You are a dear!"

He blushed at her fervor and started vigorously polishing his spectacles with a large white handkerchief. "I always wanted a daughter," he mumbled.

Miles heard an odd sort of choking splutter. It must be the eavesdropper, Snodgrass, coughing again, he decided, though it had seemed to come from the opposite direction. He'd have to have a word with the fellow!

In three swift strides he reached the passage to the servants' quarters. No one in sight.

"Miles!" Nerissa called after him. "We *shall* drive into Porchester tomorrow, shan't we? In case Mama and Papa write to bid me return to York?"

"Yes, we shall go," he promised. Let her have her pretty new clothes. If her parents then summoned her home, he would be relieved of a great responsibility—though just why he felt responsible for her was far from clear—and he'd stand to inherit the entire fortune.

So why did the possibility of her departure from Addlescombe depress him?

* * *

A week had passed since Nerissa wrote to her parents. Surely their answer must have arrived by now! As the landau pulled up outside the Stickleback Inn, she clenched her hands within her new down-filled muff. The footman jumped from his perch behind and ran in to pick up the post for Addlescombe.

Would Mama and Papa let her stay?

At least if she had to go home, she had a whole new wardrobe to take with her. She glanced down at her elegant moss-green-velvet pelisse trimmed with black braid, and at the great heap of packages beside Maud on the opposite seat.

"I have been dreadfully extravagant, Cousin Sophie," she said guiltily.

"Not at all, dear. Half of those are Miles's—well, a third, I daresay, but definitely the larger ones, since a gentleman's garments are so very bulky. Is it not fortunate that he decided to escort us on horseback today?"

"It was something of a squeeze last time, with all the parcels of reticules and fans and stockings and gloves and shawls. I had not intended to buy so much!"

"Pray do not forget, Nerissa, dear, that it is your money, after all."

"Only if I don't have to go home."

"But in that case it is Miles's money, and he has said he is very well pleased to spend a little on tricking you out in style. I believe that was his expression? Although perhaps it is not quite proper for a young lady to accept clothes from a gentleman—but he is practically a relative, you know, and Mr. Harwood said you might consider it your money, if only for a few days. Oh, I do so hope dear Anthea will not insist on your leaving!"

"I should be sorry indeed never to see you again, Cousin Sophie."

As for the rest of her relations, she doubted even absence could make her heart grow fonder. Over the past few days they had all followed Raymond's lead in making overtures to her, as Miles had predicted. Not for a moment was she deceived into thinking they resented her presence less or had ceased to hope that she would fail to observe Sir Barnabas's conditions.

How smug Cousin Euphemia had looked when Nerissa made such a cake of herself in church on Sunday! She had been halfway down the aisle, when she realized the entire congregation was staring at her. Unable to move, her breath caught in her throat, she had stood like a rabbit mesmerized by a stoat until Miles took her arm and gently led her to the family pew. Two days later the memory still made her blush.

At home everyone understood about stage fright. At home no one had any reason to stare at her. A sudden wave of longing swept over her for the close-knit world of the theater, for the community where she was an accepted and useful—if not highly valued—member.

Perhaps, in her new clothes, Lucian would notice her even if she returned without a fortune. She bit her lip. She wanted to go home!

And then Miles came out of the inn, a tankard in his hand, and smiled at her.

"I thought I'd wait here for you to catch up," he said. "Can I bring you ladies any refreshment? Miss Sophie, a dish of tea? Or will you step in for a few minutes?"

"So very considerate, dear boy," twittered Miss Sophie, quite unused to anyone attending to her comfort. "Nerissa, do you care to—but here is Ben with the post," she interrupted herself as the footman returned to the carriage with a bundle of letters and periodicals. "Ben, is there a letter for Miss Wingate?"

"Yes, miss, 'tis come. From York, 'tis the right one for sure. I put it on top, miss." He handed the bundle to Nerissa.

Maud forgot she was supposed to speak only when spoken to. "Oh, miss," she cried, "I hope 'tis good news."

Nerissa's eyes met Miles's in a look of shared amusement, and suddenly she prayed she'd be allowed to stay. The servants wanted her, if only because the alternative was Cousin Euphemia. Miss Sophie wanted her. And Miles needed her support and friendship through the long months ahead in a house full of ill-wishers. He watched anxiously as she fumbled with the seal.

"Here's my pocket knife."

"Thank you." Her hands shook. The sight of Mama's writing made her realize how much she missed her. She no longer knew what she hoped for.

Chapter Nine

Sir Barnabas glared in disgust as Nerissa entered the drawing room in her new evening gown. To be sure, his granddaughter was pretty as a picture in the deep rose sarcenet modestly trimmed with blond lace, but modesty was the word for the style, too. With its high neck and long sleeves, it displayed no more of her shape than the most wishy-washy of present-day fashions allowed. Waists right up under their bosoms! In his day a woman's waist was where it belonged, and well stayed into the bargain.

The jade was cleverer than he had allowed for. He'd been certain the purchase of new finery would tempt her to a display of garish vulgarity, but there was nothing in her appearance for the highest stickler to cavil at.

Still, all was not lost. That good-for-nothing godson of his was gazing at her like a star-stricken mooncalf.

Well, she *was* pretty, the late baronet admitted grudgingly. Candlelight glimmered on her hair, done up on top of her head in a fanciful knot. Her ingenuous, hopeful smile would have graced the most blameless damsel. Pretty—and a superb actress!

Her hopefulness merged into contented relief as

Miles came forward and bowed over her hand, his admiration evident. He was well and truly hooked, Sir Barnabas exulted.

"Delightful," Miles said. *Enchanting,* he thought. The gown showed her slender figure curved in all the right places, and the smooth, shining topknot of hair gave her an air of graceful dignity. He wondered if her mother had dressed her dowdily on purpose to disguise her charms and keep her safe. She was safe from him. As a delicate color rose in her cheeks, he grinned and added, "What excellent taste I have!"

She laughed. "And you are very fine in your new coat. I cannot thank you enough for your help, Miles. I'd have been sadly at a loss without you. As it is, even Cousin Effie has found nothing to criticize except the quantity of my purchases."

"You don't still feel guilty over the cost, do you? Since your mother sent you permission to stay, the money is as good as your own."

"It is as much Mama's and Papa's as mine, though Mr. Harwood will not let me send them any yet. Still, it seems horridly selfish to spend so much on frivolities for myself when Mama's letter is full of plans for all of us. She wants to take a house outside the city, with a proper garden, and to hire a wardrobe mistress for the playhouse so that I need not sew anymore. And, most important, to refurbish the theater so that audiences will not stay away because of its shabbiness. It needs . . ."

A sort of growling howl drowned her words. Miles swept the room with a wild glance. He was hearing things again. He turned back to Nerissa just as she exclaimed, "Oh, what was that?"

"You heard it, too?" he asked in relief.

At that moment the drawing room door opened

and Mr. Harwood came in. Miles and Nerissa both stared at him. His round face was as artlessly cheerful as ever. He turned slightly pink under their united gaze.

They glanced back at each other and shook their heads. The fearsome noise had not emanated from the inoffensive little lawyer.

"Then what . . . ?" Nerissa faltered.

"Did you hear a peculiar sound just now, sir?" Miles demanded.

"A peculiar sound?" Did Mr. Harwood look just a trifle shifty? "What sort of sound?"

"Like a dog that has been trodden on and can't decide whether to snarl at the offender or whine at the pain. A cross between fury and anguish, wouldn't you say, Nerissa?"

"Yes, that's a very good description."

"Good heavens!" The lawyer was definitely embarrassed. "No doubt one of the grooms has fallen over one of Miss Philpott's dogs in the stables. My dear Miss Wingate," he went on hurriedly, "may I say how charming you look this evening?"

Miles let him change the subject, though the stables were much too far off to hear a dog. If he was surer of his inheritance, he'd get himself a dog, he thought, but one could not keep a country dog in London.

Nerissa, blushing, was thanking Harwood for his compliment. "And I must thank you for letting me purchase this gown and so many others," she said. "I wish you were able to let me send money to my parents. I have just been telling Miles of their plans for improving the York Playhouse when funds are available."

"Ah!" With an air of enlightenment Mr. Harwood

turned toward one of the chairs by the fireplace and frowned at it, a minatory frown.

He really was behaving very oddly. Miles was about to challenge him to explain, when the door opened again, to admit Mrs. Chidwell, Lady Philpott, and Aubrey.

Euphemia Chidwell, dressed in purple, as always, bore down upon them like Lord Byron's wolfish Assyrian upon the fold. Her teeth were bared in an improbable beam of pleasure, her eyes hard and calculating behind her lorgnette.

"Well, Miles," she said with an awful gaiety, "is not our little Nerissa a beautiful sight in her new attire? Positively alluring, I vow. In fact, irresistible!" Her elbow, sharp despite the padding on the rest of her, nudged him in the ribs, and he winced as she added in a sly whisper, "A tempting morsel to a dashing blade like yourself, no doubt."

"Miss Wingate is at last dressed as befits her station," he said, coolly reproving.

"Very proper, cousin," Aubrey said, deigning to bestow his approval. "One would not be ashamed to be seen anywhere with you." His corset creaked as he turned to Miles. "Your coat is not badly cut, Courtenay, for a provincial tailor. Naturally I have mine made in London, by Nugee. At least, I did," he reflected, recalling his changed circumstances. He retired to the far end of the room to brood in silence upon his wrongs.

"It is quite monstrous," said Lady Philpott in a voice quivering with reproach, "that my poor boy is no longer able to dress as befits *his* station."

"Now, Jane," Mrs. Chidwell chided, "you know we all agreed to let bygones be bygones."

"I'm sure it is nothing to you, Euphemia, if my

unhappy children are turned out of doors as pau-
pers. . . ."

Seeing Nerissa looked distressed, Miles drew her
away and asked her about the denizens of the York
Playhouse. The rest of the family soon came in and
they went in to dinner.

Nerissa was by now used to presiding over the
dinner table. She did her best to see that everyone's
likes and dislikes were catered to, and judging by
the number of dishes sent back empty, she succeeded.

Nor had anyone objected to her substitution of a
pleasant landscape for the painting of the dog with
the dead duck in its mouth.

Among the reams of advice puzzled out from
Mama's much-crossed letter was a caution to seat
compatible guests next to each other at her dinner
parties, with due regard to precedence. Fortunately
she did not have to worry about such matters for the
moment, with only the family present. They sat
where they chose, regardless of precedence and
compatibility. So far, thank heaven, Cousin
Euphemia had not quite come to blows with Cousin
Raymond.

Yet, they were on the verge of battle again, Effie
laying down the law on some church matter and
Raymond pugnaciously quoting the prayer book to
refute her. Nerissa met Miles's eyes, at the far end
of the table, and he rolled them comically. Wishing
she could sit next to him she signaled to the rest of
the ladies. Euphemia was forced to abandon her dis-
pute and to retire with them to the drawing room.

According to Miss Sophie, Sir Barnabas had been
able to quell the combatants with a glance. Nerissa's
only recourse was to remove one of them. In six

months they would both leave the manor—
sometimes six months seemed forever!

"You learn very fast, dear," Miss Sophie congratulated Nerissa as they sat down together on a love
seat. "Already you preside at the table as if you had
been bred to it."

"Do you think so?" she asked, pleased. "There is
such a great deal to learn. I am quite comfortable
with Cook and Mrs. Hibbert now, but Snodgrass
still puts me in a quake, I confess."

"Oh, but I, too, find him utterly intimidating,
quite like dear Barnabas at his grumpiest."

"I have not found Tredgarth grumpy, though, as
you warned me he can be. He is quite willing to
grow flowers for me. If it is fine tomorrow, I shall
walk into the village and see if anyone can spare me
some seeds and bulbs. I must go anyway. Now that
I have lady-of-the-manor clothes, it's time I found
out what the lady of the manor can do to help the
villagers."

"Do you think you ought to, dear?" said Miss
Sophie dubiously. "Of course, one contributes cast-
off clothes and sends a footman with soup when
there is sickness, but neither Effie nor Jane has ever
become personally involved."

"Mama is most particular in her letter that it is
my responsibility to become acquainted with the
tenants and their needs. She even asks after some of
the people she knew long ago."

"Dear Anthea!" Miss Sophie exclaimed, and
made no further objection to Nerissa's plans. "Pray
do not forget to take your abigail with you."

However, the next morning, when Nerissa was
ready to leave, clad in her new red cloak and stout
new walking shoes, she had sudden qualms. To
thrust herself upon several dozen strangers, she

wanted more company than just Maud. Miss Sophie
was no walker. Raymond Reece was the obvious
choice, but she still did not trust him to guide her
aright. She'd ask Miles to go with her.

"Mr. Courtenay has rid out with Mr. Bragg,
miss," Snodgrass informed her. "The bailiff, that
is."

Nerissa was surprised. Miles had told her he
meant to master the estate accounts, but she had assumed his interest lay solely in ensuring he was not
cheated. To go off with the bailiff suggested he
wished to take a more active part in managing
Addlescombe.

But he was a city dweller, a gamester and a rake,
a self-confessed wastrel. No doubt he needed to
check that matters on the ground corresponded with
the reports in the account books. Nerissa wondered
whether he could distinguish a field of wheat from
a field of barley any better than she could. At this
time of year they were all plowed up anyway, so he
might as well have stayed at home and gone with
her to the village.

Disappointed, she set off with Maud, unaware of
Sir Neville reluctantly sneaking along behind.

"I shan't do it again, I tell you, Euphemia," Sir
Neville blustered. "Can you imagine what a
nodcock I must have looked when that drunkard
Bedford came upon me sneaking behind his privy?
He invited me to make use of it."

"Oh, no!" Jane moaned. Sir Barnabas grinned.

"And all she did was chat with the villagers,"
Neville went on. He gave Effie a poisonous glance.
"It was before you moved in, or you would recall
that her mother was the same, always poking and

prying into the affairs of the lower classes. The older people remember her well."

Yes, thought Sir Barnabas sadly, he had taught Anthea a feeling of responsibility toward her dependents if not toward her rank. It had been a mistake to invite Neville to live at Addlescombe. He had hoped, on his wife's death, that his sister-in-law would be a mother to Anthea, but Jane had never had the least interest in any but her own children.

Little wonder that Anthea had been eager to leave home, yet she had turned down more than one respectable offer to run off with that penniless, low-born, disreputable mountebank. Unforgivable!

His choler revived, he drifted after the three to the dining room, where a luncheon was set out. Here he found another cause for irritability. He missed his vittles, dammit if he didn't!

Miles was hungry after a morning spent on horseback. He spared a glance for Nerissa—her rosy cheeks and sparkling eyes suggested she, too, had been out and about—and then applied himself to a plateful of cold meat, pickles, cheese, and treacle tart.

When at last, his appetite satisfied, he looked up, he found her watching him.

"I trust all is to your liking?" she asked teasingly.

"Excellent. Only one thing missing."

"Missing? Oh, dear, what?"

"Not really missing, but I have a fancy for pigeon pie, and Bragg says the pigeons were a serious pest when the winter wheat was sown. I believe I shall take a gun out this afternoon."

"I'll join you," Matilda grunted.

Nerissa seemed surprised, but she said readily, "Cook will be glad of some pigeons, I daresay, and she asked just this morning whether you mean to provide any pheasants. But, Miles, I'd like a word with you in the library before you go out. Mr. Harwood, also, if that will be convenient, sir?"

"Certainly, Miss Wingate, I am at your service."

Intrigued, Miles followed Nerissa and the lawyer to the library. What had prompted her to take charge? She didn't appear vexed or distressed, simply serious.

The library had become something of a refuge from the rest of the family, who had been accustomed to avoiding it in Sir Barnabas's day. Nerissa had had the dead-fish picture replaced by a charming portrait, rescued by Mrs. Hibbert from the attics, of her mother in a riding habit. A vase of autumn leaves stood on the long table.

Nerissa seated herself behind the desk and invited the gentlemen to take chairs opposite her. Miles hid his amusement at her businesslike air.

"I wish to consult you," she said, "because I cannot spend money without Mr. Harwood's approval and I should prefer to have Miles's agreement."

"You want a new carriage," Miles guessed.

She bent a frown upon him. "Pray do not be facetious, Miles. I was in the village this morning and I discovered that several cottages had their roofs damaged by a gale last month. As my grandfather was dying, nothing was done about them, but they must be rethatched before winter comes." She turned a severe gaze upon the lawyer. "Surely, sir, this is an allowable expenditure. I understand Sir Barnabas, whatever his treatment of his relatives, always took good care of his tenants."

"Pshaw!"

Mr. Harwood whipped out a handkerchief, buried his face in it, and sneezed an unconvincing sneeze. Miles was quite certain the irascible exclamation—

that was no sneeze!—had not been produced by the lawyer, but there was nowhere else for it to have come from. He was almost ready to believe the manor was haunted, except that he didn't believe in ghosts.

"Excuse me," said Mr. Harwood, tucking away his handkerchief. "Indeed, my dear young lady, the roofs must be mended. Mr. Bragg and Mr. Reece both did mention the matter to me, but I fear it slipped my mind in the press of urgent business attendant upon Sir Barnabas's demise. Mr. Courtenay, you have no objection, I am sure."

With Nerissa's gray eyes regarding him with mixed command and appeal, Miles could not have objected had he wanted to. "Lord, no. Have the thatcher in as soon as possible, while this fine weather holds."

"I shall go and speak to Mr. Bragg at once," said the lawyer, and trotted off.

"So you ventured to the village," Miles said. "All went well in spite of the neglected damage?"

"Yes, almost everyone seemed pleased to see me, especially those who knew Mama. And do you know, Miles, everything Cousin Raymond told me was true. He appears to be genuinely concerned for his flock. I suspected he might have misled me and I was so afraid of doing everything wrong."

"You should have asked me to go with you." Yet in fact he was pleased that she had not. The morning's expedition had done wonders for her self-confidence.

"I looked for you, but you had already gone out with Mr. Bragg, to inspect *your* flocks. I was quite astonished. Has he taught you to tell the sheep from the cows?"

"My dear girl, I have known a sheep from a cow

since I was in leading strings. I was not bred up to live by the turn of a card. I expected to inherit the family estate, and I made sure I learned how to manage it."

"Oh, I'm sorry!" Nerissa exclaimed, at once abashed, commiserating, and curious. "I thought you a thoroughgoing town beau. What happened?"

"My father had not my interest in the land. He preferred the thrill of venturing all on the turn of a card. When he died, the place had to be sold to pay his debts." Miles made no attempt to hide his bitterness, though always before he had tried to conceal it, even from Gerald Thorpe. "Despite my juvenile efforts, the estate was so run-down by then that it brought in very little."

"And you were left to live by your wits?"

Her evident sympathy soothed him enough to allow him to essay an ironic grin. "Fortunately I inherited more skill and luck with the cards than my father ever had. I cannot say I don't enjoy the excitement of gambling, but I had rather by far expend my efforts on the humdrum tasks of agriculture. I *must* inherit Addlescombe!"

"You will want to live here? Oh, dear! I supposed we should sell it at the end of six months."

"Never! Don't fret, Nerissa, we shall contrive. You shall have the money and I the land, or I shall pay you rent for your share of the estate. Harwood will work out some equitable division."

"Yes, of course."

"It's dashed lucky you don't want to live here, too. That would make matters difficult!" His words did not noticeably cheer her, so he went on. "In the meantime, enjoy Addlescombe while you can. You have a riding habit now. When shall I give you your first lesson?"

* * *

Nerissa nearly succeeded in persuading herself she didn't care a bit if Miles was glad she didn't expect to live at the manor with him. He was quite right, it was out of the question, unrelated as they were, especially since Mama and Papa showed no desire to give up acting.

It wasn't exactly that she didn't *want* to live at Addlescombe. As time passed, she took pleasure in running the household, helping the tenants, even in planning a flower garden though she might never see it bloom.

She decided to take Miles's advice and enjoy Addlescombe while she could.

Her first riding lesson had to be postponed, however. Miles had forgotten that she needed a sidesaddle. He ordered one from the saddler in Riddlebourne, but by the time it was delivered, the weather had broken. A week of wind and icy rain kept even Matilda indoors.

With everyone confined to the house, tempers frayed. To escape, Nerissa started to explore the shelves in the library. Simply handling the soft calf-skin bindings was a pleasure.

She came across a history of Britain, and was fascinated by the differences between its version and Shakespeare's of the life and death of kings. It was heavy reading, though, so she sought out lighter works when she wanted to retire early to bed with a book.

To her disappointment, if not surprise, Sir Barnabas's library was devoid of novels. She found a shelf of travelers' tales, several of which proved amusing. It was among these that she discovered a set of volumes entitled *The Arabian Nights Enter-*

tainments: Excerpts Translated from the Arabic. At least, she did not so much discover it as have one of the volumes thrust into her hand.

The effort exhausted Sir Barnabas. First he had to merge with the wall behind the bookcase, which required dematerializing still further from his already tenuous state. Then he had to wait, in extreme discomfort, until Nerissa was in the right position. And then he had to give substance to one hand and provide it with sufficient energy to shove the book off the shelf.

Drained, he fell forward, passing right through his granddaughter in the most painful manner. She shuddered as if taken with a sudden ague, but she caught the book.

Pulling her shawl closer about her, she read the title as Sir Barnabas flopped flimsily to the carpet. He had just enough strength left to pull his feet out of her way; they had suffered enough without being trampled on. Aarghh, he was dying—or would have been if he were not already dead.

"Arabian Nights," Nerissa murmured to herself. "That sounds interesting." And she went off, carrying it.

Sir Barnabas's eyes would have gleamed had they been visible. Those salacious stories of Oriental beauties and their lovers were bound to inflame the jade's passions, hitherto successfully held in check. His opinion of her would be proved right long before she reached the last volume.

Chapter Ten

In her new nightgown of fine lawn trimmed with real lace, Nerissa was soon tucked up cozily in her bed, warmed for her by Maud with a long-handled warming pan. Reaching for her book, she sniffed experimentally. No sign of the cold she thought she might be catching when that horrid chill overcame her in the library. It must have been an errant draft blowing down the chimney.

Outside, the rain beat on the windowpanes; inside was an island of comfort. She opened the book and began to read.

The first part disappointed her. She skimmed over the accounts of the unfaithful queens and their dreadful ends at the hands of their husbands. Shocking, to be sure, but she had been brought up on the works of the Bard, not to mention the bawdy comedies of the Restoration and the grim vengeances of eighteenth-century tragedy. Though herself unacquainted with the sweets of illicit passion, she had long been inured to tales of lust and licentiousness and violence.

Between dire deeds were enough fascinating descriptions of palaces and treasures, of curious customs and magics, to keep her reading until the vizier's gallant daughter entered the story. Sir Barnabas would have been disappointed to know that she fell asleep more concerned over Scheherazade's loss of her head than of her maidenhead.

The following night Nerissa went to bed directly after dinner. She could not wait to find out what happened next.

During the night the rain stopped. By morning the clouds were thinning and by midday a watery sun shone. "Perfect for a riding lesson," said Miles after luncheon. "The ground will be nice and soft to land on after all that rain."

"You mean you expect me to fall off?" Nerissa asked indignantly.

"It's more or less inevitable. Are you going to cry off?"

"Certainly not. I shall go and change into my habit at once."

She hurried upstairs and rang for her abigail. At first she had felt awkward about calling on the girl, but Maud soon made it plain that she felt slighted when her mistress managed without her. She was eager to learn. Already she worked wonders with Nerissa's hair, taught by Lady Philpott's abigail, who had little chance to practice her art on her ladyship.

Maud helped Nerissa take off her morning dress and put on the riding habit. Gold-frogged *à la militaire,* it was a rich brown color that made her hair seem almost fair, Nerissa thought, regarding herself in the looking-glass. She was glad to see that the small round hat made of cork left all her side curls visible.

"Fine as fi'pence," said Maud with satisfaction.

"I hate to think I shall get it muddy," Nerissa said regretfully. As she turned away from the mirror, the long train dragged on the floor. "Oh, but how shall I walk all the way to the stables?" she exclaimed in dismay.

"Jus' drape it over your arm, miss, like so," Maud advised. " 'Member how your ma holds hers in the pitcher? There now, if you doesn't look more like to Miss Anthea than ever."

Buoyed by the thought that she was following in Mama's footsteps, she sped down to the stables.

Miles was already there, walking a dapple-gray mare around the yard, her hooves clopping on the paving stones. He led her toward Nerissa, who took a step backward.

"It's very large."

"Not really. She was your grandfather's, and he was quite a small man. She's elderly, too, sedate, and on the sluggish side. You're not afraid, are you?"

"N-no. Matilda rides, and Mama used to, so why should not I?"

"No reason at all. Here, rub her nose, like this. Her name is Vinnie, from some fancied resemblance to Dorset Blue Vinnie cheese, I gather."

"What an insult, the poor creature." Nerissa ventured to stroke her long nose with a hand gloved in fine Limerick leather. Vinnie nodded her head, her ears pricked forward, her lustrous brown eyes inspecting Nerissa with calm interest.

"Come, we'll go to the paddock."

"For a softer landing," said Nerissa with a wry grimace. She walked beside him, casting a nervous glance over her shoulder once or twice at the following horse. Whatever Miles said, Vinnie was big.

The paddock was a half-acre meadow with a three-rail fence around three sides, hedged on the fourth. The tussocky grass certainly looked more accommodating than the flagged stableyard, but if Vinnie was so placid, perhaps she wouldn't fall after all, Nerissa thought hopefully. When Miles stopped and dropped the reins, the mare stood obligingly still.

Before Nerissa had time for second thoughts, Miles turned to her. "I'll link my hands, you put your foot in them, and I'll throw you up."

"Which foot?"

He reflected. "It must be the left one. Yes, the left. Ready?"

He stooped with cupped hands. Nerissa put her left foot in them and he thrust her upward. For a horrid moment she was afraid she was going to fly right over the other side.

The reality was far less dramatic. She landed in the saddle, and promptly slid down again.

Miles steadied her as her boots met the soggy ground with a squelching thump. Beneath the curling brim of his glossy new beaver, his blue eyes laughed at her, though he managed to keep a straight face.

"How am I supposed to stay up there?" Nerissa demanded crossly.

"You hook an unmentionable part of your anatomy—"

"Don't be a nodcock, Miles! Which part?"

"Your knee." He grinned openly. "Sorry, I didn't think to explain. You hook your right knee around the horn, see, here, at the front of the saddle, and put your other foot in the stirrup. I'll guide it in for you. Let's try again. Balance yourself with a hand on my shoulder. That's it."

This time, as a still more unmentionable part of her anatomy hit the saddle again, Nerissa jerked her right knee up and forward. Impeded by her skirts, far from hooking around the horn, it cracked painfully against the protrusion. From the waist down she was immovably swaddled. Falling forward, she grabbed Vinnie's mane in both hands. The saddle horn jabbed her in the ribs.

Miles fumbled at her left leg. "I c-can't find your f-foot," he stuttered. "You're all tangled up in your t-train." Helpless with laughter, he staggered backward.

"Miles!" she wailed. The ground, glimpsed past Vinnie's dappled neck, looked alarmingly far below. Patient Vinnie moved not a muscle.

"Cowhanded clunch!" boomed Matilda's voice somewhere nearby as Miles caught his breath and came to the rescue.

"Let go and slide down, as you did before. I'll catch you, I promise."

Cautiously she transferred one hand to the horn, clung with the other to the saddlebow, then decided to trust him and let go. As she slithered down, Miles caught her to his chest and held her while Matilda, arriving just in time, unwrapped the train from her legs.

For a few seconds his eyes were close to hers, his mouth inches from her own, his heart beating against her breast. Breathless—with annoyance, naturally—she snapped, "Put me down!"

He obeyed, setting her gently on her feet and at once removing his hands from her waist. "I'm sorry." His voice still quivered with amusement. "I didn't realize a sidesaddle makes for such complications."

"Clunch," Matilda repeated, her weather-beaten face severe. "You cannot simply throw a novice up and expect her to fall neatly into place. Come over to the fence, cousin. I'll mount from that, showing you how to arrange yourself, and then you can try it at your leisure."

"Thank you, Cousin Matilda," said Nerissa meekly.

"It's just for the sake of your unfortunate mount," said her cousin, her tone gruff as she took Vinnie's reins. "But you had better call me Mattie."

Sir Barnabas snarled. Well might Miles look sheepish, trailing the women and the mare to the fence! He'd had the perfect opportunity to kiss the wench, and he'd made a mull of it.

Not that it was entirely his fault. The baronet turned his fury on his niece. What did the creature mean by interfering? For the horse's sake—pah! Call her Mattie—tchah! She had no business toadying to Nerissa just because she couldn't bear to see a bad rider.

Sulking, he watched his granddaughter master the art of mounting, first from the fence and then from Miles's clasped hands. The long-suffering mare stood stock-still or moved equably where she was bid. As Nerissa gained confidence, she sat up straight, a graceful figure in the saddle. Matilda and Miles between them taught her how to hold the reins.

"I'm off," Matilda said at last. "Hippolyta hasn't had her exercise today. Remember, Nerissa, don't go hauling on the reins and hurting Vinnie's mouth."

"I shan't," Nerissa promised, flashing her dazzling smile. "Thank you, Mattie."

"Hmph." Matilda tramped away.

"It's time we stopped, too," said Miles. "You'll be devilish . . . dashed stiff tomorrow."

Nerissa bent a laughing frown upon him. "Pray mind your tongue, sir! Please, can I not ride just a little way across the paddock? With you leading Vinnie? Very slowly?"

"If you wish." He smiled up at her.

Sir Barnabas turned his head to make sure Matilda was well on her way. She disappeared through the arch into the stables. When he looked back, Vinnie was ambling away across the paddock, Miles at her head, Nerissa erect on her back.

Reaching the hedge, they turned and ambled back. Nerissa showed no signs of being about to part company with the saddle. As her mount's late master knew very well, the mare was of far too placid a disposition to shy unexpectedly. It was up to him to ensure that Nerissa once again fell into Miles's arms. He drifted across the grass and materialized right in front of Vinnie's nose.

With a neigh of terror, her eyes rolling, Vinnie reared. Nerissa slid down over her rump, landed flat on her back, and lay still.

Dismayed, Sir Barnabas dodged the descending hooves. He did not mean the chit any serious harm. He had expected the docile old mare to sidestep, dislodging her novice rider painlessly.

Miles was horrified. Abandoning Vinnie, he rushed to Nerissa and knelt beside her, regardless of the effect of muddy grass on his new riding breeches. He leaned over her, gently taking her hand. "Don't try to move."

She gasped for breath.

Just winded, Sir Barnabas decided. Thank heaven she had fallen in the paddock, not the stableyard.

Vinnie turned and went to investigate. She lowered her head to nuzzle Nerissa's shoulder, looking as penitent as a horse can look. Nerissa struggled to sit up.

Miles helped her, and kept his arm around her

shoulders. "I cannot imagine what got into her. Roe, the head groom, assured me she's the most tranquil beast in nature."

"Something frightened her, the poor dear." Nerissa stroked Vinnie's nose. "See how sorry she is? Miles, help me up. I'm sure I heard somewhere that if one falls from a horse, one should remount at once."

"In one of your plays, no doubt," he said with a wry smile, pulling her to her feet.

"No doubt." Stretching experimentally, she winced. "Is it good advice?"

"To prevent a loss of nerve, certainly." He picked up her hat and set it on her head. "But you must be bruised even if you haven't broken anything. You'd better go straight in, to a hot bath."

"No, I'll ride, just as far as the gate. Help me to mount."

Whatever the hussy's morals, Sir Barnabas thought with grudging pride, she had bottom, his granddaughter. And, to judge by Miles's approving face as he threw her up, he recognized it.

When they reached the gate, Nerissa was glad to slide wearily down into Miles's clasp, though Matilda had taught her to dismount without aid. She ached all over. Leaning heavily on his arm, she hobbled to the stableyard. How fortunate that he was just a friend, not a beau, for she must have looked an utter widgeon sprawling on the ground, and nothing could be less graceful than her present gait. She was sure she had mud in her hair, too, as well as all over her habit.

Before handing Vinnie over to a groom, Miles gave Nerissa an apple and showed her how to feed it to the mare on the flat of her palm. Vinnie whiffled softly, all contretemps forgotten.

"I wonder what frightened her," Nerissa said as they continued into the house. "Not something that occurs often, I trust!"

"It must have been something out of the ordinary, though I saw nothing, or she would have a reputation for being skittish." He paused outside Mrs. Hibbert's room. "I'll tell Hibby to have gallons and gallons of hot water sent up to your chamber."

"A hot bath sounds like heaven. I shall go on up."

On her way to the stairs, she found three of her relatives in the front hall. Lady Philpott stared at her in horror.

"What *have* you been doing, Nerissa?"

"Learning to ride," she said with what nonchalance she could muster.

"How enterprising," said Raymond Reece. "But I regret to say that you have just missed our visitors. What a pity you did not come in a few minutes sooner."

"A great shame," Mrs. Chidwell agreed.

"Visitors?"

"General and Mrs. Pettigrew and their two daughters, our nearest neighbors, from Kingstonriddle," Raymond explained. "They called hoping to make your acquaintance."

"I am sorry I did not meet them," said Nerissa, disappointed.

"So am I," her cousin Euphemia said with unexpected fervor.

Nerissa excused herself and started up the stairs, very conscious of their eyes on her besmirched back. With an effort she held herself straight, hoping the mud did not show too badly against the brown cloth. On the landing she turned and started up the second flight. A wave of fatigue hit her, and she stopped to gather her strength to complete the ascent.

From below came Great-Aunt Jane's complaining voice. "How can you say, Effie, that you are sorry she did not meet the Pettigrews? We do not want her to become acquainted with the neighbors, and besides, I vow I should have died of shame to present such a hoydenish creature as Neville's niece."

"Exactly," said Raymond. "She—"

"You are a ninnyhammer, Jane," Euphemia interrupted. "What could suit our purpose better than having the Pettigrews meet her when she is in such a disgraceful state?"

"Exactly," said Raymond, annoyed, "as I was about to observe."

"I'm sure you need not worry," Jane said crossly. "Sooner or later the common creature is bound to commit some dreadful, ill-bred gaucherie that will put us all to shame."

So much for professed friendship. Even Mattie had helped Nerissa only for the horse's sake. Though she had mistrusted their overtures, she was disheartened.

And Aunt Jane was all too probably right. Her confidence had grown as she learned to deal with the household, but in that process there had been room for mistakes. In meeting strangers, one faux pas could ruin her chance of acceptance, and the etiquette of morning calls was not something Mama had ever felt it necessary to teach her.

"And remember, dear," said Miss Sophie, "though in town you will offer refreshments only to particular friends, in the country visitors have come several miles to see you. It is only polite to offer tea to the ladies and a glass of wine to the gentlemen."

"That will be easy to remember." Nerissa sighed. "As for all the rest, I can only hope I shall not forget when the moment comes."

"As to that, dear Miles and I decided you ought to have a little practice as well as instruction." She bounced up in a shower of hairpins and pattered over to the door. "He is waiting in the breakfast room next door, with Ben, who will play butler. I shall fetch them."

While she waited, Nerissa picked up hairpins and glanced around the morning room to see that all was neat. To receive guests in an untidy apartment, according to Miss Sophie, showed a shocking lack of respect.

The morning room was one of Nerissa's favorite rooms. Not at its best on a dull afternoon, it was little frequented, which was why they had chosen it for her lesson. Still, the poppy and cornflower chintz was cheerful, and the vase of pearly-white honesty seedcases looked very well against the peach-colored wall.

Depositing the hairpins in a small Chinese porcelain bowl on the mantelpiece, she sat down and smoothed her apple-green skirts. She was ready for her callers.

The door opened and Ben stepped in. The young footman appeared about to burst with suppressed mirth. Playing Snodgrass's part amused him, Nerissa supposed.

"Miss Datchett to see you, miss," he announced with a snigger and moved aside.

Miss Sophie bustled in. She had put on a hat—crookedly—and gloves. Her eyes twinkled with merriment. As Nerissa rose and advanced to meet her, the correct words of welcome on her lips, a second visitor swept into the room.

The intruder, in a huge, old-fashioned, all-concealing Oldenburg bonnet and a voluminous purple pelisse, struck Nerissa with consternation. She was not ready for a real caller, especially a lady of such imposing presence.

Ben opened his mouth to announce the stranger. All that came out was a cackle, and he turned away, clapping his hand to his mouth.

A pair of bright blue eyes peered at Nerissa from the depths of the bonnet. She looked down and saw that the pelisse ended a foot above the floor. Below the hem protruded a pair of ankles clad in buff morning trousers.

"Miles!" She giggled. "Oh, Miles, you nearly gave me a spasm, you wretch. Do be yourself, pray, for I shall have to entertain gentlemen as well as ladies."

"Believe me, I cannot wait to get rid of this torturous contrivance." He undid the bonnet's ribbons, wrenched it from his head, and presented it to Ben. "Here, take the dratted thing away. How you ladies can bear to wear such monsters is beyond me."

"Fashion," said Miss Sophie profoundly. "Be careful as you take off the pelisse, Miles. Effie will truly have a spasm if you damage it. Or if she finds out you borrowed it, come to that."

"No one else's would go around me. You won't peach on me, will you, Miss Sophie?"

"What do you take me for, you naughty boy? Now go back to the door and come in again so Nerissa can show what she has learned."

Trained to the theater, and with no audience but Miss Sophie and Miles, Nerissa had no great difficulty playing the part of hostess. She found being a guest still easier when they reversed the roles and Miss Sophie was hostess. Her tutors pronounced her fit to meet the world.

"I'm sure it is Jane's duty to introduce you to the neighbors," said Miss Sophie apprehensively, "but since she has made no effort to do so, I shall take you on a round of calls. You, too, Miles, for Neville will not help you, I fear, nor Aubrey nor Raymond. Effie will be angry, I daresay, but I do not care for that. I only hope people will recall who I am."

Nerissa hugged her. "Dear Cousin Sophie, how could anyone possibly forget you? I had far rather make my bows under your auspices than Aunt Jane's."

Privately she was less positive. In company, Miss Sophie must always have been overshadowed by her sister. Great-Aunt Jane, though not much more assertive, was now the wife of a baronet and thus a person of some consequence among the local gentry.

When Miss Sophie went off to sneak Effie's pelisse back into her clothespress, Nerissa voiced her doubts to Miles.

"You and I are also of some consequence," he reminded her. "We are heirs to Addlescombe. I'm sure everyone is agog to meet us."

"Then why have only the Pettigrews called?"

"Hibby told me Sir Barnabas discouraged casual callers once he gave up hope of disposing of his niece and nephews in marriage. He was not the most sociable of men. People lost the habit of dropping in, particularly as Addlescombe is somewhat out of the way. No doubt they are waiting to see whether we are more sociable than your grandfather."

"I wish I had been in when the Pettigrews came."

"Ah, but according to Hibby, the Pettigrews are more interested in meeting me than you." Miles smiled sardonically. "It seems there are two daughters of marriageable age, and I am now a highly eligible landowner."

Unaccountably cast down, Nerissa summoned up an answering smile. "If they think so, it seems to indicate that Aunt Jane has thus far succeeded in stopping the others spreading word of the conditions in Sir Barnabas's will."

"And his condemnations of the two of us. We shall be welcomed everywhere, so don't fret, my dear girl. I'll go and make sure we have the use of the landau tomorrow."

However, another storm blew in overnight and the morning dawned with rain pelting down as if it would never stop. On the second day, the groom who rode to Riddlebourne for the post reported that the lanes were a quagmire. On the third day, he could not get through—the Riddle was in flood. Nerissa began to think fate was against her meeting the terms of her grandfather's will.

She said as much to Miles, to Sir Barnabas's delight. It was time he intervened again. If the wench was giving up hope of winning, she'd be the readier to abandon the fight against her baser urges. All he had to do was entice her into Miles's arms at a suitable time and place.

The best time and place were obvious. Even his half-witted relatives had worked out that a watch kept upon their chambers at night was more likely to be productive than any amount of following them about the countryside. At the end of the short side passage where the two chambers lay was a window in an alcove. The curtain drew across the alcove rather than the window and behind it was a large early-Jacobean chest with a carved lid. Here they took it in turns to keep a vigil, well provided with cushions to protect against the ridges and bosses of the carving.

Sir Barnabas had spent many a long night hovering nearby, waiting to catch Nerissa sneaking into Miles's room, or vice versa. He didn't care which.

So far he and his fellow watchers had waited in vain. Now he decided to take an active part.

He'd wait until midnight, when the rest of the household was settled and Miles and Nerissa would believe themselves safe from observation. They'd both be in night attire, with a choice of warm beds awaiting them. What could be more natural than that, lured out into the chilly passage, they should both repair to the same bed?

The first night after he devised his scheme, the watcher was Euphemia. He had no intention of letting Effie claim the credit for catching Miles and Nerissa in flagrante. The second night Sophie was on duty, and he didn't want to frighten her. The third night was Raymond's; the possibility of the parson attempting an exorcism made Sir Barnabas shudder.

The fourth night was Aubrey's turn. Sir Barnabas watched him settle himself in the alcove, clad in a flamboyant dressing gown of scarlet Chinese brocade over his Cumberland corset. Drawing the heavy green velvet curtain across in front of him, he sighed deeply and the creak of his corset came to his contemptuous uncle's ears.

The last of the household had retired to bed half an hour since. Wafting down the main passage, Sir Barnabas saw the strips of light beneath the chamber doors go out one by one. He was fairly sure he'd be able to direct his disturbance so that none of them woke.

Only the dim illumination of the night lamp on the hall table at the junction of the passages remained. He returned to the side passage. Miles's light was out, but Nerissa's still shone. No doubt she was avidly perusing the sensuous fantasies of the *Arabian Nights.* So much the better!

At last she blew out her candle. A few minutes later came the faint, distant chime of the clock in the front hall. Midnight.

Sir Barnabas almost wished he had chains to clank. Failing that, he reached into the inmost recesses of his tenuous being and produced a series of eerie moans, bloodcurdling groans, and banshee shrieks.

Undignified but effective, he thought as Miles's and Nerissa's doors swung open.

Chapter Eleven

Dearly as she loved Vinnie, Nerissa fancied the notion of a flying horse of ebony inlaid with gold and gems. But eager as she was to read the adventures of the prince who flew off on it, she simply could not keep her eyes open any longer. She snuffed her candle, tossed her shawl on the bedside chair, snuggled down, and in no time drifted into a dream.

The prince, a dashing young man with dark hair, blue eyes, and a slightly crooked nose, mounted the ebony horse. As they disappeared into the depths of an azure sky, the wicked sorcerer revealed that he had not shown the rider how to bring his magic steed back to earth. At once the king, his wife and daughters, and all the people of the city began to lament and shriek in despair. The din was enough to wake the dead.

More than enough to wake Nerissa. She sat bolt upright. The noise was coming from the corridor just outside her chamber.

Slipping out of bed, she reached for her shawl and threw it around her shoulders as she dashed to the door. She opened it a crack and peeked out, her hand on the latch ready to slam it shut if need be.

By the light of the night lamp, nothing was visible but the opposite wall.

The dreadful outcry died away to a whimper and stopped. Nerissa opened the door a little wider just as Miles stepped out of his chamber into the passage. He glanced around with a puzzled frown. Though he was hardly dressed for action in his long, striped nightshirt and nightcap, she felt the safer for his presence. She tiptoed out to join him.

"What was that?" she whispered.

"It sounded like a dozen cats fighting a pitched battle on this very spot," he said in a low voice, "but it must have been outside. On this side of the house, no one else would hear it."

"I suppose so, though it did sound very much as if it were indoors. I don't hear anything now. Something must have frightened them away. Let's listen for a minute."

A feeble, plaintive mutter faded into silence. Then a sudden loud creak made Nerissa jump and clutch Miles's arm.

"Someone is coming!"

He shook his head, his grin reassuring. "I think not. Don't you recognize that sound?"

She strained her ears and heard another creak, much fainter. "Not Aubrey's corsets!"

"Hush, he'll hear."

"But where is he?"

"Behind the arras."

"The arr— Oh, the curtain. What on earth is he doing there?"

"What was Polonius doing behind the arras?"

"Spying on Hamlet and— Aubrey is spying on us?" she asked, shocked.

"They take it in turns. They don't want to miss catching us at our . . . hmm, naughty business."

Nerissa's face burned. She was glad the light was so dim. "Naughty business!" she said in a wrathful whisper. "There is not going to be any naughty business. My feet are cold. I'm going back to bed. My bed. Alone."

"But of course." Miles bowed as she turned away. "Sweet dreams."

She swung back. "His corset couldn't possibly have made all that noise, could it?"

"No, but perhaps he fell asleep, had a nightmare—'Dead, for a ducat, dead!'—and cried out."

"Or it might have been cats outside." Neither explanation quite satified Nerissa, but she was soon asleep again. In her own bed. Alone.

Sir Barnabas cursed his dandified, lily-livered clunch of a nephew.

"Good heavens, you are up early, Cousin Aubrey," said Nerissa in frank astonishment. Two days had passed since the arras incident, so he had made up for lost sleep, but he was rarely seen below stairs before noon. Now here he was at the breakfast table.

"Aubrey is always *up* early," Raymond observed, ponderously witty. "He is never *down* early, however, owing to the exigencies of his toilet. 'The fashion of this world passeth away,' Aubrey. 'Vanity of vanities, all is vanity.' " He got up to leave.

Aubrey flushed, looking sulky.

" 'The glass of fashion and the mould of form,' " Nerissa quoted consolingly. " 'The observ'd of all observers.' "

Hamlet again. Avoiding Miles's eye, she heard him choke on his muffin, but Aubrey was gratified.

He smoothed the sleeve of his tight-waisted mulberry coat and modestly touched the garnet nestled in his elaborately tied cravat.

"Thank you, cousin. I have always striven to win for my family a certain reputation for elegance of dress, without assistance until you came to Addlescombe." He studied Nerissa's apricot morning gown with approval, then cast a disparaging glance at Raymond's sober black-clad back at the door. "In fact, that is why I have come down a little earlier than usual. I wish to do you a service."

"A service, cousin?"

"My man tells me you intend to make a round of the neighbors today?"

"Yes. Miles and I have already been out riding and we confirmed that the lanes are rapidly drying, as the groom reported yesterday."

"I shall go with you."

A muffin-muffled groan came from Miles's direction, but Nerissa looked at Miss Sophie and saw her give a pleased nod. Aubrey, son and heir to the baronet, would make up to some extent for Lady Philpott's defection.

"Thank you, cousin. I shall be glad of your escort," she said demurely.

"Not at all, not at all. I am, of course, acquainted with everyone of importance, and I believe I may claim a degree of prominence among those with aspirations to fashion." He glanced complacently down at his mulberry-and-cream-striped waistcoat. "I must tell you, Nerissa," he continued in a burst of candor, "everyone is vastly eager to meet you. And you, too, Courtenay, naturally."

"We are vastly flattered, Philpott," said Miles with a touch of mockery that Aubrey altogether failed to recognize. "Nonetheless, your presence cannot but facilitate our entrée into local society."

Aubrey nodded graciously. Finishing his dry toast and weak tea, he departed to complete his preparations for the outing.

"It is very good-natured of him to offer to go with us," Nerissa chided Miles. "You must not tease him so."

"He doesn't notice. As for good nature—he's panting for the prestige of being our sponsor. Surely you don't believe that nonsense about his preeminence in matters of fashion!"

Nerissa giggled. "Well, no, but he might be quite a smart if only he did not dye his hair and plaster his face with white lead and pinch in his waist with a corset."

"Really, dear," said Miss Sophie, blushing, "you simply must not mention such . . . such *items of attire* in mixed company, even if it is just dear Miles. You know, you will do much better if I go simply as your chaperon and you have Aubrey to introduce you."

"As long as you are with me, Cousin Sophie, I don't mind who does the honors." She looked at Miles, laughing. "Besides, I thought Aubrey's waistcoat monstrous elegant."

"It would not be considered out of place in town," he acknowledged reluctantly, "but for country wear it's downright foppish. Anyway, if it will make you more comfortable, Miss Sophie, it will be worth the mortification of making our appearance under his auspices."

"He's not *your* relative," Nerissa pointed out tartly.

"Thank heaven!" Miles retorted.

They set out half an hour later. The sun was just

beginning to melt the sparkling frost from leafless
twig and thorn. Swathed in rugs and scarves, hot
bricks at their feet, they had the front of the carriage
open after Nerissa soothed Aubrey's protests by taking his place with her back to the horses. He entertained the ladies by pointing out landmarks in
between his descriptions of the clothes he had worn
on previous visits to the neighbors.

Miles rode alongside, or ahead when the lane nar-
rowed, on Grandee, a splendid black with a star on
his forehead. Nerissa wished she could ride with
him, but he said it was too far for both her and
Vinnie, and Miss Sophie said it was not proper for
a lady to call on strangers on horseback. Once she
had made friends, she might ride over to see them.

Friends seemed too much to hope for, Nerissa
thought wistfully. The best she dared wish was to be
accepted as a well-brought-up young lady.

From the first, the Pettigrews appeared to have no
suspicion that she might be anything else. The family was quite new to the neighborhood, as Brigadier-
General Pettigrew, a large, hearty man with a
flourishing mustache, had purchased his small estate
after Waterloo. His stiff-mannered wife seldom
opened her mouth without mentioning the "dear
Duke" and the titled officers they had consorted
with in Brussels.

Miss Anna Pettigrew was a pretty, lively blonde,
her elder sister quiet and rather plain. The latter,
upon a signal from her mother, came to sit beside
Nerissa.

A silence ensued, during which Nerissa tried desperately to think of something both appropriate and
innocuous to say. She knew how to enter a room
and greet her hostess, how to respond to civil in-
quiries about her health and how to handle a teacup

gracefully. However, Miles and Miss Sophie had not taught her how to chatter with a young lady of her own age who would presumably expect more than polite nothings about the weather.

Recalling certain conversations with Bess Rigby, Nerissa blushed. At the same moment, Miss Pettigrew blushed and said diffidently, "I understand you have lived in the north, Miss Wingate?"

"Yes, in York."

"I have heard it is an interesting city."

Nerissa contrived to describe the beauties of the medieval streets and buildings, the minster, the city walls, and the castle, without approaching the dangerous topic of the theater. Indeed, she had attention to spare for her surroundings, which included Miss Anna flirting in a shockingly forward manner with Miles.

At least it looked shockingly forward to Nerissa, but she had to admit she was no judge. Miles seemed not at all averse, and Mrs. Pettigrew watched with a doting air. No doubt she considered Mr. Courtenay of Addlescombe a great catch for her daughter.

"It sounds delightful," said Miss Pettigrew, recalling Nerissa's wandering wits. "I have never been in the north, although we lived in many different places before Papa bought this house."

"Do you like living here?"

"Oh, yes, the countryside is beautiful, is it not?"

They talked of local beauty spots and places of interest, and Miss Pettigrew offered to take Nerissa to see them in the summer, when the weather made such outings possible. Nerissa gratefully accepted, afraid that to say she would be gone by next summer might entail an explanation of her grandfather's will.

"Were you really never in Dorset before?" Miss Pettigrew flushed. "I beg your pardon, Miss Wingate, I do not mean to pry. Lady Philpott mentioned that Sir Barnabas quarreled with your mother. I am so sorry. It must be horrid to have a breach in the family."

"I never knew my grandfather, so I never missed him." To prevent Miss Pettigrew from inquiring after her mother, she rushed on. "From what I have heard of him, I cannot be sorry to have lived at such a distance."

Slightly shocked, Miss Pettigrew nodded doubtfully. "I am fortunate," she said with another blush, "in that I shall not have to remove far from my family when I marry. The gentleman to whom I am betrothed is a curate at present, but he has a promise of a living quite nearby, at Buckford."

With a silent sigh of relief at the change of subject, Nerissa pressed her for details and was treated to a rhapsody on the positively angelic young man. After such confidences, it was only natural that Nerissa and Caroline reached Christian-name terms before Miss Sophie indicated it was time to take their leave.

Nerissa was sorry she had been unable to match Caroline's openness. However, she had learned that the best way to avoid speaking of herself was to show an interest in the person she was with.

On the other hand, Miles's interest in Miss Anna appeared to be all too personal. Did he really need to press her hand in parting and assure her fervently that he could scarcely wait for their next meeting to hear her perform upon the harp? Not that Nerissa cared, but once they were seated again in the landau, Miles at a safe distance on Grandee, she asked Miss Sophie about Anna Pettigrew's coquettish ways.

"A little forward, perhaps," Miss Sophie admitted, "though I hesitate to call her *fast*. Such conduct is barely acceptable in a young lady of impeccable background, my dear, and will not do at all for you. Not that I mean to cast the least reflection upon dear Anthea and your papa!"

"I cannot fault your deportment, Nerissa," said Aubrey judicially. "I shall not mind taking you about. Mrs. Pettigrew remarked to me that you are a pretty-behaved miss."

"For that I have Cousin Sophie to thank." Nerissa leaned forward and kissed the little lady's petal-soft cheek.

At the Digbys, Nerissa was singled out by the younger son, Mr. Clive. Though not much older than herself, he had the red nose of the confirmed toper, and he wore an ancient shooting coat with sagging pockets and curious tufts of feathers stuck in the lapels. Putting her newfound wisdom into practice, she soon discovered that he was a passionate angler. The wire and feather devices were fishing flies, and the hue of his nose, she guessed, was due to sitting out in the damp in all weathers. Before they parted she knew more about the pursuit of perch, roach, tench, chub, gudgeon, and the wily pike than she could possibly have imagined there was to know.

As he handed her into the carriage, he begged permission to call on her at Addlescombe. She graciously consented, though she suspected that after a few more half-hours with him she would never be able to eat fish again.

She noticed that Miles looked sour. No pretty girls for him to flirt with at the Digby's, she thought.

The lack was doubly remedied at the Firstons', where they were invited to take a nuncheon. The young squire's two sisters gaily plied Miles with delicacies, and he blatantly reveled in their attentions. Their widowed mother, dressed in slate-gray satin overelaborately trimmed with lace and jet, discussed the finer points of fashion with Aubrey. Nerissa was entertained by the younger Mrs. Firston, a friendly young matron who was more than willing to discourse endlessly on the cleverness of her two small children.

Now and then Mrs. Firston broke off to say anxiously, "I do hope Peter will come home in time to make your acquaintance, Miss Wingate."

Mr. Firston was riding about his estate with his brother, John, who was a doctor with a practice based in Porchester. "You will like John," Mrs. Firston assured Nerissa. "The children are very fond of their uncle, and he of them." She could give no higher praise.

Nerissa had just promised to visit the nursery after luncheon when the two young men came in. John Firston, a tall, blond, handsome gentleman, was urged by his sister-in-law and his mother to take the place beside Nerissa, which he did without visible reluctance.

While he ate, he satisfied Nerissa's genuine curiosity about the life of a country doctor. She found him charming and was sorry when, after the meal, he apologized for having to rush off to see his patients.

"I must dash up to the nursery before I go," he said with a smile. "Paul and Bella would never forgive me if I failed to visit them."

"Do take Miss Wingate with you," Mrs. Firston urged. "I must have a word with Peter before I go up."

On the stairs, Dr. Firston turned to Nerissa, his face tinged with pink, and said hesitantly, "If you have no objections, Miss Wingate, I should like to bring a young lady to call on you at Addlescombe. She is Miss Herriott, daughter of the vicar of Penfold."

"I shall be pleased to make Miss Herriot's acquaintance," Nerissa told him, glad that despite his relatives' matchmaking, he appeared not to be on the catch for a supposedly wealthy wife. At present she felt far more in need of female friends than of admirers.

When they left the Firstons, Miss Sophie was wilting after the agitation and exertions of the day. Miles curtly ordered the coachman to turn the horses' heads for home. He rode ahead, and when the landau reached the manor, he was waiting to hand the old lady down and give her his arm into the house.

"I'd like a word with you in the library, Nerissa," he said with a foreboding look, "if you can spare me a moment."

"As soon as I have taken off my hat and seen Miss Sophie laid down comfortably on her bed. Now, don't argue, pray, Cousin Sophie. You will feel much better for a little rest, and Miles can wait."

Despite her resolute response, Nerissa worried as she helped Miss Sophie take off her bonnet and pelisse and doffed her own. Had she done something dreadfully wrong which everyone but Miles had been too polite to mention? She had never seen him so stern.

She tidied her hair, wishing it were as fair as Miss Anna Pettigrew's, took up a shawl, and went down to the library.

As she entered, Miles stopped pacing and turned toward her. "I just want to warn you," he said stiffly, "or, rather, to remind you, that your suitors will have to be told about Sir Barnabas's will."

"Suitors!"

"Clive Digby and the doctor fellow. They are courting you believing you a wealthy heiress. You cannot marry without explaining that your inheritance is conditional, and I cannot suppose you wish to reveal the conditions."

"For heaven's sake, Miles, I'm not about to marry anyone!" Nerissa was exasperated, and hurt by the implication that her supposed wealth was the only reason for anyone to want to marry her. She was not about to tell him John Firston already had a sweetheart—and she wouldn't have Clive Digby if he was filleted and dished up with lobster sauce, garnished with lemon and parsley. "Besides, the same goes for you," she snapped.

"For me?"

"Anna Pettigrew and *both* Miss Firstons! How do you propose to reveal the mythical nature of *your* fortune to their guardians?"

He flushed and retorted angrily, "I can wait to propose until the myth becomes reality. You cannot choose the moment when you receive an offer."

"True, nor can I stop them courting me."

"You can discourage them."

"I don't know how. As you must be well aware," she continued, her lip curling in scorn, "the only way to deter the sort of men who pursue actresses is frankness of a kind which would be certain to give offense to honorable gentlemen. And you cannot teach me, since I am sure you have never been the recipient of polite discouragement. Your success—with actresses—is notorious, is it not?"

" 'A hit! A hit! A palpable hit!' " Miles muttered as she swept from the room.

* * *

Effie's voice reverberated through the small back parlor. "Aubrey and Sophie took Courtenay and the girl to call on our neighbors."

Her denunciation brought a shocked silence.

Anticipating an enjoyable time, Sir Barnabas settled himself on a china cabinet. He would not for the world have missed this meeting of his abominable relatives.

Jane Philpott stared at her son in horror. "Aubrey, how could you! To lend that creature your countenance when I have specifically refused to take her about! You will ruin us."

"She is a credit to the family," said Aubrey sulkily, with a contemptuous glance around the drabs and dowdies crowded around him in the small back parlor. "Nothing tawdry, complete to a shade. And her behavior was perfectly decorous, too," he said as an afterthought.

"This is your fault, Jane," Effie accused. "If you had only agreed to let me tell everyone she is an actress, no one would have received her. I shall have to disclose it now."

"No-oo!" Jane bleated. "Think of the disgrace if people knew my son had introduced an actress into their homes!"

"You will keep a still tongue, Euphemia," said Sir Neville, for once supporting his wife, "if you want to live at the manor when I come into my rightful inheritance. No one must find out we have an actress in the family."

"That being so," Raymond put in, "if she never meets anyone, how can she be discredited?"

"You cannot persuade me Aubrey thought of that." Effie's furious face was an excellent match for her purple gown. "Let alone Sophie. She is a snake in the grass, whom I have nurtured in my bosom all these years."

Sir Barnabas sniggered. The bosom in question was large enough to provide every comfort, but Sophie had never rested easy there. He was glad she was not there to be tongue-lashed, and glad she had stolen a march on her sister even if she had thereby outflanked him, too.

So Nerissa had won her spurs, the clever chit. Still, the battle was yet to come and Raymond was right—unless she met the enemy, she could not be defeated. Sooner or later without fail she'd show her true colors.

He was irritated when Effie agreed with him. "No matter," she said, calming down. "Nerissa was bound to meet people in the end, and with her upbringing she will soon come to grief without our intervention. Let us concentrate on Miles Courtenay for the moment."

"I don't see what we can do about Courtenay," Neville grumbled. "You can't force a man to seduce a wench."

"We could invite an opera dancer to seduce him," Effie suggested outrageously, "since Nerissa is playing the prude."

"Do you know any?" Raymond asked with an interest most unbecoming to his cloth.

"No doubt such creatures can be bought. Oh, stop wringing your hands, Jane. I know you will not allow it, though I am certain it would work. He has been celibate for nearly two months now."

Matilda came in just then, in a muddy riding habit as usual. "Nerissa's in high dudgeon with Miles," she announced.

"How do you know?"

"I asked where he was just now when I met her

in the hall, and she stuck her nose in the air and said she neither knew nor cared."

Neville gloomed. "No hope of her succumbing to Courtenay's charms, then."

"Don't be a lobcock, Neville," said Effie, "it won't last long. And you are forgetting the other condition in Barnabas's ridiculous will. Miles has also been deprived of the excitement of gambling for two months. If he sees us wagering real money on a game of cards instead of playing for fish as we usually do, he will be unable to resist joining in."

Matilda shrugged. "I shan't play. I don't know the first thing about cards and I'm going up early anyway. There's a meet tomorrow."

"As a man of the church, I cannot condone gambling," Raymond said sanctimoniously.

"Fustian! If you prefer, you may be the one to fetch Harwood once Miles is on the hook, but we shall not place real wagers. We shall agree to return all stakes after we have lured him into placing his."

"Suppose we lose to *him?*" Aubrey protested. "He will never agree to return his winnings."

"Wantwit," Effie snapped, "what does losing a few shillings matter when you stand to win Addlescombe and a fortune?"

About time they recollected the gambling clause, Sir Barnabas thought. Effie's notion made sense, though, blast the woman. After a few weeks' deprivation, Miles must be all the more likely to succumb.

Under normal circumstances Sir Barnabas wouldn't put it past his granddaughter to warn Miles away from the cards even though she stood to gain all he would lose. However, since she was miffed at him, he'd have nothing to distract him from the fatal fascination of the game.

Chapter Twelve

Miles was surprised at how bereft he felt. The peagoose was still in a pet with him, and all over a few words of friendly advice. Seated at the other end of the dinner table, she studiously avoided his eye—and glowered if she chanced to catch it.

Toying with food which had lost its savor, he signaled to Snodgrass to refill his wineglass. The ruby claret was the same color as her gown, and how well it suited her!

Maybe he had phrased his advice badly, leading her to believe he thought Digby's and Firston's only interest in her was her money. Nothing could be further from the truth. She was a deuced pretty girl—though not to his taste, he hastily reminded himself—and her artless manner of looking up at a man was enough to win any heart.

If only the rest of her devilish family would go away, he'd sort things out with her in no time. Instead, she rose and led the ladies out, leaving him with her grandfather's excellent port and no congenial company in which to enjoy it, since Harwood was abed with a cold.

How was he to explain to her that he had only been flirting harmlessly with Miss Anna and the

Firston girls, without implying she had a right to an explanation?

Three glasses of port, on top of the wine and very little to eat, made everything seem easy. All he had to do was reassure her that she had charms enough to make her fortune irrelevant. Then they could spend a comfortable evening together, discussing plays, or the estate, or, like Miranda and Ferdinand, playing chess, the one game not associated with gambling.

Somewhat surprised to discover Sir Neville, Aubrey, and Raymond had departed unnoticed while he brooded over his glass, Miles made his way through to the drawing room. Nerissa was not there.

At the near end of the room a card table had been set up for the usual game of quadrille or casino, played for ivory fish. Miles had never been able to summon up any enthusiasm for either game, nor for the winning of worthless counters from inexpert players.

By the farther fireplace, Lady Philpott was occupied with her endless embroidery. Opposite her, Miss Sophie wielded a netting shuttle, her plump little hands remarkably nimble and dextrous. She smiled at Miles. If Mrs. Chidwell had read her a scold on account of their outing, she did not seem to have taken it to heart.

Beside her sat Reece, reading aloud in a monotone from what sounded alarmingly like a collection of sermons. Miles glanced back at the card table, where the parson was generally to be found of an evening, with Sir Neville, Aubrey, and Mrs. Chidwell. The other three were there, an empty chair in Reece's place. Mrs. Chidwell was dealing for vingt-et-un, her hands as nimble with the cards as her sister's with the netting shuttle.

Miles felt a stir of interest. He had always been lucky at vingt-et-un. Perhaps, since Nerissa had deserted him, he should try his skill against Mrs. Chidwell, though a deft dealer was not necessarily a proficient player.

As he moved toward the table, Sir Neville and Aubrey each placed their bets, and the stakes were not fish but shillings. A faint thrill raced through Miles's veins.

He reached for the back of the empty chair.

"Miles?" Nerissa's soft, hesitant voice came from behind him.

The spell broke. That innocuous game meant not the possible loss of a few shillings but the certain loss of Addlescombe.

Wild with relief, he swung around and sped to meet her, both hands held out. As she clasped one, her other holding a book, he blurted out, "I'm not going to marry Anna Pettigrew, nor either of the Firston girls. I'm not going to marry anyone, or not for years and years, at least."

She smiled. "And I'm not going to marry Dr. Firston, who gave me a very strong hint that he is already promised elsewhere, nor Clive Digby."

"You don't care for Digby? Don't worry, I'll find you others more to your liking."

Nerissa did not appear to find his offer inspiriting. She ignored it in favor of answering his question. "Mr. Digby has absolutely nothing on his mind but dace and bream, and I do not care to be wooed with fish."

"Fish!" The word struck Miles as exquisitely funny. "There's no harm in fish. It's shillings are the danger."

"So you *were* about to play. I feared it."

He drew her to a confidante midway between the

two groups. "I was tempted, I confess." His head was clearing. At the card table, he saw, the three players were muttering together, their expressions disgruntled. "Do you know, I suspect they made a deliberate attempt to entice me. Not that they invited me to join them or even looked at me, or I might have guessed. But I have never seen them play for money before, and since neither you nor Harwood was here to restrain me . . ."

"I went to fetch my book." She held it up, and he read the title: *The Arabian Nights' Entertainments.* "I fell asleep in the middle of a story last night. Miles, do you want to play cards with me? I don't know many games, but I am quite good at picquet."

"Picquet! That's a gamester's game if any is. Look, having failed to hook me, they are pocketing their shillings and bringing out the fish."

She glanced around. "Oh, dear, it does seem they were trying to trick you into gambling. How underhanded!"

"Did you play picquet for money?"

"No, only for fun because it was a revolving game, backstage. Whoever was offstage for long enough would play for a while and then give up his hand to the next. I used to play in between helping people change costumes and mending rents."

Miles laughed. "A test of concentration indeed. But I wouldn't dream of playing for money with you even if there were no chance of anyone catching me, and it's dull work playing for fish."

"Oh, not fish! I thought we might play for imaginary riches." Her eyes sparkling, she held up her book. "Carnelian and sardonyx, jacinth and spinel, gold-broidered brocade, Damascene nenuphars—whatever they are—and even talking dogs and flying horses."

"Good Lord!" Startled, he reached for the book, flipped it open at random, and skimmed a page. "Why be so modest? I wager 'a palace of Sumaki marble with pillars of alabaster and mosaics of lapis lazuli and gold' that I can pique, repique, and capot you. What *is* a nenuphar?"

"I don't know, but is it not a splendid word? I have been meaning to look it up in Sir Barnabas's dictionary. Shall we play?"

"Yes, but you must lend me the book or you'll have the advantage of me in knowing what stakes are available."

"This is the second volume. I'll show you where the first is, in the library. Or we could read aloud to each other," she suggested shyly. "I cannot remember half the exotic treasures, and I shall not mind starting at the beginning again."

"A splendid notion. Neither of us could possibly read as badly as your cousin." He nodded toward the parson, who was still droning on, his face sour. No doubt he had been involved in the failed plot, too.

"Raymond is reading a shockingly dull sermon, which is part of the reason I went to fetch my book."

Miles did not inquire as to the other part of her reason, being fairly sure she had simply wanted an excuse to continue avoiding him. Only her concern for him, to stop him ruining himself, had made her relent.

He smiled at her. "Most fortunate, or you might not have thought of such magnificent stakes. We shall keep a list of treasures, roughly sorted by value so we don't find ourselves wagering marble palaces against mere pearls."

"In that case, you had best read whilst I write. I

have seen your hand and I doubt there is enough paper in the house."

"My writing does tend to sprawl a bit," he admitted with a grin. "Let's go and find the first volume."

When, having discovered that nenuphars were mere water lilies, they returned from the library, Miss Sophie wanted to talk to them. With a defiant air she insisted she was eager to take them next day to visit two or three more families living at a somewhat greater distance from Addlescombe.

"Effie may say what she pleases," she said stubbornly, "if she and Jane will not introduce you, then I am determined to do so. It is my duty and my pleasure, though it was a great help to have Aubrey with us today, was it not?"

Nerissa pressed her hand. "I was happier to have you beside me, Cousin Sophie, but I daresay Miles and I might contrive without you if we must. I don't wish to cause you trouble with your sister."

"Oh, no, pray do not regard it. You are such a comfort to me, Nerissa dear. I feel quite bold now that you are here, I vow. To tell the truth," she added in a puzzled voice, "though Effie was vexed because I had gone against her wishes, she did not seem disturbed by your having met people. She did not forbid me to present you to the rest of our neighbors."

"How odd!" Nerissa said with a smile. "Cousin Euphemia is so accustomed to laying down the law, I am surprised she missed such an excellent opportunity."

"So we shall go tomorrow?"

"Miles?"

"Yes, certainly. I have no urgent business on the estate."

"Then let me tell you whose acquaintance you shall make," said Miss Sophie happily.

As she began to describe the Nidds, the Loftings, and the Hazlitts, Miles resigned himself to a postponement of his reading with Nerissa. Listening with half an ear, he wondered whether Mrs. Chidwell was truly unperturbed by Nerissa's introduction to the local gentry. Surely she was not so blind as still to believe Nerissa was a wanton slut. Complying with Sir Barnabas's third clause would be no trouble to her, so her greedy relatives must count on her failing to win acceptance.

That was it. They were sure that however well she started, sooner or later, one way or another, she would forfeit the neighbors' esteem. By not introducing her themselves, they hoped to insulate themselves from her coming disgrace.

Miles's surmise was bolstered when Aubrey left the card table and came to join them.

"We shall pay more calls tomorrow?" he said. "Splendid, splendid. All went very well today, did it not? I knew my influence would suffice to insure your welcome."

Aubrey must be included in the others' scheming. Such was the man's conceit, he was unable to imagine his standing affected by his young cousin's downfall. Miles fumed.

He decided not to relay his guess to Nerissa. Her confidence was shaky enough without knowing her ill-wishers expected her to fail. They might be right, alas. Her upbringing had been deficient, and he and Miss Sophie could not possibly cover every contingency.

The worst threat was from her suitors, he reckoned. How the devil was he to protect her from them?

The next day added a third to their number—for Miles was not inclined to dismiss the handsome Dr. Firston, whatever the fellow had hinted to Nerissa. Jeremy Lofting showed a decided interest in Nerissa, and he could not be dismissed as a fortune hunter, as he was heir to a very pretty property between Riddlebourne and Porchester. He had progressive ideas about agriculture, too, many of which Miles resolved to copy. It was difficult to disapprove of him. He just was not quite right for Nerissa.

Miles racked his brain all the way home, without success. Though he came up with plenty of ways to stop any courtship in its tracks, all were liable to ruin Nerissa.

Snodgrass met them at the front door, looking even more impassive than usual.

"The Digbys called in your absence, miss," he told Nerissa.

"Oh, I am sorry to have missed them."

"Mr. Digby—Mr. Clive Digby, that is—left a . . . an offering, miss. Perhaps *gift* is the correct word."

"A gift? Where is it?"

"I took the liberty, miss, of having it conveyed to the kitchens. Cook, I may say, was delighted but awaits your instructions on the precise disposition of . . . the gift."

"Snodgrass, what *is* it?"

"A basket of fish, miss. Very fine perch, I understand, fresh caught this morning."

Nerissa burst into peals of laughter. Miles caught the butler's eye and was prepared to swear he saw the corner of that very proper servant's mouth twitch.

"Oh, dear," Nerissa said unsteadily, "I must confess I expected only monologues on fish from him,

not baskets of fish. How very kind, to be sure. I'll
go and see Cook."

As she and Snodgrass went off and Aubrey
started up the stairs, Miss Sophie said to Miles in a
perplexed tone, "I daresay it is unexceptionable for
a young lady to accept a gift of fish from a gentleman? If it were jewelry or clothes, one would know
it must be sent back."

"I'd say a basket of perch is on a par with a box
of bonbons," he reassured her.

"But it is not quite proper to give any gift when
they have met only once."

Miles had to agree that Clive Digby's courtship
was proceeding with indecorous celerity. "Next time
we see him," he said, "you and I must each thank
him for the fish as though we considered it a present
to the household."

"Dear Miles, how clever you are."

"You had best warn Nerissa, and advise her as to
what gifts are acceptable."

"No doubt actresses are willing to take anything
they are offered, poor things," said Miss Sophie
with an air of worldly wisdom.

"They don't always wait for an offer," Miles told
her sardonically. He paused, then continued hesitantly. "Since Digby appears to be making Nerissa
the object of his attentions, she needs to know how
to conduct herself with an admirer, and not only
where gifts are concerned. I cannot claim to be able
to advise her. Can you?"

Miss Sophie turned scarlet. "Oh, yes, dear. I was
not without suitors in my youth. Though Effie did
not consider any of them suitable," she added wistfully.

They both started and looked around as an angry,
wordless mutter filled the air.

"Such odd noises the wind makes sometimes," said Miss Sophie. "Yes, I will speak to Nerissa about her beaux. I do believe Mr. Lofting is quite *épris* also, do not you? And perhaps Dr. Firston. It is not to be wondered at. Nerissa is a delightful girl."

Miles smiled as he watched her go, but his smile soon changed to a frown. The rules of propriety changed at a snail's pace compared to niceties of etiquette and fashion, so Miss Sophie should be able to advise Nerissa adequately. However, trouble still lay in wait if any of the gentlemen in question decided to propose to her before she was assured of her inheritance.

Though she could avoid explanations by refusing a proposal, some inexplicable feminine whim might actually lead her to wish to marry one of the fellows. Miles—nobly, he felt—wanted her to be able to accept if she so chose. Thus the difficulty was reduced to preventing too early an offer.

A stroke of genius hit him. All he had to do if Digby, Firston, or Lofting showed signs of serious intentions was to remind him that though forbidden to put on blacks, Nerissa was in mourning for her grandfather. Under the circumstances, a proposal of marriage would be crassly insensitive.

On the other hand, no gentleman with the slightest claim to sensitivity would regard *fish* as an appropriate present for the young lady of his choice. . . . He'd have to keep an eye on Clive Digby.

The perch were served at dinner, breaded and fried in butter, garnished with parsley and lemon slices. The delicate white fish was delicious, and Miles saw Nerissa eating some with every evidence of pleasure. She cast him a quizzical smile the length of the table.

Forgoing port, he followed the ladies out after the meal. "You enjoyed the perch?" he asked, pulling up a chair beside Nerissa at a small Pembroke table near the confidante.

"I don't know when I have tasted better fish," said Nerissa. "One could never buy it so fresh in York. I am sorry I laughed at Mr. Digby. After all, I believe I shall quite like to have a beau who is a dedicated angler."

"I used to fish when I was a boy," Miles informed her, displeased by her change of heart toward Clive Digby. "In a river near my home or the Addle when I visited my godfather. Maybe I shall try my hand again when I have time to spare. I wonder whether the fishing rod I had here is still about."

"Mr. Harwood would let you buy one, I expect. Will you teach me to fish?"

"You might do better with lessons from Digby."

"Oh, no! I had rather learn from you."

"Very well, then," Miles agreed, gratified, "provided we have a spell of weather neither too wet nor too cold. It's not usual for a female to fish, but I see no objection."

"Perhaps I had best ask Miss Sophie."

"Not now," he protested as Nerissa began to rise. "Let us read, before we are interrupted. I put the first volume on the mantelpiece before dinner."

While he retrieved the book, she took from the table's drawer several sheets of paper and two pencils. Returning, he sat down and opened the book. Nerissa moved a tall branch of candles so that the light fell on the page and on her paper.

"This will be a change from my usual reading," Miles remarked.

"What do you read?"

" 'Words, words, words.' "

She laughed. " 'What is the matter, my lord?' "

" 'Between who?' "

" 'I mean, the matter that you read, my lord.' "

"Sheep and turnips. Aubrey suits the role of Polonius better than you do."

"Lucky for him that you are no Hamlet. I suppose they will watch us closely once we begin to play, hoping to catch you making real wagers."

"We shall leave our lists lying about for them to peruse. I doubt any of them is quite crack-brained enough to believe I have actually staked a talking dog. Are you ready? Good heavens, I'll skip the apostrophe to Allah and Mohammed if you don't mind. Here we go."

He began to read. The first part of the story had few treasures worthy of note apart from saddles of gem-encrusted gold, which sounded, as he commented, deuced uncomfortable. With nothing to write, Nerissa started to sketch Oriental-looking figures as she listened.

Miles broke off to say, "Those are good. I didn't know drawing was one of your accomplishments."

She looked up, her face flushed in the candlelight. "Only costumes. Turbans and veils and draperies. As you see, the faces are blank. I cannot draw portraits or landscapes or other ladylike subjects, but I found it easier to make costumes if I sketched them first. We once put on Racine's *Bajazet,* in translation of course, and that has a Turkish setting, you know. It was not a success."

"Not because of your costumes."

"I hope not," she said with a smile. "No, Mr.

Fothergill, our manager, was forced to conclude that
Racine seemed stilted to audiences used to Shakespeare. Do go on. You read well."

Pleased, he continued. A few lines later he came
to the young king's discovery of his wife's infidel-
ity. The brief passage was finished before it struck
him that he should not be reading such things to an
innocent young lady.

But Nerissa appeared unconcerned, continuing
her sketching without a pause. Of course, she had
been brought up on *Othello* and the like, he reminded himself. He read on.

The description of the carryings-on of the second
queen and her attendants was another matter, not a
trifle warm, not even merely indelicate, but positively ribald. Miles, his face hot, found himself
reading faster and faster in a softer and softer voice.

Nerissa's face was in shadow, her head bowed
over her drawing. As far as he could tell, she was
oblivious of the indecency of the story. He ought to
warn her of the utter impropriety of listening to
such stuff, but he could not bring himself to speak
of it.

Instead, he said, "I should never make an actor,
I'm already growing hoarse. Is it too early to ring
for the tea tray?"

"No, of course not." She jumped up and went to
ring the bell.

While she was gone, Miles skimmed through the
next part of the book and was horrified to find it going from bad to worse. Yet when he opened it at
random, the page he read was entirely innocent. For
the most part, it consisted of a list of exotic fruits
and flowers, including the Damascene nenuphars
and such delicacies as Osmani quinces and Omani
peaches.

He decided the only thing to do was to read ahead each night and mark, to be omitted the next evening, those passages that were unfit for a delicate female's ears.

Nerissa did not return to Miles. She did not see how she could ever face him again. The indecorous stories that had seemed unimportant when read to herself became shocking from the lips of a handsome rake. Shocking and disturbing, leaving her with the most peculiar quivery feeling.

She could not possibly tell him she didn't want him to read anymore. He would want to know why. She should never have started the business. What was she to do?

For the present, she told Snodgrass to bring in the tea tray, and then went to speak to Miss Sophie, hoping her face showed none of her agitation. By the time she was ensconced behind the tea things and Miles came to fetch his cup, she was calmer. Nonetheless, her heartbeat sped up on his approach.

"I've found an account of the preparations for a feast," he said. "Instead of reading further tonight, shall we play a game, wagering—let's see—Sultani citrons and musk-scented fritters on the outcome?" He pulled a face. "Though I'm not sure I fancy musk-scented fritters."

Suppressing a sigh of relief, Nerissa wrinkled her nose. "Nor I. And have you come across coffee flavored with ambergris? It sounds quite horrid. Still, it scarcely matters, since for us they exist only in fancy."

"Quite. The immaterial is immaterial," Miles agreed, and took his cup of tea, smiling at her in a way that made her feel shaky all over again.

Immaterial! Sir Barnabas pursed his invisible lips

in annoyance at this cavalier dismissal. He'd show them the importance of the incorporeal.

His sharp eyes had not missed Nerissa's perturbation when Miles read that disgraceful story. He must strike while the iron—or in this case the hussy's passion—was hot. Tonight she'd not resist Miles's advances if he sought her bed.

Fortunately Aubrey was not on watch tonight. Last time his dead uncle had succeeded in luring the pair out of their rooms, the numbskull had been too terrified to budge an inch yet had given away his presence and ruined the plan. This time Sophie was on duty. As Sir Barnabas was well aware, the poor dear always sank into a deep slumber within half an hour of concealing herself behind the curtain. She would not interfere.

As before, he watched the lights go out one by one, until only the night lamp still burned. Then he slithered around the edge of the curtain to make sure Sophie was sleeping.

She was still wakeful, shivering as she tried to pull her shawl around her shoulders and hung a rug about her knees at the same time. It was a cold, clear night, the moon shining in at the window. By morning there would be a heavy frost.

Sir Barnabas wished he could tell her to go to bed. He was still able to make himself seen and understood only to Harwood, and whenever he did, the lawyer read him a lecture on the folly of his will. If he touched Sophie, he would only make her colder, so he pressed into the corner of the alcove, making himself as small as possible.

At last her eyes closed and her face relaxed in sleep. The lines of anxiety smoothed away, she looked years younger. As Sir Barnabas gazed down at her, his immaterial heart twisted painfully within him. If only . . .

Nonsense! It was far too late for regrets. He slipped out into the passage.

And he groaned and he howled and he screeched and he bawled and he bellowed, and finally he gnashed his teeth. Not the slightest sign of life from either Miles's or Nerissa's chamber. Maybe he had left it too late and they were fast asleep, or else they had convinced themselves that he was nothing but a horde of squabbling cats.

How dared they so insult him!

Gibbering with rage, he squeezed under Miles's door. Miles lay sprawled on his back, the bedclothes spread over him in a loose, disorderly heap.

Sir Barnabas grinned nastily. It was a cold night. If Miles was sufficiently chilled, he'd seek warmth, and the nearest source of warmth was in Nerissa's bed. Gathering his strength, the baronet pulled and pushed the covers onto the floor—counterpane, blankets, sheet, and all.

Exhausted, he sank down onto Miles's bare feet, adding the cold of the grave to that of the frosty night.

Miles shivered, woke, and felt for his blankets. His groping hands met nothing. He sat up, dislodging Sir Barnabas, then swung his legs off the bed. Sir Barnabas landed on the floor. Miles reached for his dressing gown and thrust his arms into the sleeves. Candlestick in hand, stumbling across the room, he raised the latch, opened the door, and stepped out into the passage.

Painfully, Sir Barnabas crawled after him and reached the threshold just in time to see him cast a yearning look at Nerissa's chamber door.

Chapter Thirteen

Miles found it hard to sleep after seeking out and marking the naughtiest bits of the first few stories. Two months without a woman and four to go! No wonder his awareness of Nerissa just next door was such an aching temptation however hard he tried to persuade himself he looked upon her as a little sister.

At last he fell into a restless sleep, tossing and turning and tangling with his blankets. His dreams were filled with a horrid caterwauling, but he was awoken by frozen toes.

He must have kicked his bedclothes onto the floor. Well, he was quite capable of remaking the bed without waking a servant, but he needed light to do it. Rather than wrestle with a tinderbox, he'd go out to the night lamp in the passage.

Tying the cord of his dressing gown, he picked up his bedside candle and felt his way to the door. His teeth chattered. Simply climbing back into a cold bed would never warm him up, he thought. As he stepped out into the passage, he cast a longing look at Nerissa's chamber door, behind which she lay curled in slumber, warm as toast.

Sternly admonishing himself, he went to light his

candle with a spill from the vase by the lamp. He decided to go down to the kitchens to see if he could find and heat a couple of bricks or a warming pan, and perhaps a hot drink.

First he returned to his chamber to put on his slippers, which were hiding under a chair, and to make the bed ready for whatever heating device he could procure.

When he returned to the passage, he suddenly wondered who was hiding behind the curtain, spying on his comings and goings. Though it made no difference to his actions, he was growing tired of the surveillance. Perhaps it was time to disabuse the watchers of the notion that he and Nerissa were ignorant of their presence.

He strode past Nerissa's chamber to the end of the passage and flung open the curtains.

The rattle of the curtain rings roused Miss Sophie. She huddled there, wrapped in an inadequate shawl, blinking up at Miles, shivering convulsively.

"Good gad, what folly is this?" He took her bluish, icy hand. "My dear Miss Sophie, you'll catch an inflammation of the lungs. To bed with you!"

"I d-don't think I c-can m-move, M-Miles."

"That doesn't surprise me in the least. Here." He picked up her rug from the floor, where it had slipped, and draped it over her, then took off his dressing gown and tucked it around her shuddering shoulders. "Wait just a moment."

He went to bang on Nerissa's door and, when that brought no immediate answer, opened it. Holding his candle high, he saw her sitting up in bed, huge dark eyes fixed on him.

"Miles!" she squeaked, pulling up the covers.

'Don't be missish. I need your help. Miss Sophie's out here freezing to death.''

"Oh, Miles, I'll come at once." She scrambled out of bed, treating him to a brief glimpse of one slim white leg. He turned away, returned to the alcove, and a moment later she joined him, decently swathed in her dressing gown. "Dear Cousin Sophie, what a sorry pickle you are in. Miles, can you carry her to her chamber? I shall go ahead to open the door."

He gently deposited Miss Sophie upon a chair by her smoldering fire, which did little on such a night to drive the chill from the room. Nerissa chafed the poor little lady's hands.

"I shall d-d-do very well now, d-dear," said Miss Sophie. "I am s-so s-sorry . . ."

"Nonsense," said Nerissa firmly. "I shall help you into your night rail. Miles, do you go down and wake Lil—the kitchen maid. She sleeps on a pallet by the kitchen fire. Have her prepare a warming pan or hot bricks. Or better, both, and a mug of hot flannel besides. Here is your dressing gown." She blushed as she handed it to him without looking at him.

Miles put it on and went down as ordered, but he had no intention of waking Lil if he could help it. The fewer people who knew about the night's alarms and excursions the better—except that he was determined to confront Mrs. Chidwell and forbid her to make her sister stand watch. If the widow chose to do so herself, that was her own affair. She was well enough padded to survive the cold.

The kitchen maid was fast asleep on her straw pallet by the hearth, snuggled beneath a tattered blue and yellow patchwork quilt, her rosy cheek pillowed on her hands. Probably it was cozier there for such a slip of a girl than up in the servants' garrets, but Miles resolved to ask Nerissa about it.

He must also explain to her that "hot flannel" was no drink for a lady. Though the combination of gin and beer, heated, sweetened, and spiced, was certainly warming, Sir Barnabas would never have allowed a drop of blue ruin in the house. A negus of wine and hot water was what Miss Sophie needed. However, since Snodgrass locked up the wine cellar every night, she would have to make do with chocolate.

The kitchen's warmth drove the chill from his bones as he crept around, setting a pan of milk on the range and two bricks to warm on the hearth. He found a gleaming copper warming pan hanging on the wall and quietly filled it with hot coals, one by one with the fire tongs instead of the shovel. He made the chocolate in the pantry so as not to wake Lil with the chink of spoon against mug. It was as he stood gazing down at the hot bricks, wondering how he was to transport all his impedimenta upstairs, that he realized the child was staring at him with wide brown eyes.

He sighed. "Go back to sleep, Lil."

"Lor', sir, howdja know me name?"

"Miss Wingate told me."

A light of fervent devotion entered Lil's eyes. "Aye, miss knows it, she do." Sitting up, her skinny shoulders clad in red flannel, she regarded his preparations with curiosity. "You cold, sir? I coulda done that for you."

"I didn't want to wake you. Now I don't know how to carry everything upstairs."

She considered. "You c'd drink the choc'lit here. Or I c'd carry summat for you, 'cepting Mrs. Hibbert says I'm not to go 'bove stairs. I know what, sir, I'll getchera towel and you c'n tie the corners in a knot and carry it over your arm wi' the bricks inside."

As she started to push her quilt aside, Miles said, "Stay there, don't get cold. That's a clever notion. Just tell me where to find a towel."

Lil directed him to a back kitchen. Returning, he gathered up his burdens, bade her good night, and set off for the upper regions. He nearly told her not to mention his nocturnal visit to anyone; on second thought, to keep it secret he'd have to take everything back downstairs again. It would be easier just to make sure he removed the evidence from Miss Sophie's room to his own.

This he explained to Nerissa when she answered his soft tapping.

"Yes," she assented, relieving him of the warming pan, "I'll bring it all to you as soon as I have her settled. But we can only hope to keep the secret from the servants. I mean to speak quite plainly to Cousin Effie in the morning. Miss Sophie is not to be set to watch us again."

"We think alike. I had already planned to issue an edict on the subject, so you need not. It's best if your involvement is not revealed to anyone at all."

"Come now, Miles, you cannot expect Miss Sophie to lead her sister to believe *you* helped her to bed!"

"No, perhaps not," he conceded, grinning. "All the same, let me tackle Effie."

"I shall be glad to," Nerissa admitted. "One way or another, she is sure to kick up a dust."

Sir Barnabas made sure he was present to witness Euphemia's discomfiture. He followed her from the morning room when Miles sent Snodgrass to request an interview in the library.

Though answering a summons, Effie swept into the library like a high and mighty duchess. Miles rose and came around the desk to seat her courteously in a shield-back chair. Then he went to close the door. Settling on a corner of the desk, Sir Barnabas noted that the click of the latch made somewhat of a dent in Effie's assurance.

Miles returned to his seat. Regarding her sternly, he asked in a deceptively mild voice, "Have you spoken to your sister this morning, ma'am?"

"To Sophie?" said Effie, startled. "Not this morning."

"Have you asked after her? I take it you have noticed that she is not yet come down?"

"Naturally. I suppose you do not expect me to carry her breakfast to her!"

Miles matched her sarcasm. "I might expect you to be concerned at her lying late abed, since she is usually an early riser. As it happens, Nerissa persuaded her to stay there to try to ward off the effects of her unpleasant experience last night."

"What unpleasant experience?" Effie asked uneasily.

"When I found Miss Sophie, ma'am, concealed in the alcove on your orders, she was so cold as to be unable to move her limbs. We can only pray that she will not take an inflammation of the lungs."

"You cannot blame me because she has not the sense to wrap up properly." Now she sounded like a sulky child.

"I blame you for setting her to watch Nerissa and me. For yourself and the others I care not. You are capable of deciding for yourselves whether to do anything so crack-brained. Miss Sophie obeys your command."

"She certainly does not, if she told you I commanded her to spy on you!"

"My dear Mrs. Chidwell, I have known for some time that Nerissa's loving relatives are willing to expose themselves to extreme discomfort in the hope of catching her—and me—out."

"Then no wonder no one has seen anything!" Effie burst out in disgust. "I might as well call the whole thing off for all the good it's doing."

"You might indeed, though what *you* do is a matter of indifference to me." Miles stood up and leaned with both hands on the table. "However," he said grimly, "I forbid you to involve your sister in any more midnight vigils."

Quite like the head of the family, thought Sir Barnabas, surprised. Who would have thought such a here-and-thereian could put on such a show of authority?

"Trust Sophie to make a mull of it," Euphemia snapped. Flouncing from the room, she slammed the door behind her so vigorously that Sir Barnabas only just dodged past without being squashed.

She returned to the morning room, where Jane was at her eternal stitchery and Aubrey flipped idly through *The Gentleman's Magazine*.

"They have found out!" she announced.

Jane dropped her needle, looking as terrified as if she had been party to a conspiracy to assassinate the prince regent. Aubrey turned his head as far as his overstarched cravat permitted and stared at Euphemia.

"Who found out what?" he inquired.

"Miles and Nerissa know we have been keeping them under surveillance."

"Good," said Aubrey. "Then we need not do it any longer. As Raymond said, if they know we are watching, they will take care there is nothing to be seen."

"We shall lull them into a false sense of security. I made sure Miles knew I thought it pointless to continue. For a week or two we shall abandon our post, lest they check. Then, when they believe themselves safe from observation, we shall resume the watch."

Much as Sir Barnabas hated to acknowledge Effie as his chief ally, he had to admire her cunning. Not that it was anything new. He was still not quite sure how she had weaseled her way into his household when her husband died. Of course, if she had not brought Sophie with her, he'd not have been so poor-spirited as to yield.

Miles and Nerissa were good to Sophie, he had to admit. At present he felt almost kindly toward them. Ah, well, he would leave them free of midnight alarms for a while, at least until Euphemia decreed a renewed vigil.

Aubrey groaned. "Not until after the Christmas assembly in Porchester," he protested. "I simply must look my best for that, and *nothing* is so devastating as a night without sleep."

"Pah!" said Euphemia, silently echoed by Sir Barnabas.

"That reminds me," Aubrey continued, "I must tell Nerissa she will need a new gown. I wonder whether she knows how to dance respectably or only the sort of cavorting performed by opera dancers."

"You will *not* teach her the country dances and cotillions," Euphemia commanded.

"Aubrey," his mother wailed, "surely you do not mean to take that girl to the assembly?"

"Of course he does, Jane. Do pull yourself together. Everyone will be there. It will be a splendid opportunity for her to ruin herself."

"It will cause no end of talk if she does not go," Aubrey pointed out.

With a heavy sigh, Jane resigned herself.

"It's too late to get in a fidget," said Effie. "You already lend her countenance by joining her to receive visitors when she is queening it in the drawing room."

"It would look excessively odd if I did not," Jane said petulantly. "I cannot snub old acquaintances just because of the wretched girl. How I wish she had never come to Addlescombe."

"So do we all, except my gullible widgeon of a sister. I'm off to see what she has to say for herself."

Once again Sir Barnabas followed Euphemia from the morning room. Her determined, heavy-footed tramp boded ill for Sophie. As she stumped up the stairs, he slid up the banister beside her, one of the few joys of ghosthood, he had discovered.

She gave a single peremptory knock on Sophie's door and stormed in. Quelling his qualms at entering a lady's bedchamber, Sir Barnabas sailed in on the wind of her passage. Sophie was sitting up in bed, a bundle of shawls with a round pink face peeking out, topped with a pink-ribboned nightcap.

"How kind of you to come, Effie," she quavered hopefully. "I am really fit as a fiddle, but dear Nerissa—"

"Traitor!"

"Oh, dear, you do not think I—"

"I think you revealed our plans to the enemy. . . ."

"Oh, no, Effie, not enemy!"

"The enemy," Euphemia repeated firmly. "Now that Miles and Nerissa know we have been watching them, how shall we ever catch them creeping into each other's rooms?"

"But they don't," Sophie protested with the air of one prepared to go to the stake for her beliefs. "I mean, yes, they know, but they don't creep. Besides, what difference does it make if we watch the passage, when there is a connecting door between their chambers?"

Effie's lower jaw fell until all her chins were squeezed together like a stack of undercooked dropscones. Not a pretty sight—Sir Barnabas turned away his eyes with a shudder.

She recovered herself. "A connecting door?" she exploded. "For pity's sake, why did you not tell me?"

"I forgot. And then when I came to know Miles and Nerissa, I realized they would never use it, so it did not seem to matter."

"Ninnyhammer! Is it locked?"

"I'm sure I have not the least notion, Effie."

"Then go and check. No, you are not to be trusted, I shall go myself."

Sir Barnabas hurriedly withdrew as Sophie scrambled out of bed, shedding shawls like hairpins. She scurried after Effie; he brought up the rear.

Around the corner Effie charged, past Miles's room, and drew rein at Nerissa's door. Her imperative knock was unanswered. Marching in as if she owned the place, she stood staring around.

"Really, Effie, I cannot think you have any right in Nerissa's chamber uninvited. Do come away." Sophie plucked at her sister's sleeve, to no avail. "See, the bolts are shot on this side."

"Naturally she would bolt it afterward," said Effie scornfully, "to mislead the servants." She went to the connecting door, opened the bolts, and tried the handle. "Locked."

"I *told* you they would never use it." Poor Sophie was almost crying with vexation.

"The key must be on the other side." With a last suspicious glance about the room, Effie returned to the passage and knocked on Miles's door.

"Surely you are not going into Miles's chamber!" Sophie gasped.

"Of course."

"Pray do not! Well, I am going back to bed."

Sophie sped away round the corner, followed by Effie's stentorian, "Deserter!"

Effie invaded Miles's room with no less boldness than she had Nerissa's. She went straight to the connecting door. Sir Barnabas saw that on this side the bolts were open, the key in the lock. A wave of fury overcame him. Had his granddaughter and his godson been indulging themselves with impunity all this time?

Checking that the door was indeed securely locked, Effie removed the key from the keyhole and concealed it somewhere about her ample person. Then, instead of making a quick escape, she moved to the bed. She picked up a book from the bedside stand and opened it, fanning through the pages as if in search of incriminating evidence.

No lascivious love letter fell out, no damning list of gambling debts. About to close the book, disappointed, Effie stopped and stared at a page in horrified fascination. Peering around her bulk, Sir Barnabas saw a passage marked in pencil, but before he could see what it was about, Effie slammed the volume shut. Her face scarlet, eyes popping, hand pressed to heaving bosom, she dropped the book on the table as if it burned her fingers.

"Disgusting!"

"Well, what a surprise." Miles's suave voice made Effie jump visibly and Sir Barnabas jump invisibly.

Effie swung around, catching Sir Barnabas a blow in the ribs with her elbow that would have left a spectacular bruise on a living body. "You!" she said in tones of utter loathing.

"It *is* my bedchamber you are in. Good Lord, my dear Mrs. Chidwell, never say you have come to give your all—and a more than adequate all it is—to save the family fortunes? Fair Euphemia, can it be that you wish to seduce me?"

Her face took on an alarming hue, her breathing became stertorous, and she backed away. Sir Barnabas dodged. The nightstand crashed to the floor.

Miles smiled mockingly. "Such maidenly modesty," he marveled. "But come now, you and I both know a certain license is permitted to widows of a certain age."

"Ravisher!" she yelped.

"By all means, ma'am. Do you wish to make an assignation for later, or shall I . . . er . . . ravish you on the spot?"

This polite question caused some remnant of common sense to revive in Effie's tumultuous breast. "I came," she said haughtily, "to retrieve a key."

His eyes went straight to the connecting door and his lips tightened. "I don't pretend to know what you are about, but if you have unlocked the door anticipating that I will therefore ravish Nerissa—"

"No, no!"

"Or vice versa, perhaps?—you are sadly out in your reckoning."

"Nothing of the sort," said Effie in a sulky huff. "I was making sure it is locked."

Miles crossed to the door and checked. "Very well. I suppose you merely want to be sure that when we ravish each other, one of your spies observes us."

"I told you I am calling off the watch."

"Ah, yes," he agreed with a cynical look. "But I don't trust your mischief. Give me the key, if you please. It will be safest with Mr. Harwood, I believe. You may come with me and see me hand it over."

He held out his hand and Effie put the key into it, with a bad grace. Holding the door for her, he swept her a low bow as she sailed out, nose in the air.

Delighted, Sir Barnabas hurried to escape while the door was open. His godson had undoubtedly had the better of the exchange, he thought, yet nonetheless the result was that the door was definitively locked. Most satisfactory.

Besides, he wouldn't have missed the look on Effie's face for a monkey.

Miles, too, cherished the memory of Effie's face. However, the incident left him dissatisfied. Not that he gave a tinker's curse for the loss of the key. He had no desire to use the door, but he wished he had not spoken so casually of Nerissa's using it.

On the other hand, the old harridan was so determined to think ill of Nerissa that any protestations of her innocence would have fallen on deaf ears. As it was, as long as Effie Chidwell lived in hopes of catching them in flagrante, she was unlikely to try any other tricks.

He was sure she was the ringleader of the efforts to discredit them, though the others were just as bitterly resentful. Raymond Reece's clerical calling, which he appeared to take seriously, ought to hold him back from desperate measures. Aubrey and Matilda had other absorbing interests. Sir Neville and Lady Philpott were too weak to act on their own account, though they must expect to be the principal heirs if Miles and Nerissa were out of the way. All of them would follow Mrs. Chidwell's lead.

What she hoped to gain from the alternative will was debatable. From what Miles had learned of the animosity between her and Sir Barnabas, the late baronet was not at all likely to have left her a larger share of his fortune. The puzzle was why the old curmudgeon, though firmly in control, had ever let her reside at the manor.

In comparison, coercing Sir Neville into giving her a home would be child's play, whereas she must know Miles was not to be intimidated. Nerissa, of course, was not going to be at Addlescombe.

He was going to miss her, Miles realized. The pleasures of having a little sister far outweighed the pains. Perhaps she and her parents would visit him sometimes.

Unless she married a Dorset gentleman. Surely not Clive Digby!

The following day did not bring Clive Digby, but the Loftings called at the manor. Miles scarcely allowed Jeremy Lofting to exchange courtesies with the ladies before he whisked him off to the estate office to discuss agriculture.

What with one thing and another, not until the following evening did Miles remember to ask

Nerissa about the kitchen maid's sleeping quarters. She had just won from him a dozen slave girls dressed in Mosul silk embroidered with gold stars and playing upon flageolets and psalteries.

"Maybe we could teach some of the maids to provide music for my dancing lessons," she said, giggling.

"With tambourines and cymbals? I suspect lutes and flutes are beyond them, and I wouldn't know where to find a psaltery, or recognize one if I saw it. By the way, I have been meaning to ask you about the kitchen maid. I found her sleeping on the hearth the other night. Is there no proper bed for her upstairs?"

"She prefers to be in the kitchen. It is warm there, and the other girls tend to tease her for being such a scrawny little thing."

"She has enough to eat?"

"Plenty, and Cook is no slave driver. Many children her age have voracious appetites yet remain thin because they are growing. I can see you are going to ask whether the rest of the maids are comfortable and well fed. I assure you I would never allow anyone working for me to go cold or hungry. I inspected their quarters, and you must have noticed how plump and cheerful they are. Mrs. Hibbert told me Sir Barnabas believed well-treated servants work harder."

"Trust Sir Barnabas to have any motive but philanthropy. Dash it, where did that draft come from?" he cried as their pack of cards and lists of stakes slithered across the table and fluttered to the floor.

As he picked up the cards, Miles thought how much Nerissa had changed since her arrival at Addlescombe, when she had been downright timid with Hibby and Snodgrass. As her self-confidence had grown, so had a sense of responsibility for her dependents.

He had indeed noticed the buxom, cheerful maids, several of them decidedly pretty in a countrified way. The rural nature of their charms, otherwise just what he preferred in a *chère amie,* must be the reason he had admired from a distance without being the least tempted. Not that he was the sort to seduce an honest serving maid, yet it was odd that those lush figures awoke in him no hint of desire.

Only Nerissa roused his senses, but of course that was solely due to the suggestive circumstances of Sir Barnabas's wretched will. She was no more to him than a little sister to be advised and protected.

Chapter Fourteen

"Out of the question," said Miles.

"Oh." Nerissa blinked back tears of disappointment that momentarily hid the page of the *Ladies' Magazine*. The evening gown depicted there was quite the most beautiful dress she had ever seen. She had asked Miles, who had been out all day, to come down to dinner early so that she could show it to him.

The frock of white British net over a rose satin slip had a very high waist trimmed with lace and tiny puff sleeves with knots of rose ribbon. The skirt, fuller than the ordinary, boasted a deep lace flounce embroidered with roses and seed-pearl rosettes. "I daresay it is too elaborate," Nerissa said sadly. "Mr. Harwood will never agree to pay so much."

"The cost has nothing to do with it. I'll engage to talk Harwood into whatever you please."

"Then you think it will not suit me?"

Miles took the magazine and studied the fashion plate more closely. "No. Though the girl in the drawing is too plump for the style, it would look very well on you. All but the—" He cleared his throat. "All but the neckline."

Silly tears rose to Nerissa's eyes again. Miles thought she had not enough bosom for the glorious dress.

But he hastily went on. "Not that it will not suit you, only the décolleté is far too extreme for a country hop."

"No, it is not. When Miss Firston lent me the magazine this afternoon, she showed me what she and her sister will wear to the Christmas assembly. Here, look, these are just as low."

"Possibly." He frowned. "However, the Firstons are well established as a respectable family. You are still in the process of establishing your reputation, so you must be particularly careful not to offend even the highest stickler."

Nerissa sighed. "I suppose so," she said.

He continued to frown at the plates, turning from one to another. "You know, I believe the shape of the one you have chosen makes it appear lower. These ... er ... sort of scoops in the bodice ..." His voice trailed off and he flushed.

His embarrassment surprised and amused Nerissa. After all, he was a rake! When she realized he had expurgated the *Arabian Nights,* she had been grateful for his kindness but had not imagined he might find the stories equally disconcerting.

She agreed with him about the gown, though. The shape of the neckline was the one thing she did not care for. The satin bodice was scooped out on either side, rising to a knot of ribbon between the breasts. It looked too much like something Bess Rigby would wear hoping to suggest the possibility of her voluptuous bosom popping out of its confinement.

She was not about to enlighten Miles on that subject, however. "I'm sure the shape can be altered without spoiling the gown," she assured him.

"Cousin Sophie and I are going into Porchester tomorrow to the dressmaker, so I shall see what she has to say. This wide V is prettier, is it not?"

"It will do, if it can be made a bit higher and with a wide fall of lace above it."

"I expect so," she conceded. After all, he had her best interests at heart. Besides, the girl in the picture was wearing a rose-garnet necklace to fill the expanse of skin above the corsage. All Nerissa owned by way of ornament was her plain gold locket, worn on a ribbon for lack of a chain, which held tiny miniatures of Mama and Papa and a lock of Lucian's hair.

"Not the toque," said Miles. "It's hideous."

"Toques are all the rage."

"Hideous," he repeated firmly, "and you have no cause to hide your hair. All you need is a wreath of silk roses. No, rosebuds."

"Yes, sir." She smiled at him. "I daresay rosebuds are less likely than a toque to fall off in the middle of an energetic dance. Miss Firston thinks there may be waltzing this year. You will teach me to waltz?"

"We shall try it after dinner tonight. Perhaps Miss Sophie will play the harpsichord for us, since she and Aubrey will not be needed to make up a country-dance set. I tell you, it's not easy to whistle and teach you the steps at the same time."

"I must say it's a trifle confusing when you take up a different tune after correcting my errors!"

A few minutes later Miss Sophie joined them in the drawing room.

"Miles is going to teach me to waltz this evening," Nerissa said. "Will you play for us?"

"Oh, no, dear, not the waltz. A shocking dance!"

"It's not considered shocking nowadays, Miss Sophie," Miles informed her. "Everyone does it."

"In town perhaps, but not in Porchester," said Miss Sophie with unwonted firmness.

"Cecily Firston told me it will be danced at the Christmas assembly," Nerissa said.

"Wishful thinking, I fear. I spoke to Mrs. Nidd, who is on the ladies' committee, just the other day, you recall, when we called on the Nidds, and she said the waltz will on no account be approved."

"I should like to learn it anyway, in case it is allowed after all."

"I cannot like it, Nerissa dear. Even if Mrs. Nidd should be overruled, those young ladies who take part will be thought fast."

Nerissa sent a look of appeal to Miles, who shrugged his shoulders. "Miss Sophie knows better than I what is acceptable to the local biddies."

"Here is Aubrey now," said Miss Sophie. "Do you ask him for his opinion, my dear."

Aubrey concurred with Miss Sophie. "Porchester society is sadly old-fashioned, alas. There is no appreciation for the latest modes. The waltz is still frowned upon. I should not care to see a young lady under my care bring censure upon—" He came to an abrupt halt as he heard Cousin Euphemia's elephantine tread entering the drawing room. Casting a nervous glance behind him, he hurried on in a louder voice. "You are going into Porchester tomorrow, are you not, cousin? I shall go with you. I have a coat which will at a pinch suffice for the assembly, but I simply must order a new waistcoat."

"You are welcome to come with us," said Nerissa sincerely, though her lips twitched. She appreciated his willingness to give her good advice, even if he strove to conceal the fact from Euphemia.

Aubrey went to meet Euphemia and herded her away from the others.

"He's afraid we may reveal his defection from the ranks," said Miles, "though I rather suspect it was inadvertent. Good gad, Nerissa, when he says his coat will suffice 'at a pinch,' do you suppose he means it is even tighter than his usual?"

She laughed. "I trust not, or he may burst his stays in the middle of the assembly."

"Now, now, children," Miss Sophie reproved them. "I am sure dear Aubrey has a good heart beneath his fashionable clothes. So that is settled, Nerissa? You will not waltz?"

"No, dear cousin, I can see it would be frowned upon." A horrid thought struck her. "Oh, dear, perhaps I should not dance at all because of being in mourning for my grandfather!"

Miss Sophie clapped her hand to her mouth in dismay. "Heavens, I quite forgot. Which goes to show the importance of wearing mourning, does it not? I wonder whether you should even attend the assembly."

"Gammon!" said Miles roundly. "Sir Barnabas forbade us to observe mourning, not just to wear it. We shall ask Harwood, but I believe he will say the will virtually *requires* you to dance, Nerissa. Leave him to me."

Mr. Harwood came down too late to be consulted before dinner, but afterward he and Miles joined Nerissa and Miss Sophie.

"Mr. Harwood agrees that you must dance," Miles announced.

"That is not precisely what I said," the lawyer admonished him, but his eyes twinkled. "However, I see no reason why you should not, my dear young lady. I understand you wish to order a new gown?"

Nerissa had the magazine ready. "This one, sir, if you do not think it too extravagant."

He set his spectacles on his nose and gravely examined the colored plate. "Charming, charming. You will be quite the belle of the ball, Miss Wingate."

"Oh, no, I know several much prettier girls who will be there. But I shall have the prettiest gown, I vow, if you consent."

"How can I refuse? I must make one stipulation, however. If the dancing continues much past one o'clock, which it generally does not, for we keep country hours in Porchester, you will have to leave before the end. Two hours must be allowed for the journey in darkness, and Sir Barnabas was most particular that neither you nor Mr. Courtenay is to spend a single night absent from Addlescombe."

"One o'clock, not midnight, like Cinderella?" Nerissa asked, laughing. "You are generous, sir."

Mr. Harwood beamed. "One o'clock, ma'am, or your gown will turn to rags, your carriage to a pumpkin, and the horses to rats. No doubt you will not wish for glass slippers, but be sure to buy yourself dancing shoes. Do you need anything, Courtenay?"

"Nothing, sir. Thank heaven we gentlemen are not required to show off new finery at a ball, Aubrey notwithstanding. But there is a small matter I should like to discuss with you, if you please."

The two gentlemen drew away. Nerissa watched them for a moment and saw Mr. Harwood listening intently to Miles's hushed yet vehement exposition. She wondered briefly what made him so earnest, then forgot as she turned to Miss Sophie to debate the relative merits of bows and rosettes on dancing slippers.

* * *

Nerissa stared at the elegant young lady in the looking-glass.

"Oh, miss, 'tis beautiful," sighed Maud ecstatically, clasping her hands.

The gown was indeed just as beautiful as she had hoped. The silk rosebuds in her hair were perfect, the rosetted dancing slippers pretty and comfortable. But even with the raised neckline, the expanse of visible chest looked alarmingly bare.

"My locket, please, Maud."

She had bought a length of narrow ribbon to match the gown, and the locket suspended about her neck much improved matters. She refused to admit, even to herself, a hint of dissatisfaction. Mr. Harwood had been truly generous; she could not put him in the difficult position of having to refuse a request for jewels.

Jacinth and chalcedony, tourmaline and chrysoprase, spinel and sardonyx; those were fantasies to amuse Miles with at cards. Reality was half a yard of pink satin ribbon and a small oval of gold—and the most beautiful gown in the world, she reminded herself.

"It is splendid, is it not? Miss Sophie will want to see it. Pray see if she is in her chamber."

Miss Sophie came in and clapped her hands. "Enchanting! I cannot wait to watch you dancing."

"Only three days to wait." Nerissa smiled at her fondly.

"How this reminds me of my youth, my first ball! Only our fashions were quite different, of course. Such great wide skirts we wore, it's a wonder how we ever managed them. I wish I had still my gold chain to lend you for your locket, Nerissa. I sold it some years past to buy my jet beads, which Effie says are far more suitable at my age. Not that your ribbon is not very pretty, my dear."

Nerissa did her best to banish renewed doubts as to the adequacy of the ribbon. "Now that Miss Sophie has seen my gown, I shall take it off, Maud," she said. "I don't want to risk any damage."

Maud carefully unpinned the wreath of rosebuds and set it on the dressing table. Nerissa took off the locket. Somehow, as she handed it to the maid, it dropped to the floor and popped open. A yellow curl fell out.

"Oh, miss, I'm that sorry." Crouching, Maud picked up the locket and tried to restore the separated snippets of hair into a smooth lock. "I've spoilt your pa's hair."

"It was my fault," Nerissa said, hot-cheeked. "Never mind about it now." She had not spared Lucian a thought in weeks, she realized. She could scarcely bring his handsome face to mind.

As Maud stood up, she glanced at the two minuscule portraits in the locket. The knowing glance she threw Nerissa showed all too clearly that she had noted Mr. Wingate's hair, as dark as his wife's. Nerissa felt her cheeks flaming.

With exaggerated care the abigail placed the locket and the blond curl beside the rosebuds. "Right, miss, let's get that gown off and hung up safe," she said. "It's a good job you won't have to wear it in the carriage all the way to Porchester."

"Yes," Nerissa agreed as the rose satin rustled over her head. "It would be horridly crushed."

Miss Sophie nodded. "I am glad Mr. Harwood has hired chambers at the Cross Keys for us to change in. Your grandfather was always wont to do so when we stayed at Addlescombe for Christmas in the old days. Poor Barnabas became quite unsociable after your mama ran off." She sighed. "What a pity dear Anthea will not be here to see her daughter attend her first ball."

Nerissa echoed her sigh. It would indeed be wonderful to have her mother to chaperon her, and in her last letter Mama had expressed a wish that she might do so. However, she was equally wishful that Nerissa had been there to see her triumph in the comic role of Mrs. Heidelberg in *The Clandestine Marriage,* with Papa as a splendid Lord Ogleby. For Anthea Wingate, the present was the world of the theater. The life of a young lady making her bow in country society was relegated to a half-forgotten and little-regretted past.

For Nerissa it was the all-important present and near future. However, she still had not revealed to her parents the insulting terms of her grandfather's will, nor the resentment of most of her relations. If Mama knew, she would be deeply concerned—but rather than find a way to attend the assembly, she'd probably order Nerissa home.

And, despite the difficulties, Nerissa did not want to go home. She just hoped the family would let her enjoy her first ball without seizing the occasion to disgrace her in the eyes of all the local gentry at once.

Miles had said Cousin Euphemia was the only one likely to try, the others being too afraid of sharing her disgrace. So Nerissa was relieved when Effie came down with the first symptoms of a cold on the day of the assembly and decided to stay abed to avoid a putrid sore throat.

"To avoid watching your triumph, more likely," said Miles.

Whatever the reason, in her absence Nerissa took

her place beside Miss Sophie in the landau with un-alloyed anticipation of pleasure. With Miles, Raymond, and Matilda riding alongside and Mr. Harwood's chaise following, they set off in the early dusk of the winter evening.

It was pitch dark long before they reached Porchester, but the Cross Keys was brightly lit with lanterns and flaring torches. As the landau turned under the archway into the yard, General Pettigrew was handing his wife and daughters down from their carriage. Ostlers dashed about, and the rotund landlord of the inn stood in the doorway to welcome his guests, a beam on his red face.

The Pettigrews waited for the party from Addlescombe. An unknown gentleman stood with them, whom the general introduced as his prospective son-in-law, come on a Christmas visit. The Reverend Paul Simmons was a large, jolly young man, to Nerissa's surprise, for the shy Caroline's paeans on her betrothed's saintliness had led her to expect a pale, weedy creature.

Miss Anna Pettigrew attached herself to Miles like a limpet, and Nerissa found herself going into the Cross Keys on the general's arm. The landlord handed her a dance card as she entered.

"I hope you will save me a dance, Miss Wingate," the general boomed. "M'wife don't dance, but there's life in the old dog yet, and I mean to stand up with all the prettiest girls tonight. Courtenay, I say, Courtenay, what d'ye think, shall we dine together before the hop?"

"Pray let us, Mr. Courtenay," Anna added her appeal, fluttering her eyelashes.

Miles agreed with altogether too much alacrity before turning to Jane Philpott with a token request for her consent. "You don't mind, do you, ma'am?"

"Pray do, Lady Philpott," urged Mrs. Pettigrew, whether because of the love of titles Nerissa had noticed or for the sake of throwing her daughter and Miles together.

They did not appear to need throwing together. Miles smiled down at the girl as Lady Philpott graciously assented. As a result, Nerissa greeted Mr. Clive Digby, on his entering the hall, with warmth enough to embolden the angler to beg the honor of the first dance and to take her to supper.

Trained by Miss Sophie in the etiquette of the ballroom, she knew she had no excuse to refuse him. Not that she wished to, for today his nose was only a little pink and he wore respectable evening dress with just one single, modest artificial fly in the lapel. If Miles preferred the company of the coquettish Miss Anna, it was up to Nerissa to show him she was perfectly capable of enjoying her first ball without his support.

She was about to voice her acceptance, when Miles intervened. "Beg your pardon, my dear fellow, Miss Wingate is promised to me for the first dance and for supper."

Mollified, though indignant at his presumption, Nerissa cast him a speaking glance but did not deny his unjustified claim. Anna pouted. Clive Digby settled for the second dance. Before Nerissa had to grant him another later in the evening, more people came from the inn yard and those already in the lobby moved on to their various apartments.

The Addlescombe ladies tidied themselves in the chamber reserved for them and repaired to the private parlor next door to take a dish of tea.

Miles was not in evidence. Nerissa suspected that having done his duty by her, he was dancing attendance on Anna Pettigrew, or perhaps the Firston girls had arrived by now, or the dashing Miss Nidd.

Wherever he had disappeared to, she was soon too busy to miss him as the parlor filled with visitors. Miss Sophie and Aubrey introduced her to those she had not met before because they lived on the far side of Porchester from Addlescombe, too far for morning calls. Lady Philpott was kept fully occupied in agitated explanations of the lack of mourning for Sir Barnabas. Nerissa acquired a new admirer, a homely but amusing gentleman who exacted a promise of a dance before he was ousted from her side by Caroline Pettigrew and her betrothed.

Mr. Simmons's good-natured heartiness strongly reminded Nerissa of the general. She decided Caroline had been attracted by his likeness to her much-loved father.

"How now, Miss Wingate," he said, "you'll visit us at Buckford, I hope? I've just received word the old vicar will retire in the New Year, so I expect to be wed to my dear Caroline before Easter." They exchanged such a fond look that Nerissa was suddenly filled with envy.

There was envy mixed with her curiosity, too, when a few minutes later Dr. Firston brought his sweetheart to meet her. Miss Herriot was a tall, statuesque redhead whose gown of cheap green silk with but a single flounce did not detract from her striking appearance. She and John Firston made a handsome couple.

"I have been quite longing to make your acquaintance, Miss Wingate," she said, adding candidly, "John's family are in hopes that he will marry you, but I trust we may be friends for all that."

Nerissa laughed. "Certainly." Matching candor

for candor, she asked, "Is your family also opposed to a match between the two of you?"

"Not exactly, though of course they had rather I married a gentleman of twenty thousand a year, if I could but find one! No, Papa says we may be betrothed as soon as John's practice allows him to take a house for us. At present he alternates between his brother's house and horrid lodgings here in Porchester, poor dear. It's a dreadful thing to say, but what we need is more people falling sick."

"Dr. Firston, pray call at Addlescombe tomorrow," said Nerissa promptly. "You are sorely needed. My cousin, Mrs. Chidwell, is laid up with a desperate case of the sniffles."

They laughed, and he said, "I will come to Addlescombe tomorrow if you will stand up with me this evening, ma'am."

So when Miles at last returned, already in evening dress, just as Nerissa was going to change, she was able to wave her dance card at him in triumph and announce, "I shall not be a wallflower tonight."

"No fear of that. Who is on your list?"

"Mr. Digby, and General Pettigrew, and Caroline Pettigrew's curate, and Dr. Firston and—"

"Firston!" Miles frowned. "What the deuce is he doing here already? He lives in Porchester, so he has no need to come early, and his family is not yet arrived."

"He came to meet Miss Herriot. He brought her to see me and I like her, even though she is quite beautiful."

"Oh, his sweetheart," said Miles dismissively, cheering up. "I wasn't sure he hadn't invented her. Have you any blank spaces on your card? I've been down in the taproom, talking to some fellows, and they all begged for introductions."

"Because they believe me to be an heiress." She sighed.

"Well, yes, but once they see you, your fortune won't be the only reason."

With that meager comfort Nerissa went to change. More comforting was the discovery that Miles had not, after all, been dallying with some pretty young lady. He probably preferred barmaids anyway, she thought wryly, given his known taste for actresses. Though why she should care, she was sure she didn't know.

Maud was waiting to help her into the glorious gown, to place the locket about her neck, and arrange the rosebuds in her hair. "There's to be a bit of a jollification in the kitchens while the gentry's dancing, miss," she said. "You won't mind if I go? If you was to need me, any of the inn servants'll find me quick."

"Go, and enjoy yourself, Maud. I never thought I needed an abigail, but I don't know what I should do without you."

She kissed the girl, who flushed with pleasure. "You look pretty as Miss Anthea in the pitcher tonight, miss. All the gentlemen'll be begging for a dance."

Nerissa glanced at the mirror. She knew she would never match Mama's beauty or presence, but tonight, her cheeks pink with excitement and her eyes sparkling, she did look quite pretty. Of course, most of it was due to the gown. Recalling Miss Herriot's shabby green dress, she was ashamed of ever having wished for a finer necklace.

She went through to the parlor. All the others were there, Miles with his back to her, talking to Raymond. Mr. Harwood came up to her.

"My dear young lady, worth every penny, I do

declare." Fumbling in his breast pocket, he drew out a small velvet-covered box. "And here's a little something to add the final touch."

Nerissa held her breath as she undid the tiny brass catch. Everyone was watching her now, but they were family, no more disturbing to her than being surrounded by the playhouse company.

"Pearls! Oh, perfect! How did you guess? 'A kind overflow of kindness,' indeed."

Mr. Harwood shook his head, leaned forward, and whispered in her ear, "Not I, my dear. Entirely young Courtenay's notion, only it would not be proper for him to give them to you himself. However, the cost is to come out of his share when your inheritances are confirmed." He put a finger to his smiling lips. "Not a word to anyone. He asked me not to tell."

She looked at Miles across the room, trying to put all her gratitude in her eyes. He grinned and gave her an insouciant wave.

Aunt Jane, sallower than ever in her topaz necklace, bracelet, earrings, and aigrette, pursed her lips. "Shocking extravagance," she lamented to Sir Neville in a scarcely lowered voice, "and with *our* money. Barnabas must be turning in his grave."

At that moment Sir Barnabas was wandering disconsolately through the empty halls and passages of his home. The malicious pleasure he found in listening to Effie honking into a handkerchief had soon faded. He was bored.

Truth to tell, he rather wished he were at the Cross Keys watching his granddaughter dancing the night away. He wished he had seen her face when Harwood presented the pearls. The more she enjoyed herself now, the greater the inevitable fall, he told himself.

He had been furious at first when Harwood gave in to Miles's pleas to buy the hussy those pearls. Perhaps it *would* look odd for a reputed heiress to wear no jewels, but to claim it was unfair to make her look odd was sheer twaddle. When Sir Barnabas went to the immense effort of materializing to the lawyer to forbid the purchase, the credulous fool insisted he had misjudged the girl. Harwood was bound for disillusionment. One of these days she'd let down her guard and damn herself from her own mouth.

Sir Barnabas had given in over the pearls but made Harwood promise to tell Nerissa they were Miles's gift. Gratitude might yet lead her into his bed. Her self-control was stronger than Sir Barnabas had reckoned on, though. None of his efforts in that direction had borne fruit.

Before he turned to other methods, he decided, he would provide one more irresistible opportunity for debauchery.

Chapter Fifteen

Dinner with the Pettigrews was a merry affair. They all sat at a long table in the coffee room, which was full of other parties fortifying themselves for an energetic evening. Waiters dashed to and fro with laden trays, dodging between the chairs and somehow never spilling a drop.

Only Sir Neville and Lady Philpott wore long faces. Mr. Simmons, seated beside Nerissa, kindly put their soberness down to the need to uphold the dignity of their titles. Raymond, on her other side, and Aubrey seemed to have set aside any pique over the pearls, at least for the present. Matilda had joined a group of cheerfully loud-voiced hunting friends.

Even Mrs. Pettigrew's stiffness melted somewhat. Her husband's importance as a general officer was confirmed by the presence at his table of the only titled personages in the room. One of her daughters, the less promising, had her betrothed at her side, even if he were a mere curate; the other was captivating the heir to Addlescombe.

However captivated by Miss Anna, Miles did not neglect Miss Sophie, Nerissa noticed. He made sure she was not overlooked by the busy waiters and frequently turned to exchange a few words with her. He was a true gentleman, whatever his past misdemeanors.

And he was a thoughtful, generous friend. Nerissa had to stop herself from constantly raising her hand to touch the pearls. She had not had a chance to thank him yet, but already the musicians could be heard tuning up in the assembly room at the back of the inn.

People began to abandon the remains of their dinners and leave the coffee room. Nerissa was in a fever of impatience. She did not want to miss a single step of her dance with Miles. But General Pettigrew was in the middle of a long and involved story that made him chortle frequently though it raised not a hint of a smile from Lady Philpott.

Catching Nerissa's anxious gaze, Miles nodded toward a clock on the wall. Plenty of time, she realized, wondering how he had read her mind.

At last they moved. Miles joined her, offered his arm, and they entered the crowded passage to the assembly room. As they made their way slowly along it, Nerissa looked up at him.

"How can I ever thank you for the pearls?"

"I told Harwood most particularly not to say they were a gift from me." Blue eyes laughed at her. "It's no money out of my pocket since the money has yet to reach my pockets. Besides, it would be highly improper to accept jewelry from a gentleman unrelated to you."

"You are my god-uncle, remember, and besides, I won a crystal coffer full of amber and amethysts from you just last night. Oh, Miles, they are quite perfect, the very thing to wear with this gown."

"I must say, you look complete to a shade," he said approvingly.

"Spanish coin makes a change from Arabian dinars and dirhams."

"I'm not offering Spanish coin. I'll be the envy of every man in the room."

She clutched his arm as panic clutched her heart. "No, Miles, will everyone stare when we go in? When we dance?"

"Why the deuce should they? You're a pretty girl, not a jinni summoned by a magic lamp."

"Because we are strangers?"

"There are bound to be other strangers, and I wager you have met most people already anyway. Look, there are the Loftings just ahead of us, and the Digbys behind. I'll tell you what, if people do stare, it will be at Aubrey, not at you."

For the first time, Nerissa looked properly at Cousin Aubrey's evening clothes. With pantaloons of a delicate primrose hue, he wore a coat of russet velvet adorned with huge gilt buttons, pinched at the waist and padded at the shoulders in his usual exaggerated manner. His true glory, however, was his new waistcoat, a marvel of chocolate-brown silk embroidered with gold stars and a border of gold curlicues.

With his dyed hair and painted face, he suddenly struck Nerissa as a larger-than-life stage figure, an older version of Lucian Gossett. Of course, Lucian had talent to excuse his vanity, but he, too, would probably one day dye his hair when the gold began to fade.

Miles, elegant in black and white at her side, would never stoop to such stratagems. He was not as handsome as Lucian, but his dark hair would gray naturally, giving him a distinguished air. Then his crooked nose would lend a hint of whimsicality that accorded far better with his character than the slightly sinister impression Nerissa had originally received.

She flushed as his quizzical smile told her she was staring. As for anyone staring at her, lost in thought she had entered the assembly room, entirely oblivious of the rest of the world.

"Aubrey's waistcoat is quite dazzling, isn't it?" Miles said. "Like something out of the *Arabian Nights*. Pray rest your gaze on my eye-soothing profile as long as you wish."

Nerissa laughed. "When I first met you, I thought your profile made you look like an Iago or a Cassius."

" 'Yond Cassius has a lean and hungry look,'— probably because you were feeling lean and hungry at the time, though admittedly the sister of a friend of mine once called me piratical."

"You saved my life with an apple and biscuits, so I knew you were no pirate."

"I have never plundered a ship, but I admit to stealing the first dance from Digby."

"I am glad you did. I shall need you to remind me of the steps at first, until I grow accustomed to dancing among so many people and with proper music."

"Madam, you insult my whistling! Come, let us stand next to your friend Miss Pettigrew. She will not mind if you go astray."

They followed Caroline and Mr. Simmons onto the floor as the fiddlers struck up the first country dance. At first Nerissa had no attention to spare from her feet, but she soon found it was easier to watch what everyone else was doing instead of trying to recall the steps. If she faltered, Miles or Caroline steered her right. They united to steer Mr. Simmons, too, as he bumbled through the pattern of the dance like a good-natured puppy, with more willingness than skill.

By the end of the set, they were all breathless with laughter and exercise. Nerissa was glad of a few minutes' respite, sitting with Miss Sophie while the gentlemen hunted out their next partners.

Before Mr. Digby claimed her hand, she had time to look about her. The dark coats of the gentlemen formed a background for the rainbow hues of the ladies' gowns. Here and there a jewel glittered, but most of the ladies wore jet or amber beads, gold chains, or, at most, pearls. Lady Philpott's topazes were the finest gems to be seen, as she was obviously aware, however sallow they made her. Nerissa realized her pearls were perfect not only for her gown but for the occasion.

The long room was decorated with scarlet-berried holly and fragrant evergreens, and three bunches of mistletoe hung from the ceiling. As couples took their places for the second dance, Nerissa saw several snatched kisses, pecks on the cheek that left girls blushing and young men grinning.

Mr. Digby appeared before her, bowed, and escorted her to join a set. She prayed he would not use the mistletoe as an excuse to try to kiss her.

On the other hand, she found herself quite indignant when he waxed eloquent on the subject of a particularly fine pair of trout he had caught the previous day. Her first ball was no place for a parade of piscatorial prowess!

She saw Miles, in the next set, twirling Anna Pettigrew directly beneath one of the clumps of mistletoe. Anna glanced up, fluttered her eyelashes, pouted. Miles ignored the suggestive byplay, but Nerissa guessed from his sardonic look that he was aware of it. He caught her eye and gave her a suspicion of a wink.

Did she want Miles to kiss her? Not under the mistletoe, she decided. Not just because the mistletoe was there. That was just like a stage kiss. A proper kiss, though, the kind she had sometimes glimpsed when Mama and Papa thought she wasn't looking . . .

"Our turn, Miss Wingate," said Clive Digby, and swung her on his arm.

She threw herself into enjoyment of the dance, and she did enjoy it thoroughly, and those that followed. The general was the only gentleman to venture a kiss, at which she could not possibly take offense. Always conscious of Miles's whereabouts, of whom he was dancing with, she never actually witnessed him succumbing to the lure of the mistletoe—so perhaps he did not. He arrived promptly to take her in to supper, just when she was sure she could not possibly dance another step.

It was after supper that she saw him standing up with the plainest young lady in the room, a pudding-faced, awkward miss who had scarcely danced all evening. That was when Nerissa realized Miles had made a point of alternating between the prettiest girls and the wallflowers.

And that was when she realized she loved him.

Had something happened at the assembly to subdue Nerissa's usual cheerful spirits? Miles frowned unseeing at the trampled saplings, nodding automatically as Bragg asked his permission to chastise the tenant-farmer whose cattle had wreaked the havoc.

"Have him replant come spring," he ordered the bailiff, "and he's to fence the plantation."

For three days now she had been quiet, almost listless. Had some impudent sprig of the squirarchy dared take advantage of the mistletoe to kiss her? His blood boiled at the thought.

Yet she was no milk-and-water miss. He doubted she would let such an occurrence overset her—unless she happened to find herself in love with the fellow concerned. His frown deepened. None of them would do for her, but there was no accounting for feminine whims and crotchets.

". . . Unless you had rather not . . ." Bragg's uncertain voice trailed away.

"Not what? I beg your pardon, my mind was elsewhere."

"I thought we might drop in at the Addled Egg, sir, and drink a wassail, seeing tomorrow's Christmas Eve. It'll be dark in half an hour and the men'll be coming in from the fields."

"A splendid notion." He turned Samson's head toward the village. "I have a distant memory from my childhood: Was not Sir Barnabas used to give a Christmas party every year for his tenants and dependents? On Boxing Day, I think."

"Aye, sir, in the great barn at the home farm, but it ha'n't been done this twenty year and more, since Miss Anthea's been gone."

"Miss Anthea's daughter is back now and Sir Barnabas is gone. It's too late to arrange for this year, I daresay, but we'll see about next year." It was a good tradition, even though Miss Anthea's daughter would be gone again long before next Christmas. Perhaps she and her parents might come for a visit for the festivities—unless she married a Dorset man.

Bragg on his cob at his side, Miles rode into Addlescombe village in the early winter twilight.

Lights shone in the windows of the flint cottages trimmed with brick and roofed with elaborately patterned thatch. The clock on the square tower of the little flint-and-stone church struck half past four as they dismounted before the alehouse. By the light of a lantern hanging from the inn sign, a cracked egg, they tied the horses.

The low-ceilinged black-beamed room fell silent when Miles entered its smoky warmth and doffed his hat. Then came a murmur of respectful greetings. An old gaffer nodding on the wooden settle by the fire was forcibly removed to give place to the master. Miles knew better than to protest.

"What'll you 'ave, zir?" The innkeeper's buxom daughter Nancy swayed her hips and flaunted her bosom, tugging down her bodice as she dodged between the close-set tables.

"Bring out the wassail bowl," Miles commanded. "It's mulled ale all around, and chalk it up to me."

A cheer went up. Old men nodded knowingly to each other: This was something like the old days, when the lord of the manor had not disdained to drink his cup with his people.

The first bumper arrived, a brimful pewter tankard with spicy steam rising. Miles raised it—"To Addlescombe and all who dwell therein!"—took a hearty swig, and almost choked. Mine host's recipe for mulled ale apparently included a bottle or three of gin.

Nancy dashed about with half a dozen tankards in each capable hand, blond curls flying. She looked prettier to Miles with every toast he joined in, to the crops, the beasts, a merry Christmas, the New Year. Then she was seated on his knee, a cozy armful, giggling as he accidentally drank to his own health. His empty tankard miraculously refilled itself. The fumes rose in his head and Nancy's warm breath caressed his cheek. Her breast was soft and full beneath his hand. His loins stirred.

Someone whispered in his ear, "If you was to take our Nancy upstairs, zir, you wouldn't be the first, not by a long chalk."

Wriggling, Nancy wound her arms about his neck and pressed closer.

Miles took a deep draft of mulled ale. A cacophony of shouts, song, and laughter shook the rafters and resonated in his head. His hand found its way beneath the willing wench's petticoats.

A cry arose. "We ha'n't drunk 'the young mistress.' A health to Mistress Wingate, Lord preserve her."

"And the old maister. Here's to Sir Barnabas, God rest his soul."

Miles froze, his befuddled mind screaming a warning. Sir Barnabas's soul might or might not rest in heaven. His will unquestionably stalked the earth, threatening disaster to those who indulged in a little harmless pleasure. To one of those, at least, namely himself.

He was among friends. They were drinking his health again, this time with sly winks and nudges. No one would give him away to the dastardly crew up at the manor. Nancy was eager, breathing in his ear now, and stroking the nape of his neck.

She slipped down from his lap and urged him to his feet. He had to steady himself with one hand on the settle back as she took his arm to lead him to the delights of her bed.

Was it worth the risk? He was far too top-heavy to reckon the odds, yet surely Lady Luck would smile just this once if he broke his rule and gambled while jug-bitten!

He glanced down at Nancy—but he must be even boskier than he thought, for his gaze failed to focus on her face. Instead, an image of another face interposed, Nerissa's, disconsolate, a plea in her great gray eyes.

Gad, he was foxed if he was seeing visions! Only drunkenness could explain why he felt he'd be letting her down if he had his way with Nancy. After all, should he be betrayed, Nerissa's inheritance would instantly double.

And he'd have to leave Addlescombe, leave her to the tender mercies of her ever-loving family.

Nancy tugged on his sleeve. He shook his head regretfully.

"It's time I was getting on home." Bussing her cherry-ripe lips in farewell, he patted her ample behind and weaved his way to the door.

"G'night, zir."

"Merry Christmas, zir."

"Happy New Year."

Someone handed him his hat. He waved it at the company, cried, "Merry Christmas!" and stepped out into the night.

The cold air made him stagger. Bragg appeared at his side and gripped his elbow.

"I'll see you home, sir. Should have warned you about the daffy in the wassail bowl."

"The more the merrier," said Miles, his head rapidly clearing. "Thank you, but I'll do now. You be off to your family."

By the light of a waning moon he rode Samson home at a walk, listening to the night sounds. An owl hooted nearby and another answered in the distance. As he crossed the bridge over the Addle, an otter whistled. In the dark of a spinney a badger raised its white-striped head and stared at him before returning to its rooting for grubs. Then he was out in the moonlight again, the fertile fields spreading on either side.

Lord, he loved Addlescombe! Thank heaven he had not lost it for the sake of a brief moment's bodily gratification.

Reaching the house, he went straight to his room, sprawled on the bed, and sank into oblivion. When Simpkins woke him to change for dinner, the last wisps of gin had cleared from his brain and he knew just how to drive off Nerissa's blue devils.

The valet helped him dress and bore off his riding clothes with a sigh. Miles was proving a sad disappointment to Simpkins, as his wardrobe grew more and more countrified with every purchase.

Miles went down to the drawing room and found Nerissa already there, listlessly turning the pages of a magazine lent by one of her new friends. She looked up, flushed, and gave him a wan smile. He had to take her mind off whichever popinjay had caught her fancy.

"Nerissa, I've just recollected that Sir Barnabas used to give a party for the tenantry and servants every Boxing Day."

"Boxing Day!" She was dismayed, but he had her interest.

"I know that's impossible. Hibby and Cook would collapse in spasms if we suggested such a thing. But why not Twelfth Night? Could you organize it by then?"

"Twelfth Night? I shall have to consult Cook and Mrs. Hibbert, but I don't see why not. Oh, Miles, that does sound like fun."

The sparkle had returned to her beautiful eyes, and he was satisfied.

* * *

"Parties for peasants!" snorted Euphemia Chidwell. At last recovered from the indisposition that had kept her abed for a fortnight, she lolled on the sofa in the morning room, stouter than ever. "Pearls before swine! And talking of pearls, I can scarcely credit the unmitigated impudence of that man Harwood spending our—well, Neville's—money on pearls for that Paphian. Why, my own are not half so fine!"

Sir Barnabas grinned. If Harwood was so brazen as to disregard the intent, if not the letter, of the will, at least the fellow had the sense to let Nerissa's pearls outshine Effie's.

"Dear Nerissa looked quite charming," sighed Sophie, guiltily retrieving a hairpin from her lap and shoving it at random into her hair.

"The hussy has thoroughly gulled you, as well as Harwood. You appear to regard her as a daughter!"

Sophie pinkened. "Oh, no, not a daughter, Effie. I am much too old. More as a granddaughter, perhaps."

Something caught in Sir Barnabas's throat, and he had to clear it in a way that would have emerged as a loud "Harrumph!" had it been at all audible.

"Pah! You always were a sentimental nodcock, Sophie. If we don't make shift to send your 'granddaughter' packing, and Miles with her, we shall find ourselves struggling for existence in a tumbledown shack."

"Tumbledown shack?" Sophie faltered.

"Tumbledown shack," said Effie firmly.

Sir Barnabas wished he could reassure Sophie. Vague as ever, she had no idea that the four hundred a year he had left the sisters, together with Effie's two from her husband, would allow them a comfortable if not luxurious life.

Effie continued. "We must act. Merely watching and hoping will get us nowhere. Barnabas was a looby to suppose the two of them are not clever enough to outwit his paltry rules."

Looby, indeed! Who was the only one to make any positive effort to encourage Miles and Nerissa to succumb to their lecherous propensities? His momentary lapse into sentiment banished, the late baronet snarled with frustrated fury. Whatever he did, Effie would never know.

"I cannot imagine why I did not think of it before," Effie was saying. "Just because Miles and Nerissa have not indulged their base passions where we could observe them, there is no reason why we should not report to Harwood that we caught them misbehaving."

"Oh, Effie, no! Bearing false witness . . . I am sure dear Raymond would not approve."

"Drat Raymond! Between his piety and Jane's fear of social ostracism, we shall never oust the usurpers. We shall not tell them. Lawyer Harwood will scarcely have the impertinence to doubt my word."

Will he not? thought Sir Barnabas gleefully. Much she knew of the little man's stubborn willfulness. It wouldn't work, and who'd be the looby then?

"Don't sit gaping at me, Sophie. Ring the bell. And pass me those comfits. I must keep up my strength."

Unhappily, Sophie obeyed.

Effie managed to crunch up a dozen sugared almonds before a footman appeared. "James," she directed him, "find Mr. Harwood and tell him I wish to speak to him at once."

As the door closed behind him, Sophie raised her voice in timid protest. "That was Ben, Effie, not James."

"Fiddlesticks. All footmen are called James."

"Only recollect, Nerissa told you most particularly that the servants are to be called by their proper names in her house."

"Nerissa is not here," said Effie, displaying with a savage crunch her opinion of Nerissa's reproof. "And Addlescombe Manor will not be her house much longer!"

The dish of comfits was empty by the time Mr. Harwood came in. "I'm sorry to keep you waiting, ladies," he said genially. "I was in the middle of an important letter when your message reached me. Now, what can I do for you?"

Effie's scowl showed what she thought of the lawyer's letter being more important than her business, Sir Barnabas thought, amused. However, rather than taking Harwood's words as a warning, she smoothed the ill temper from her face and replaced it with what he guessed to be an attempt at disillusioned sorrow.

"Effie, pray don't," Sophie pleaded.

As usual, her sister ignored her. "Mr. Harwood, I deeply regret being the bearer of sad tidings. Your trust in Miss Wingate and Mr. Courtenay has been shockingly abused. With my own eyes"—she produced a shudder that made her look like a singularly unappetizing purple blancmange—"I saw them together,"—here her voice lowered dramatically—*"in bed!* In the very act!"

"Indeed." Harwood's voice was a very pattern-card of skepticism. "When did this distressing incident occur?"

Effie obviously had not prepared her story. "Oh, last night," she said with a dismissive wave of her pudgy white hand. "I would have told you earlier, but Sophie begged me to keep it secret. Naturally, I know my duty to the truth and to Sir Barnabas's will."

"Naturally. Might I inquire where you saw the . . . hmm . . . aforementioned spectacle?"

"In Nerissa's chamber. Sophie and I went to look at the gown Nerissa intends to wear for the tenants' party and—"

"Oh, no!"

"Be quiet, Sophie."

"So this event occurred during the hours when the household was up and about?"

"Yes. Well, er . . ."

"I never saw anything!" Sophie burst out.

The lawyer nodded to her kindly and turned his stern, contemptuous regard on Effie. "Mrs. Chidwell, I should be remiss in *my* duty to the late Sir Barnabas's wishes were I to accept the unsupported word of one who hopes to gain from the disgrace of his putative heirs. I must advise you not to repeat this improbable tale to anyone else. Should you do so, I shall advise Miss Wingate and Mr. Courtenay to enter a suit for slander. Good day to you, ma'am."

He stalked out, every dignified inch of his short, round figure aquiver with righteous indignation.

"I have never been so insulted in my life!" Effie gasped. "Sophie, my smelling salts!"

"You do not possess any," her sister said reproachfully. "You have always decried the use of a vinaigrette as a milksop's remedy and you made me throw mine away."

Sir Barnabas nearly laughed his immaterial head off. Who was the looby now? A proper cake she had made of herself, and in the process she had once more proved him right, as always.

In time he'd be proved right about Miles and Nerissa, too, but time was rapidly passing. Three months gone already. Once the six months he had specified were up, the pair could thumb their noses at him and fornicate to their hearts' content.

He dared neither rest on his laurels nor leave it to Euphemia to contrive a better plan. He would proceed with one more haunting of the bedroom passage before resorting to sterner measures.

Chapter Sixteen

Nerissa's giggle turned into a hiccup.

"Too much cider," said Miles severely, hunting on the doorstep for the key he had just dropped. "Hush, we don't want to wake anyone."

"They must be sound asleep by now. How feather—hic—brained of them all to leave early! It was a wonderful party, was it not? Quite as much fun as the Por-hic-chester assembly. I'm not bosky, it's the bubbles."

"Here it is." As he turned the key in the lock, Sir Barnabas hastily removed his ear from the keyhole. "Come on, quietly now."

Entering the hall, Nerissa tossed back her hood and untied the ribbon of her cloak. "Hic."

"Take a deep breath and hold it as long as you can." Miles tore his gaze from her expanding chest with a visible effort, Sir Barnabas noted. "I must say, Old Amos's one-legged hornpipe was worth a fortune to behold," he said in a carefully casual tone, lighting their waiting night candles at the lamp on the hall table.

"Your demonstration of the waltz with Mrs. Bragg was worth seeing, too. I do think you might

have let me dance it, as no gentry were there to disapprove."

"Word gets about. If you have finished hiccuping,
let's go up."

"Oh, yes, I cannot wait to get into bed." She
clung to his arm as they ascended the stairs.

An invisible gleam in his invisible eye, Sir
Barnabas slid up the banisters. This was the night.
All he had to do was make them feel safe from the
spy in the alcove—that ninny Jane tonight, reluctantly, on Effie's insistence—in case they guessed
they were still watched.

They reached the junction of the passages. In a
single swirl of frigid breath, Sir Barnabas blew out
the night lamp and both their candles.

"What a draft!" Nerissa exclaimed. "Did you
close the front door?"

"I did, and locked and bolted it. Shall I find a tinderbox, or can you manage without a light?"

"I can manage. Since I told Maud I should not
need her, I put on a gown that is easy to take off."

"Good." There was a laugh in Miles's voice.

Footsteps. A door clicked shut.

At last Sir Barnabas's ghostly night vision ad-
justed to the sudden darkness. He saw the alcove
curtains stir. Jane emerged and fumbled and stumbled her way along the passage. Ah-ha, so the implication of the extinguished lights was so obvious,
even she was able to draw the correct inference! He
followed her to her own chamber.

"Neville, wake up! They blew out their candles."

"Huh?" Neville emerged from the blankets, his
striped nightcap askew.

"They blew out their candles. Miles and Nerissa.
And the lamp on the table."

"Huh?"

"Oh, do wake up. They did not want me to see that they both went into the same bedchamber!"

Neville was suddenly very much awake. "Quick, go and rouse the others. We'll want as many witnesses as possible. But quietly, mind. We don't want to warn 'em." He jumped out of bed and felt around for his dressing gown.

"I have no light!"

"Wake Aubrey first."

Sir Barnabas remembered his nephew kept a candle lit at his bedside, whether for fear of the dark or for admiring himself in his hand-glass if he woke in the night, no one knew.

In no time the hall was filled with dressing-gown-clad people, Aubrey's scarlet brocade standing out against the practical blue and brown woolens of the others. Each held a candle lighted at Aubrey's. In a body they moved toward the side passage, only Sophie trailing unwillingly in the rear.

Floorboards creaked under the mass of slippered feet. Perhaps that was what alerted their prey, or perhaps Euphemia's commanding and far from hushed "Hush!" was to blame. In all events, as they turned the corner, Miles stepped out of his chamber.

The war party shuffled to a halt.

Miles pulled the door to behind him and lounged against the doorjamb. "How kind of you all to come and make sure that we are safe returned from our rustic romp," he said sardonically.

Euphemia marched forward. Brushing past him, she burst into his room. The rest took heart and streamed after her.

Miss Sophie stopped beside Miles. "I'm so sorry," she whispered, tears trickling down her lined cheeks.

He put his arm around her shoulders and hugged her, grinning. After that, Sir Barnabas was resigned to finding the rest of the family, candles held high, staring down in baffled spleen at the empty bed.

Sir Neville halfheartedly opened the clothespress and peered inside. Raymond Reece checked under the bed. Jane tried the connecting door, rattling the latch irritably.

"She escaped through this door! I know she came in here."

They all jumped as Miles remarked in a caustic voice, "I'm sure Mrs. Chidwell will be happy to confirm that the key to that door is in Mr. Harwood's safekeeping."

Looking anything but happy, Effie nodded. Disgruntled and sheepish, they filed out, eyes lowered to avoid the sight of Miles's derisive smile. Sir Barnabas followed the embarrassed retreat, more than happy to be invisible.

As everyone fled around the corner, Sir Barnabas turned the other way. Nerissa's door was ajar, just a crack. No wonder neither he nor Jane had heard it close. She must have pushed it shut behind her, too sleepy to check that the latch caught. He slithered uncomfortably through the narrow gap. Her gown lay in a crumpled heap on the floor by the bed. Her nightgown was still spread across the foot of the bed, where her abigail had laid it out before leaving for the party. Nerissa had not bothered to change out of her chemise.

She lay lost in childlike slumber, a slight smile curving her lips.

Sir Barnabas felt a most peculiar tightness in his chest. Damn that rascally mountebank for running off with Anthea and robbing him of innocent grand-children he might have loved!

But it was the mountebank's butter-wouldn't-melt-in-her-mouth daughter he was looking down upon. Born and bred to the dissolute world of the theater, he reminded himself. Actress or wardrobe mistress, she played the role of virtuous maiden to admiration. Somehow he had to trip her up, make her bungle her lines and forget her part.

Thus far, for all Sir Barnabas's efforts, Miles had held her in his arms only once, and that at a moment when she was angry with him for laughing at her efforts to mount the mare. The way matters were between them now, if they found themselves embracing, the job was as good as done.

Somehow he had to trip her—that was it! He had failed to trick her into Miles's arms, so now he'd try to trip her.

Though Nerissa's unfortunate weakness had pre-vented her taking her place upon the stage, her par-ents had raised her in the expectation that she would follow in their footsteps. She had never been more glad of their training.

The role of Miles's friend and little sister, natural before the Christmas assembly, now had to be acted with every ounce of skill she possessed. For another three months they must live in the same house. She could not embarrass him—and herself—by letting him learn, from a word or a glance, how much she loved him.

So she laughed and teased him, won giant rocs' eggs and lost palaces of onyx and jasper at cards, willed herself not to blush at the casual touch of his hand. It was all easier than she expected. Mama and Papa had taught her well.

After Twelfth Night, the January weather turned foul, throwing them together indoors even more than usual. Nerissa decided to give a dinner for the neighbors once the lanes were passable again. She had enjoyed organizing the Twelfth Night party, and the necessary consultations with Cook, Mrs. Hibbert, Snodgrass, Miss Sophie, and even Aunt Jane took her out of Miles's way.

She had truly been too busy to spend much time with him. Nonetheless, one evening about the middle of the month he finished reading aloud to her his expurgated version of the *Arabian Nights* stories.

"What shall we read next?" he asked.

"I don't know. Would you mind if I invited Miss Sophie to join us?"

"For the next book? Not at all," he said, adding wickedly, "though we had best choose something a little more suitable for maiden ears."

Nerissa laughed, but she knew she failed to suppress a blush. Still, in the circumstances, any young lady might be forgiven for pink cheeks, even if no truly proper young lady would have landed herself in a similar situation.

"Mr. Harwood might like to read with us, too. Let us go and see what we can find," she proposed. "We can choose several and see which they prefer."

Miss Sophie and the lawyer had already retired to bed, as had Aunt Jane and Matilda, so she'd have to ask them on the morrow. Uncle Neville, Aubrey, Raymond, and Cousin Euphemia were absorbed in their cards and did not so much as glance up as Nerissa and Miles left the drawing room. They had all been oddly subdued recently.

In the library, Nerissa recollected a book on one of the upper shelves which she thought might be suitable. Miles moved the library steps into position for her and gave her his hand to mount them. At the top, some two feet and a half above the floor, she took hold of a shelf to steady herself, hoping he had not felt her hand tremble in his. A moment passed before she was able to focus on the titles before her nose.

Miles took a book from the shelf beside him. "Here, this might do." Turning toward her, he opened it at the title page and read: *"Personal Travels and Vicissitudes of four years and a half in America, being the Struggles of a Man in pursuit of Independence and a Settlement.* By John Davis, Esquire."

"Yes, that sounds interesting."

She had found the volume she was looking for, a *Historical Survey of the Customs, Habits, and Present State of the Gipsies.* As she started down the steps, Miles moved away, book in hand.

"I noticed the memoirs of Frederick the Great's sister the other day, somewhere along here," he said.

Nerissa's foot caught in her skirt. The book flew from her hand as she twisted and grabbed at the shelves, trying to save herself.

"Miles!" she cried, landing crookedly on one foot. An agonizing pain shot up her leg. She crumpled. Her head met something solid, and merciful blackness descended.

"But, Nerissa dear, Dr. Firston said you are on no account to put any weight on your ankle for at least a week," said Miss Sophie dubiously.

"I know, but I simply cannot bear to spend another day in bed, even with the novels Caroline and Mrs. Firston so kindly brought me. Surely between them Miles and the footmen can carry me down to the morning room without any desperate affront to propriety."

"There is a sort of chair with poles your grandfather used when his gout was troublesome. It always seemed to me a shockingly precarious contrivance."

"If Grandfather entrusted himself to it, so shall I," Nerissa declared.

So an hour later she was ensconced on the sofa in the morning room. Clucking, Mrs. Hibbert tucked a third pillow behind her and dispatched Maud after another shawl. Snodgrass directed the placement of a small table at her side, set a handbell and her book upon it, and even deigned to poke up the fire with his own august hand. Cook sent in enough hot plum turnovers to feed an army, to "keep up her strength." And Tredgarth, the gardener, had picked and brought up to the house enough yellow aconites and dainty snowdrops to fill half a dozen small vases.

"*Pampered* is the only word for it," Miles exclaimed, helping himself to a turnover as the last of the servants left the room.

"They are all very fond of Nerissa," said Miss Sophie, "and I am sure you deserve it, dear."

"I don't know what you deserve for being such a peagoose as not to fall ten seconds earlier, when I was close enough to catch you!" He shook his head, smiling. "You gave me the fright of my life."

"I assure you such was not my intention,"

Nerissa said indignantly. "The hem of my skirt just wrapped itself around my feet."

"Dangerous things, long skirts." Miles gave a reminiscent sigh. "I always did prefer the shorter hems of a few years ago. Ah, well, I must be off. I told Bragg I'd meet him in the office at eleven. Shall we read this afternoon? *Not* the book that brought about your downfall—I have taken it in dislike."

Nerissa agreed, and he went off whistling "My Heart Was So Free" from the *Beggar's Opera,* slightly out of tune, as usual. She was glad to see him cheerful. Miss Sophie had told her how devastated he had been when she fell. He had roused the entire household and sent a groom through darkness and sleet to fetch the doctor with orders to bring him back come hell or high water. Then, forbidden her chamber while she was confined to her bed, he had moped about the house, refusing to go out despite suddenly fine weather lest she should have a relapse during his absence.

"You are a little pale, dear," said Miss Sophie anxiously.

"I have the headache a little," Nerissa acknowledged.

"I knew I should not let you come down. I shall send for Dr. Firston at once!"

"Pray do not, Cousin Sophie. He said I showed no signs of a concussion, but the lump on my head is still tender and brushing my hair did not soothe it! I shall be better directly if I just sit quietly for a while."

"Then I shall leave you in peace. I believe I shall take a stroll in the shrubbery since the sun is shining. Here is the bell Snodgrass brought—so thoughtful. You must ring if you wish for company and send for me. I shall come at once."

"Bless you, Cousin Sophie. What should I do without you?" Nerissa closed suddenly tearful eyes. Dear as Miles was, she thought, without Miss Sophie's support she would have given up and run back to York long ago.

Her headache faded quickly, before the plum turnovers were quite cold. She ate one and was licking her fingers, when the door opened. Hurriedly she reached for a napkin.

"Mr. Digby, miss," Ben announced in a voice of deep disapproval. "He *would* see you, miss." His tone declared that he had tried in vain to stop the intruder.

Nerissa had no desire whatsoever to see Clive Digby. However, a rapid review of the rules brought to light no excuse to deny a visitor who was already halfway across the room. "Thank you, Ben," she said, swallowing a sigh. "Good day, Mr. Digby. How kind of you to call. Will you not sit down?"

Ignoring her invitation, he blurted out, "I came yesterday, Miss Wingate, as soon as I heard of your accident, but I was not allowed to see you. So I spoke to your uncle instead." To her astonishment, he dropped to his knees and seized her hand. "Miss Wingate—Nerissa, if I may be so bold—I have Sir Neville's permission to address you."

"To address me?" She tried without success to retrieve her hand.

"To beg you to be my wife. I opened my creel—budget to him, and he obligingly agreed that—"

"Mr. Digby, Sir Neville is my *great*-uncle, a distant relative and in no respect my guardian."

"He is not? Surely that fellow Courtenay . . ."

"Certainly not."

"Then who must I apply to?" he asked plaintively.

"That is scarcely relevant, sir." At last she wrenched her hand from his ardent clasp. "Since I fear I cannot accept your most flattering offer."

Her rejection rolled off his back like water from a fish's scales.

"Sir Neville said you would be happy to rise to my fly—I mean, to entertain my suit. At least let me cast my line—spout my speech, that is."

"It would be most improper of me to listen," she pointed out, half amused, half flustered by his persistence, "as you have not, in fact, applied to my . . . guardian."

"Who *is* your guardian? I will travel to the farthest end of the country if you will only give me a hint that you regard my lure—er, my offer—with favor."

"But I do not! Pray stand up, sir."

"Dearest Nerissa!" This time he possessed himself of both her hands, so that she was unable to reach for the bell. "I have taken you by surprise, but I must assure you of my undying devotion. Without you I am a fish out of water. You have hooked my heart . . ."

"Sir, I beg of you . . ."

Abruptly he let go of her hands and lunged at her like a pike at a minnow. Somehow she dodged his arms. His wet lips skimmed her forehead as she slithered past him and off the sofa. Inelegantly and all too slowly she hobbled toward the door, her ankle agony at every step.

And Miles was there.

She stumbled into his arms, gasping, "Miles,

pray tell Mr. Digby I am not going to marry him!"

A bewildering wave of relief and unreasoning fury deluged through him. How dare the cloddish oaf force his attentions upon her! How dare the brute drive her to escape on her sprained ankle! Miles wanted to take Clive Digby by the collar and the seat of his riding breeches, presently conveniently upraised, and hurl him headfirst through the window.

But such vigorous action, while soothing his feelings, would only distress Nerissa.

Instead, he swept her off her feet and said in his driest tone, "Digby, Miss Wingate is not going to marry you. If you will kindly stop floundering upon the sofa, I shall return her to the place she ought never to have left. Perhaps you are unaware that she has an injured limb?"

When a crimson-faced Digby had departed and Nerissa's ankle was swathed in a hot poultice of bran and comfrey, Miles sat down beside her. She was still a trifle pale and shaken. He felt an overwhelming desire to take her in his arms and comfort her. Only the possibility that she might interpret such a move as something other than brotherly affection and protectiveness deterred him.

"Well?" he said with a quizzing smile. The only thing to do was to turn the whole affair into a joke. "A coarse fisherman indeed."

"Oh, no, Miles, you have it the wrong way around. He said I had hooked his heart, and that without me he is a fish out of water!"

"A pity I hadn't a gaff handy."

Her giggle delighted him. "Thank heaven you came, with or without gaff."

"Ben was uneasy. He told Snodgrass, and

Snodgrass came straight for me." Now he wanted to shake her and demand to be told what she meant by entertaining a gentleman alone. He refrained. She was still not altogether up to snuff. Doubtless she had not known how to deal with the situation. In fact, her best course of action would have been to leave the room, which she was unable to do. It was all Digby's fault. "What the deuce did the fellow think he was up to, intruding upon you without a chaperon?"

"That, at least, was not his fault. He said Uncle Neville gave him permission to pay his addresses, and I daresay gentlemen do not habitually propose marriage with a chaperon present?"

"I wouldn't know. I told you, I'm not the marrying sort. So Sir Neville allowed Digby to believe he is your guardian?"

"Yes, and suggested I would favor his suit!" Nerissa said tartly. "I don't understand why."

"He must have hoped that one way or another the situation would lead to your downfall. I fear they are beginning to grow desperate. We must beware!"

"Matters are desperate!" Euphemia announced. She dropped heavily onto the sofa beside her sister, making Sophie bounce.

Sir Barnabas silently agreed, glad Effie would never know of the infuriating fact that for once his views were in accord with hers.

His attempt to precipitate Nerissa into Miles's arms by entangling her feet in her hem had been a mortifying failure. He hadn't meant to hurt her. He was prepared to acknowledge that he regretted the pain he had caused. But he was also disgusted by the way his servants, disloyal to his memory, had rallied around her. And the stream of callers, from as far away as Porchester and even beyond, braving the wintry roads to come and express their sympathy!

That was not what he had intended. Worse, the unexpected result had made him chary of further efforts which might go equally astray. His mind was devoid of promising plans.

So he listened with interest to Euphemia.

"There are only two months left. We must do something."

"But last time we did something, it all turned out to be a mistake," Sophie timidly reminded her.

"Because Jane made a mull of it. She made a cake of herself and in the process succeeded in making us all look foolish. Even me! We cannot rely on the others. This time it will be just you and me. I suppose I can trust you, Sophronia?" She glared at Sophie, whose mouth opened to emit an inarticulate squeak.

"Good! Now, this is what you are to do. Miles is working in the estate office. You must tell Nerissa he wants to see her. Then you follow her there and lock them in together. The only window is small and high. You will put a ladder against the wall outside and check on them now and then. No one will hear them away down at that end of the house and a few hours confined in that little room—"

"But, Effie, I have no key."

"Ninny! The office is kept locked when no one is there, and Miles always leaves his key in the outside of the door when he goes in. I checked."

"Oh. And what will you do, Effie?"

"I shall wait here for you to bring me the key," said Euphemia majestically, "and then to come and tell me when the naughty business begins."

"Oh," said Sophie.

Chapter Seventeen

Nerissa's ankle was very nearly recovered, but she still tended to favor it. She limped down the passage toward the estate room. Behind her sneaked Sophie, with Sir Barnabas close at her heels. Trust Effie to make her sister do the dirty work.

The door to the office was ajar. Nerissa went in.

"Miles, Cousin Sophie said you wish to see me? Oh, good day, Mr. Bragg. I hope you do not look for my advice on estate business, for I know nothing of it, I fear."

Sophie heaved a sigh of relief and scuttled off back down the corridor. Sir Barnabas followed, a sour smile on his face. Effie's plot had failed before it was well under way. She'd have to think again.

He heard Bragg, the unwitting marplot, say, "Good day, Miss Wingate. I'm sure I don't know—"

"Miss Sophie told you I need you?" Miles's voice interrupted, sounding puzzled. "She has muddled something someone else said to her. I have not seen her since breakfast. But since you are here, let me just show you . . ."

Eager to witness Effie's discomfiture, Sir Barnabas passed out of earshot.

"You have locked them in?" Euphemia avidly greeted Sophie. "Give me the key."

"I have not got it, Effie."

"You haven't? Why not?"

"I did not lock the door."

"Dolt, can you never do anything right?"

"Mr. Bragg was in the office with them." Sophie's delight was barely disguised. "I did not think it would serve to shut them in with him."

"You should have contrived a pretext to lure him out. Go back and do it at once, before Nerissa leaves."

"But I cannot think of any pretext, Effie."

"Must I do everything myself?" Irritably Euphemia surged up from the sofa. "Come, quickly. I shall lure Bragg out. You hide, then as soon as I have him well out of the way, lock the dratted door."

She stalked off, Sophie scurrying after and Sir Barnabas once more bringing up the rear.

Just before they reached the office, Effie stopped at the door to a storage room on the opposite side of the corridor. "Hide in here," she ordered her sister in a whisper. "Leave the door open just a crack. The moment you hear my footsteps and Bragg's go past, nip out silently and turn the key."

Her face doleful, Sophie disappeared into the storeroom.

Euphemia continued to the office. Without knocking, she pushed the door wide open, stepped into the room, and announced peremptorily, "Bragg, I want a word with you."

"We are just finished," said Miles cheerfully, "so we shall leave you to it."

Nerissa slipped through the gap between Effie

and the doorpost. Miles followed as Bragg courteously inquired, "What can I do for you, ma'am?"

Effie moved forward, spluttering, "But I . . . I did not mean . . ."

Miles pulled the door closed behind him, and he and Nerissa set off along the passage.

"What on earth does she want with your bailiff?" Nerissa asked.

"Who can guess? But Bragg is quite capable of taking care of himself. Here, take my arm."

"My ankle is perfectly all right, really." She sounded absurdly guilty. "I limp only because I half expect it to hurt."

Miles laughed. "Still, you ought not to ride or walk far as yet. Should you like to go for a drive this afternoon?"

"Yes, that will be delightful. My preparations for the dinner party are well under way, and I still have a couple of days for the final arrangements. You and Snodgrass have settled on the wines, have you not?"

"Yes. The old man kept a pretty decent cellar, even if he was a spiteful old surlyboots."

Sticking out his tongue at their retreating backs in a lamentably childish manner, Sir Barnabas moved up to the door and laid his ear against it. He was dying to know what excuse Effie was offering for her peculiar behavior, but the voices within were muffled, indistinct.

He had to dodge when Sophie suddenly darted out of the storage room, dashed across the corridor, turned the key in the lock, and triumphantly removed it.

"There," she said to herself with a look of such mischief as he had never thought to see on her sweet, compliant face, "just as Effie ordered." And she trotted after Miles and Nerissa.

* * *

Two days later, the memory of her afternoon in the estate office and the humiliation of her subsequent release still had the power to bring howls of rage from Euphemia. Sir Barnabas listened with pleasure.

"That blockhead Bragg simply announced he could always find work to do," she stormed, "and then ignored me. Six hours I spent looking at the top of his head. His hair is thinning, and so I told him."

"That was not kind, Effie," her sister remonstrated.

"Kind! I was not feeling kind. How even you could be so featherbrained as to lock up the wrong people and not realize it for six hours . . ."

"I heard footsteps passing, and voices in the room." Sophie patiently repeated her story. Sir Barnabas thought she was rather proud of her cunning, and certainly Effie did not seem to suspect—or simply could not believe—that the worm had turned. "The door was shut, so I could not see who was there. When I could not find you to give you the key, I put it on your dressing table."

And how finding it there had puzzled one and all! Sir Barnabas chuckled.

"But then you forgot about the ladder and the window and went out for a drive with Miles and Nerissa without ever realizing that meant someone else was in the estate office! Only you could be such a complete knock-in-the-cradle. You and Sir Barnabas. The clunch was wrong this time. That will was the biggest blunder of his life, and his rightful heirs are going to be done out of a fortune. Miles and Nerissa are too clever for him by half."

A clunch was he? Sir Barnabas's bellow would have shaken the rafters had it been audible. Indeed, had he not been dead for several months, an apoplexy might well have borne him away. A knock-in-the-cradle was he? His will a blunder? Miles and Nerissa too clever for him?

He'd show the harridan. He'd show them all.

For the dinner party, Nerissa wore a new gown with a short train. The amber crepe over a white sarcenet slip was modestly trimmed with rouleaux of white satin, wide at the bottom of the skirt and narrow around the neckline. Miss Sophie had suggested that it was uncivil in a hostess to dress much finer than her guests, and Nerissa agreed.

"A vulgar display of wealth," Miles had added, "though you'd be surprised how many do it anyway."

Though simple, the gown was quite becoming, Nerissa thought hopefully before she was overcome by last-minute nerves.

What did she, a theater wardrobe mistress, think she was doing entertaining the gentry at a formal dinner? This was no casual morning call, potluck nuncheon, or afternoon tea. She was bound to make a mull of it.

"Why did I ever invite them?" she wailed as Maud put the last touches to her hair. "I shall do something dreadful, and they will all know I am a mere seamstress aping her betters."

"Nonsense, child," said Miss Sophie quite severely. "You are Miss Wingate of Addlescombe, granddaughter of a baronet, and all your guests are aware of it."

" 'Tis every inch a lady you are now, miss,"

Maud put in encouragingly. "What's past is past, and it don't do to dwell on it."

"Besides," Miss Sophie went on, "a formal occasion is often easier than an informal, because the rules are laid down for you and all you need do is follow them."

A knock on the door was followed by Miles's voice. "Nerissa, are you ready to go down?"

"Just coming." How typical of him to be there when she needed his support. The very sight of him, handsome and elegant in black and white, gave her confidence—and awoke her pride. She wasn't going to let him or anyone else see her trepidation.

She smiled up at him, then noticed his worried look. Surely he had no reason to be nervous! She touched his arm. "What is the matter, Miles?"

"I've been thinking. You arranged with Snodgrass to provide cards and card tables after dinner, did you not?"

"Yes. Miss Sophie said gentlemen, and ladies, too, often like to play. But they will not be set out unless they are needed."

He ran his hand through his hair. "The trouble is, while Clive Digby may be satisfied playing for fish, the rest will play for money, even if it's only shillings. And if I'm asked to join in, I'm dashed if I can see a polite way to avoid it. I've never hosted anything but a card evening and supper for gentlemen before."

"But you have been to plenty of dinner parties, or you could not have helped Miss Sophie teach me how to go on. You must have seen what your hosts did in that situation."

"Sat down and played."

"Oh." She thought hard, then gave him a quizzing smile. "You know, I don't believe you need be concerned. No one will wonder if you prefer flirting to cards, and between Anna Pettigrew and the Firston girls, there will be plenty of competition for your company."

Miles laughed ruefully. "True, though I am a cox-comb to say it. Bless you." He dropped a swift, light kiss on her forehead as Miss Sophie came to join them.

"I was just reminding Maud of what she must do to look after the visiting ladies. Heavens, Miles, you have not combed your hair!"

"Wait for me." He dashed into his chamber and reemerged a moment later, once more impeccable. "Let us go down, ladies."

The Pettigrews, the Firstons, and the Digbys all arrived right on time. In the bustle of greetings, Nerissa lost what remained of her anxiety. She knew these people, and though there were one or two she could not like, she counted several as friends. It was a pity Clive Digby was so obviously in the sulks, but at least he had turned up and not spoiled her numbers.

She was glad that General Pettigrew's rank enti-tled him to be seated on her right. He consumed his bowl of lukewarm soup without the least sign that anything was amiss, chatting cheerfully the while. Nerissa did her best to respond, but she abandoned her soup in dismay and she noted many another bowl being taken away half full. She was puzzled. They had come into the dining room on time, not kept the dinner waiting. Admittedly the kitchen was some distance away, but Cook usually managed to serve food hot. No doubt providing a formal meal with several removes to each course had flustered her, though she had extra help in the kitchen.

All the rest of the first course was equally cold.

Nerissa caught Snodgrass's eye. He made a helpless gesture and discreetly disappeared, to remonstrate with Cook, she hoped. Fortunately the main dishes were a fine turbot in aspic and a ham, and the lobster salad was delicious.

The second course hot dishes—game and vegetables and a fricassee of veal—arrived steaming, and the cakes, pastries, and jellies all looked most appetizing. In relief, Nerissa reached for her wine, which she had scarcely tasted.

The glass toppled over—before she even touched it, she could have sworn. A red stain spread across the white damask tablecloth.

General Pettigrew stopped the flood with his napkin just before it reached the edge of the table and dripped onto his trousers. He patted Nerissa's hand. "No harm done, my dear," he assured her.

But people were staring—in surprise, sympathy, or disdain, according to their natures.

Snodgrass quickly covered the stain with clean napkins. Flurried, Nerissa turned to the gentleman on her left, Clive Digby's father, and offered him the gravy for his roast pheasant. As she passed it to him, her sleeve caught on thin air. The gravy boat emptied its contents into Mr. Digby's lap.

He sprang up with a cry. Once again Snodgrass was there, his soothing murmur promising clean inexpressibles, gently urging the ruffled gentleman from the room.

Nerissa began to think she must be asleep in her bed, dreaming. Any moment she would wake up, go down to breakfast, laugh with Miles over her dreadful nightmare. But there he was at the far end of the table, determinedly making conversation with old Mrs. Firston. In between, on face after face, surprise turned to dismay, sympathy to pity, disdain to contempt.

She could not eat another bite. Somehow she stopped herself rushing out. When everyone seemed to have finished eating, she caught Miss Sophie's eye, Caroline Pettigrew's eye, and rose to lead the ladies out.

As if the movement loosened them, her hairpins started to come out. A tress flopped down to her shoulder and she felt the rest begin to uncoil.

Her foot tangled in her train. She stumbled, all but sprawled across the besmirched table, saved in the nick of time by General Pettigrew's strong arm and swift reaction.

"Bosky, by Jove!" said a male voice farther up the table.

"Disgraceful!" said a female.

Head held high, face burning, Nerissa moved toward the door. There she met Mrs. Pettigrew, who regarded her with unconcealed disapprobation and not a little alarm.

And somehow Nerissa's foot landed on Mrs. Pettigrew's train just as that lady stepped forward. There was a horrid ripping sound. A gaping hole appeared between bodice and skirt.

"What can you expect of an actress?" inquired Euphemia in the smuggest of tones.

"General," said Mrs. Pettigrew frigidly, "Caroline, Anna, we shall leave at once."

Nerissa fled.

Miles found her in her chamber. She stood half concealed by the flowered chintz window curtains, forehead pressed against the glass, white-knuckled hands clenched on the sill, disheveled hair about her shoulders.

"Have they all gone?" she asked dully as his footsteps sounded on the polished floorboards.

He stopped just behind her. "Yes, all of them. Caroline Pettigrew and young Mrs. Firston wanted to stay but . . ."

"Caroline had to obey her mother, and Jenny her mama-in-law. They are right, I am not fit for well-bred young ladies to consort with."

"Balderdash!" Miles exploded. "Such a string of disasters didn't happen by chance. I know perfectly well you were not bosky, and far from being clumsy, you move with exceptional grace."

"Theatrical training." She turned and gave him a wavering smile, her gray eyes swimming in tears.

"It was your dear relations. They set it up, I'll be damned if I know how, but I'd wager a fortune on it. Don't cry, Nerissa," he said helplessly as the tears spilled over. "I'll share your grandfather's fortune with you, you know I will."

He took her in his arms and held her while she wept into his shoulder, his heart aching for her.

"It's not the m-money," she said through sobs. "It's knowing my family h-hates me, and being sh-shamed before all those people."

"I'll bring 'em back," he vowed. He'd think of a way. He had to. "I shall convince them none of it was your fault if I have to go from house to house on bended knee, I promise."

"Oh, Miles!" She raised her head and those lovely eyes gazed up at him. "How very, very kind you are."

Kissing her was the most natural thing in the world. Her lips were tender, sweet, with a tang of salt tears. Her hair was silken-soft beneath his hand. Her body fitted to his so perfectly, he could not believe he had ever wanted a shorter, plumper woman.

And want her he did. Desire burned through him, flamed in his loins. She clung to him and he clasped her tighter, her breasts crushed against his chest, the thunder of her racing heart echoing his own. Her lips parted . . .

"Stop, Sophie, you sapskull!" hissed a venomous voice. "Not yet!"

"Stop!" cried Miss Sophie, dashing into the chamber all atwitter, leaving a ribbon from her sleeve in her sister's grasp. "Oh, dear, you simply must not, my dears."

Miles found himself several feet from Nerissa, staring at his flushed face in the mirror. He smoothed his ruffled hair with a shaking hand, turned, and said with the best attempt at amused nonchalance he could manage, "I shan't ravish her, you know, ma'am. Not with the door wide open."

"I did not think so," she said uncertainly, and crossed to the bed, where Nerissa sat with bowed head, shoulders hunched, hugging herself. Patting Nerissa's shoulder, Miss Sophie explained, "But Effie was so sure . . ."

"Mrs. Chidwell is all too apt to believe her own fantasies. I was merely comforting Nerissa. It was a friendly kiss, brotherly, not the sort that leads anywhere."

"Of course, Miles, dear."

He appeared to have persuaded Miss Sophie of the innocence of their embrace. What Nerissa thought, he could not guess. He himself was quite aware he was lying. If they had not been interrupted, in another few moments he might well have carried her to the bed and let the tides of passion sweep him away—to ruin him, and doubly to ruin her.

He *had* to act as if the kiss had never happened.

Chapter Eighteen

"You *said* we were to rush in, Effie."

"Not until they were actually in the throes of passion!" Having summoned Sophie to her chamber, Euphemia sat solidly on her dressing table stool like a magistrate on the bench, her erring sister standing before her. "I was just about to send you for Harwood, when you ruined everything," she added, exasperated.

"I misunderstood. Besides," said Sophie spiritedly, "I was never married, so how do you expect me to recognize when the right moment came?"

Bravo, Sir Barnabas silently applauded. If only he had persisted when Euphemia bullied Sophie into refusing his offer. Pride had refused to let him risk another rejection, or perhaps he could have been married to the dear girl these many lonely years. What a wife she would have made, what a gentle mother for Anthea, instead of dwindling into an old maid as unpaid companion to her fat, selfish tyrant of a sister.

Nerissa's arrival had given Sophie a new lease on life. She had welcomed the child with an open mind and come to love her enough to defy Euphemia for her sake—while he, her own grandfather, had done his best to ruin her.

Wincing, he recalled the dreadful dinner party. In an unreasoning fury he had wreaked havoc, left Nerissa's dignity and self-respect in tatters, and again pride was to blame. He would not be proved wrong.

But he *was* wrong!

Nerissa had been brought up in the immoral world of the theater, yet Anthea and the fellow she married had somehow succeeded in preserving her innocence. Nothing lacked in her conduct but a few paltry tricks of etiquette. She recognized Sophie's worth, so long disregarded, and returned her affection. The servants—even Snodgrass!—respected and defended her. In spirit she was a lady through and through.

As for Miles, gamester and rake though he undoubtedly was, he had the self-control to keep his appetites in check when necessary. The boy was also a diligent landowner, a fair but compassionate landlord, and a staunch, generous friend. His offer to share a fortune with Nerissa, which had brought a mist to Sir Barnabas's eyes, was all of a piece with his constant support and protection of his rival for the inheritance.

She had helped him, too. They would make a splendid couple, man and wife, but no, it was too much to hope for. Miles had more than once firmly stated that he was not a marrying man.

Sir Barnabas sighed. He should have put a clause in his will to ensure that in the event of Miles dying without legitimate issue, Nerissa's eldest son should have Addlescombe. Of course, when he wrote the damned thing, he had been so very sure neither would inherit the place.

They still might not, if Euphemia had her way.

"Nerissa is out of the way," she was saying, "but it just means Miles takes the lot unless we stop him. I fear it is futile to try to lure him into gambling. That nonsensical make-believe game Nerissa has him playing seems to suffice him. No, it must be a woman."

"I am sure Mr. Harwood will not permit you to invite a . . . a woman of easy virtue to the manor, Effie."

"A pity, but you are right." Effie ruminated, then brightened. "What has hampered us so far is Nerissa's resistance, I am certain of it. Men are by nature more lustful than females, and Miles is a gambler. If he could have persuaded Nerissa to lie with him, he would have risked the consequences."

"Oh, surely not!"

Rapt in her scheming, Euphemia ignored this negativism. "However, now Nerissa has nothing to lose by giving in to his importunities. All we have to do is confine them together for a few hours . . ."

"That is what you said before," Sophie dared to point out.

Effie glared at her. "But it was I who was confined for an entire afternoon, due to your incompetence. Besides, everything is different now that Nerissa will not care if she is caught."

"What do you mean to do?"

"I have not decided yet. We must wait for an opportunity."

Sir Barnabas no longer supposed for a moment that Miles would make advances or Nerissa succumb to them however long they were shut up together. Nonetheless, he resolved to throw every impediment within his power in Euphemia's way. It would be a pleasure.

* * *

After a wretched night of miserable dreams, Nerissa awoke to find reality no improvement. She was not sure which she dreaded most, facing her relatives after the catastrophic dinner, or Miles after his kiss. To him, it had been no more than an offer of brotherly comfort. To her, it had been a devastating revelation.

At last she understood all the warnings, the prohibitions, the insistence on chaperons. Held close in Miles's arms, enveloped by his virile strength, the heat of his body permeating her, his mouth on hers, she would have done anything he asked of her. So experienced a gentleman must have been aware of her response, her racing pulse, the strange weakness in her limbs accompanied by a burning tension within.

Her grandfather was right. At heart she was a wanton, and worse, an ill-bred wanton who had disgusted all her guests.

For all Miles's kind words, he'd never be able to reestablish her reputation—if he still wanted to after her disgraceful display. In any case, Mr. Harwood would probably demand that she leave at once. Even the good-natured little lawyer must have been scandalized by her deplorable blunders at the dinner party.

She had failed. There was no hope of taking home a fortune to Mama and Papa, and far more painful, she was dreadfully afraid she had forfeited Miles's respect and friendship.

In her purse was enough of the pin money Mr. Harwood allowed her to take her home to York. She could sneak out, ride Vinny down to Riddlebourne, and catch the stagecoach. But no, she would not cry craven. She must show those who hated her that they had not crushed her spirit. And since she had to face them sooner or later, let it be sooner. She would go down to breakfast as if nothing were amiss.

She rang the bell for Maud. The maid bustled about with even more than her usual alacrity, silent sympathy radiating from her in waves. It found expression at last as she draped a blue-and-gray-Paisley shawl about her mistress's shoulders.

"There, miss, that'll keep you warm. Oh, miss, we'm all on your side, even Mr. Snodgrass. He don't hold wi' pixies and such, Mr. Snodgrass, but he said it were like some mischeevious imp stood at your elbow and kept ajogging of it."

"That is what it felt like, Maud." She shuddered. "Every move I made led to another mishap."

"Cook's going to start putting out bread and milk for the Little Folk every night."

That made Nerissa smile, and she went down to the breakfast parlor buoyed by the servants' support. Not that her situation had changed, but it was a little easier to bear.

Matilda and Raymond were already down. Both wished her good morning with an air of commiseration, not the triumphant scorn she expected.

"Came a nasty cropper last night," said Matilda gruffly. "Want you to know I didn't have anything to do with it. Bad as shooting a fox."

Raymond gave her an approving look. "Not my idea of fair play," he agreed. "To seek out transgression is a duty; to induce it a sin. 'A good name is rather to be chosen than great riches,' but you have been cheated of both, cousin."

"Aubrey disapproves, too. Shocking bad taste, he said."

Before Nerissa could express her surprised gratitude for their sympathy and ask how they supposed she had been tricked, if not by a pixie, Ben rushed in.

"I'll have the fresh tea for you in just a minute, miss, and hot toast, and Cook says d'ye care for an omelette, that's best not kept on the sideboard, or aught else she can do for you special."

Nerissa developed a sudden craving for potatoes fried with onions and ham, a favorite after-theater-supper treat. By the time she had finished with the footman, Raymond and Matilda had gone out together, and a moment later Miles and Miss Sophie came in.

"Have those two been crowing over you?" Miles inquired acidly, seating Miss Sophie beside her.

"No, not at all." Glad of Miss Sophie's presence, Nerissa tried to match his lack of embarrassment. Obviously the kiss that had shaken her to the core meant little to him, accustomed as he was to the practised embraces of Cyprians.

He was still her friend, and angry on her behalf. "The wretches cut you?" he demanded as he moved to the sideboard and served Miss Sophie with her usual cup of chocolate and a muffin with strawberry jam.

"No, no, Miles. In fact, they almost apologized. They apparently agree with you that someone caused all my . . . my faux pas." She had to joke about it or cry. "The servants believe it was a mischievous pixie."

He grinned, shaking his head. "Perhaps it was, for I've lain awake half the night, trying without success to work out how it was done."

"If it was, I am safe in the future, for Cook is to leave bread and milk every night to propitiate the

Little People. Only perhaps I have no future. Mr. Harwood will probably ask me to leave now that I am no longer an heir."

"Oh, no, dear," cried Miss Sophie in distress. "Surely not!"

"He will be justified in doing so," Nerissa said gently.

"I'll talk him out of it." Miles sat down with a heaped plate. A wakeful night had not diminished his appetite. "Are you not eating, Nerissa? You must keep up your strength for the fight to clear your name. What will you have?" He started to rise again.

"Ben is bringing me a special treat," she said with a smile just as the footman came in with her fresh tea and hot buttered toast.

"The rest'll be a minute or two, miss," he apologized.

"Hot buttered toast!" said Miles enviously. "It's almost worth being persecuted for such a treat."

"I cannot eat so much." She offered him the plate. "What do you mean, fight to clear my name? It is surely hopeless after the dinner party, and Cousin Euphemia told everyone that I am an actress. . . ."

"And I told them you are not," Miss Sophie declared, "as did Jane, though for quite different reasons."

"No one will care, if my plan works," Miles said. "I spent the other half of the night thinking it up, and it is foolproof, except that it does depend on one or two people and Harwood will have to— Ah, speak of the devil. Good morning, sir. Is it too early for a legal consultation?"

"I fear I cannot disregard the terms of Sir Barnabas's will," said the lawyer heavily, "much as

I might wish to do so. My dear Miss Wingate, it is impossible to express my regret—"

"Hold, sir! Allow me to put the case to you while you eat your breakfast. No irrevocable decision should be made on an empty stomach. Now, for a start, Nerissa has not positively broken one of her grandfather's commandments, has she?"

"She has lost the goodwill of the local gentry," said Mr. Harwood hesitantly.

"A mere negative. Sir Barnabas gave her six months to win them over. . . ."

" 'To prove herself an acceptable acquaintance to the gentry of this neighborhood,' " Mr. Harwood quoted. "Yes, yes, I see what you mean. There are two months left before she can be said to have failed."

"Just as I thought. My second question is whether you will allow me to invite a few friends for a short stay at the manor."

"That will not help," Nerissa said sadly. "Sir Barnabas said most particularly 'the gentry of this neighborhood.' "

He gave her a reassuring smile. "Wait until you hear the rest of my deep, dark plot. Well, sir?"

"A deep, dark plot, hey?" The lawyer's eyes twinkled. "A small house party seems a reasonable expenditure, unless you mean to refurnish the manor from top to bottom in their honor."

"A house party!" Miss Sophie bubbled with excitement. "Whom are you going to invite, Miles?"

"And why?" asked Nerissa.

"I'll come to that in a minute. What made me think of my plot is a letter I received the other day. I didn't tell you about it, Nerissa, because you were in a fidget over the instructions for the groom you sent down to the coast for the fish and lobsters."

"An excellent turbot," murmured Mr. Harwood reminiscently.

"For heaven's sake, Miles, who was the letter from?" Nerissa demanded.

"From my friend Gerald Thorpe. He's in Devon and he asked if he could drop in to see me on his way back to town in the middle of February."

"I recall your speaking of Mr. Thorpe more than once, but how can he help me?"

"Lord Thorpe," said Miles in a weighty voice. "Viscount Thorpe, heir to the Marquis of Haverford. Poor Gerald has gone and got himself betrothed to Lady Beatrix Desmond, the Earl of Allerleigh's sister, and he's been staying at Alley's place—with his parents and his sister, Lady Charlotte. And Lottie's engaged, too, to Ferdie Merrick—Viscount Merrick—who's also at Allerleigh."

Nerissa realized she was gaping and closed her mouth. Then she opened it again to stammer, "B-but ..."

And shut it again as Ben brought her breakfast. As soon as the footman left, Miles explained.

"They are all returning to London for the Season and they plan to spend a night in Dorchester, so I'll invite them to stay here for a few days instead. I can count on Gerald and I'm pretty certain of Alley and Ferdie. Lady Allerleigh will come with Alley, of course; they were married quite recently. Dashed if there hasn't been a positive epidemic of it! And they'll bring Lady Bea. I can't guarantee the Haverfords, I'm afraid, and they would be the crowning glory, but I shouldn't be surprised if they accept."

"But, Miles, why should any lords and ladies other than your particular friends wish to stay at Addlescombe Manor? It is an excessively comfortable house but hardly grand enough for a marquis and a marchioness!''

"Oh, did I not tell you? Lady Haverford is my godmother and she's fond of me in her way, though all too liable to rake me over the coals."

"Your godmother! She must have known my grandfather, then."

"I daresay they met at my christening. At the time I was not sufficiently *compos mentis* to notice. But she was my mother's friend and Sir Barnabas my father's. I doubt if they ever really knew each other."

Miss Sophie was looking thoroughly bewildered. "I am sure it will be delightful to make the acquaintance of your friends, Miles, but how will they help poor Nerissa?"

"Why, as bait, ma'am, as gaudy flies to—"

"Please!" said Nerissa, "not fishing metaphors! You mean everyone will wish to be presented to them?"

"Precisely. Send out invitations to a dinner, or a tea, or what you will, and our country gentry will come flocking to meet the grand lords and ladies."

"Miles, dear, how prodigious clever you are!" Miss Sophie was in raptures.

Mr. Harwood took his spectacles from his pocket and thoughtfully polished them on his napkin. "Hmm, yes, an ingenious plot. It may well work, yes, I should not be a bit surprised if it does."

Nerissa's heart was too full for words. Miles was willing not only to make her known to his tonnish friends but to enlist them in her cause. Though he had now and then mentioned his forays into the beau monde, she had not realized he had so many good friends among the nobility. Gerald, Ferdie, Alley—he even called an earl by his nickname!

Lady Bea, Lottie. A pang shot through Nerissa's breast. The Ladies Beatrix and Charlotte were betrothed, but how many other titled young ladies did Miles count as close friends? If none of them could tempt him to consider marriage, the tiny whisper of hope she had been unable to suppress became utterly absurd.

"I'll write an invitation right after breakfast," Miles was saying. "Don't breathe a word to anyone until I know for certain they will come."

Miss Sophie and Mr. Harwood agreed. They both finished their breakfast and left, but Nerissa lingered over a third cup of tea. Oddly, the destruction of her last hope that Miles might not be irreversibly set against marriage made her feel less embarrassed about her response to his kiss. His plan to introduce her to his noble friends proved he did not regard her as a lightskirt. To him the kiss had been no more than a mark of friendship, as he had told Miss Sophie.

He helped himself to another slice of cold beef, sat down again opposite her, and said, "You don't believe it will work, do you? At first you looked dazzled by my brilliance, but then you turned thoughtful and down in the mouth."

She could not tell him her gloom was caused by the realization of his friendship with any number of charming, elegant, beautiful, and blue-blooded young ladies.

"It is a brilliant plan," she said sincerely. "I am just afraid whoever ruined the dinner party last night will do the same when your friends are here."

Miles frowned. "I don't believe they will dare. I rely upon Mrs. Pettigrew, who was most put out last night, to lead the returning horde. Look how she fawns on a mere baronet! But Sir Neville and Lady

Philpott have still more reverence for a title, since their exceedingly minor title is their only claim to distinction. In my opinion they will be *aux anges,* and nothing is less likely than for them to do anything to spoil the visit."

"Perhaps, but there is still Cousin Euphemia."

"Alas. I'll tell you, what we really need to win over the populace is buckets of ducats to strew in the streets, the way Aladdin did it."

"Dinars," Nerissa reminded him, laughing, "though I daresay ducats or guineas would serve as well."

"Undoubtedly. Failing that, if you don't mind, I'll have a word with Lady Haverford beforehand—"

"You will not tell her everything!" she said, horrified.

"Lord, no. Just enough so that if there is trouble she is ready to put the blame where it belongs. She is as dictatorial as any sultan in Arabia, but there's a soft heart underneath."

"I do hope she will accept your invitation. Miles, even if only your particular friends come we shall have to open up the bedchambers in the unoccupied wing. I cannot leave it to the last minute to consult Mrs. Hibbert."

"I suppose not. Well, it will not hurt for her to know we shall have visitors, but don't tell her yet who they are."

As a result of Nerissa's consultation with the housekeeper, the maids were set to dusting, polishing, scouring, and airing featherbeds. The bed linens for the spare chambers, long unused, had been stored in cedar chests in the attic. The maids were fully occupied, so Nerissa had Ben set up a folding stepladder, climbed up to the attic, and started opening chests.

Besides sheets, blankets, quilts, and counterpanes packed away in still-fragrant lavender, Nerissa found all sorts of interesting objects. There were clothes in the extraordinary fashions of the last century, including several wigs. There were pictures— she recalled that her mother's portrait had been kept here, safe from Sir Barnabas's wrath—several of which she set aside to take down and hang. There were toys and children's books, and still a half dozen chests she had no time to check.

"I daresay it will take me another two or three days to explore everything," she told Miss Sophie at teatime. "It is rather dusty but great fun. I wish I had had some of the old clothes at the Playhouse. They would have saved me a great deal of work."

Sir Barnabas sighed for the good old days when a gentleman could wear velvets and satins, lace and ribbons, crimson, lilac, and peacock without appearing a popinjay like Aubrey. In those days, ladies had kept their waists where nature intended, and Sophie had possessed one of the smallest. Admittedly, there was no sign of it now, but she had a comfortably plump figure, whereas her sister was simply massive.

Glancing at Euphemia, he saw a gleam in her eye which he did not care for at all. She was plotting again.

Alerted, he followed as she propelled Sophie before her to the back parlor after tea. "This is most fortunate," she declared, sinking onto the creaking sofa.

"What is?" Sophie asked, for once with good reason to be bewildered.

"Nerissa's peculiar notion of 'great fun.' Can you imagine anywhere better to shut her up with Miles for a few hours? You will take a message to Miles

saying Nerissa has found something vastly interesting in the attics and wants him to join her. As soon
as he is safely up, you will take away the ladder."

"What if the ladder is too heavy for me, Effie? I
am not as strong as you."

"Oh, very well, I shall remove the ladder. Then,
when they begin to misbehave, you must go for
Harwood."

"But how shall I know the right moment?"

"You will be hidden up there, spying on them."

"Then I cannot fetch Mr. Harwood, because you
will have carried off the ladder."

"Must you be constantly raising objections?" said
Euphemia impatiently. "You can always bang on the
floor as a signal, and I shall fetch Harwood."

"Ye-es." Sophie was still doubtful. "Except, if
you can hear me from below, will not Miles and
Nerissa hear and stop . . . whatever they are doing?"

Euphemia was forced to stop and think. Sir
Barnabas waited with the ghostly equivalent of
bated breath for her next preposterous command.
Her plots were growing wilder and wilder, so absurd that even Sophie saw the holes in them.

"You will make a hole in the attic floor. I shall
wait below, and at the right moment you wave your
handkerchief."

"What if someone sees the hole?"

"Not if you make a very small hole, ninny, just
big enough to drop something through. Spills will
do. All right, do you understand what you have to
do? When Nerissa is safely up there, you find
Miles . . ."

"Oh, dear, Effie, I am sorry to be so stupid, but
if I am to find Miles, how am I to get up before him
to hide?"

"For pity's sake, *I* shall take the message to

Miles!" howled Euphemia. "You will have to go up early, before Nerissa. Come on, we shall go there now to make the hole and to arrange a place for you to hide. Fetch a lantern."

The trapdoor to the attics was located above the landing leading to the upper servants' rooms. When Nerissa came down for her tea, a footman had left the trapdoor open but folded the stepladder and put it out of the way against the wall, ready for the morning.

In their ignorance, Euphemia and Sophie failed to unfold the ladder. After a struggle with the unwieldy object, they set it up leaning against the edge of the trapdoor. It only just reached, in an almost vertical position, balanced on the tips of its back legs.

Regarding it dubiously, neither lady noticed the little kitchen maid emerging from one of the abigails' rooms, carrying three or four empty hot-water jugs. Sir Barnabas saw her hurriedly conceal herself in a doorway as she caught sight of Euphemia. She peeked out, her eyes round.

"Go on, Sophie," Effie said irritably. "We shall not defeat Miles and Nerissa by standing here."

"Oh, dear, it does not look very safe."

"What a hen-hearted poltroon you are! I shall hold it steady for you. Don't forget the lantern."

Sir Barnabas moved to the other side of the ladder and gripped it in tenuous fingers, ready to exert all his powers should it so much as quiver as Sophie climbed. Step by step, the lantern swinging wildly in one hand, she clambered up and disappeared thankfully into the attic.

After calling her sister a coward, Effie could hardly complain that the way was precarious. She started up. At first her weight on the lower half anchored the ladder, but as she continued, it tottered.

Effie flung herself forward. From the waist up, she landed on the plank floor of the attic.

The temptation was too much for Sir Barnabas. Still, he never knew whether the ladder would have fallen of itself, nor whether his strength was enough to topple it—for as it oscillated, the little maid darted forward and gave it a hearty shove.

"That's for Miss Nerissa and Master Miles, y'owld sow," she muttered as the ladder crashed to the floor.

Bawling like a stuck pig, Effie hung from the trapdoor, legs waving wildly. The child fled down the stairs, screeching at the top of her voice.

"Burglars! Burglars!"

Sir Barnabas's ribs ached from laughing. In fact, he thought he was going to die—a second time— laughing. Exhausted by laughter and by the strain of pushing on the ladder, he almost faded away.

He made a supreme effort to gather his dissipating substance together. He was going to stay around until the end of the six months if it killed . . . well, if he never did another thing in his li—in his death.

Chapter Nineteen

"They are all coming," Miles announced, running Nerissa to earth in the library. He waved Gerald's letter at her.

She abandoned her household accounts. "All of them? Your godmama, too? Oh, Miles, how splendid! How many is that?"

"Four ... seven ... eight with Ferdie, and their servants, of course. We have enough rooms?"

"Plenty of bedchambers. Only I am not at all sure how to fit everyone into the dining room if we invite all those who were here that night."

"At least you need not fret about Effie causing trouble. She has been downright subdued since she got stuck halfway into the attic. But devil take it, we must invite everyone to dinner."

Nerissa pursed her lips. "Sir, pray mind your tongue," she said primly.

Laughing, he applauded. "Perfect."

"That was the first lesson you taught me. How long ago it seems!"

"You have learned so well you are more than ready to entertain the crème de la crème, but what— Ah, I have an even better notion. The Pettigrews are undoubtedly the first in consequence of our neighbors. We'll have them to dine on the second day, and the rest to afternoon tea later on. Don't tell me Mrs. Pettigrew will be able to resist the chance to brag! And the others will be the more eager at least to meet our guests."

"I hope so. When do they come?"

He consulted the letter. "The eleventh, till the sixteenth."

"The eleventh!" Nerissa jumped up, picked up her skirts, and sped to the door. "Heavens, I must see Mrs. Hibbert and Cook and write invitations and . . ." She disappeared.

Grinning, Miles followed at a more dignified pace. Truth to tell, he had been a little worried about expecting the marquis and marchioness to dine with a horde of awed yokels. They could not object to a general and his family.

Miles had his own preparations to make. Most important, he must make sure the servants all understood the exalted status of the visitors and gossiped about them as much as possible. He relied especially on the groom delivering the invitations to spread the word.

Then he had to consult with Snodgrass about wines, whether the cellar held what was needed or more must be bought in Porchester. Lastly, he must prepare to entertain the gentlemen. He had scarcely glanced into the seldom-used billiard room in months; there were enough shotguns to allow all a chance at his plentiful game, but they must be checked, cleaned, and oiled; and he would have to provide a couple of dozen unopened packs of cards.

He winced at the thought of what his friends would say when he refused to bet on the cards.

In the event, he need not have worried. The cards remained unopened, the shotguns unfired. Miles himself and the marquis were the only ones to make use of the billiard room. His friends were all far too busy billing and cooing with their beloveds to need outside entertainment.

Miles was disgusted. Gerald, Ferdie, and Alley had all appeared perfectly sane last time he saw them, and now here they were dancing attendance on three chits scarcely out of the schoolroom! Ferdie had no idea whether the book at White's had seen any interesting wagers lately. Alley had exchanged his high-perch phaeton for a tilbury because the phaeton made his new wife nervous. Gerald looked at Miles blankly when he asked after Suzette.

"Who?"

"Your *chère amie!* You kept her for three years. Have you found another?"

"Lord, no, Bea wouldn't like it."

"You are not married yet."

"Bea wouldn't like it," Gerald repeated. "Excuse me, old chap, I promised to walk in the garden with her."

If that was what the approach of parson's mousetrap did to a fellow, Miles was more determined than ever to avoid the fate. His freedom was far too precious to him.

He had been looking forward to showing off Addlescombe to his friends, and their defection left him disconsolate. He wanted to grumble to Nerissa, but she was far too busy. Not only had all the invitations been accepted with alacrity, but acquaintances from as far away as Porchester, unseen since the disaster, found excuses to call at the manor.

Nerissa was in seventh heaven as she entertained caller after caller, enjoying comfortable cozes with her particular friends. Of course Miles was happy for her, but she had no time to spare for him.

His godmother noted his downcast face. "Rusticating has done you good, my boy," she said with a considering gaze the evening before their departure. "You have lost that wishy-washy, dissipated look. But I daresay you have missed your friends and the fleshpots of London. Come up with us tomorrow and stay for a week or two."

"I should like to, ma'am, but I cannot leave Addlescombe until April. My godfather's will was a trifle odd in that respect—among others."

"Decidedly odd! Well, come in April, then, and do bring Miss Wingate with you. I daresay she will like to see the sights of town. A charming girl."

Miles brightened. It would be fun to show Nerissa the sights of the metropolis. "I'm sure she will enjoy that. Thank you, ma'am."

Then he recalled that if she stayed in London it would be on her way back to York. Devil take it, he was going to miss her damnably!

Lady Haverford summoned Nerissa with a glance and repeated her invitation. Nerissa accepted gratefully and gracefully.

Later she said to Miles, "I expect Mama and Papa will let me stay a few days in London. Maud insists on going with me, so I shall have someone to go about with."

"*I* shall take you about!"

"A tour of the gambling hells and theater greenrooms?"

"Of course not," he said, hurt.

She laid her hand on his arm. "Oh, Miles, I am sorry. If it were not for you, I should have to scrape a few shillings together to spend the night at an inn on my way home empty-handed."

"Fustian," he growled, uncomfortable with her gratitude. "If it weren't for you, I'd be seriously contemplating taking the king's shilling."

How long ago that evening when she had saved him from playing cards for money, in spite of having quarreled with him that very afternoon. She had also saved him from Nancy at the Addled Egg, though she did not know that, thank heaven! And her very presence had kept him from boredom, kept him from giving up in disgust under the pressure of unrelenting hostility.

"Neither of us could have done it without the other," he said.

"We have six weeks left," she reminded him. "Do not lower your guard."

"Six weeks to freedom!"

She nodded silently and went off to talk to Gerald and Lady Bea.

For her, six weeks to dread losing the neighbors' acceptance again, he realized. Well, Lady Haverford's invitation would come in useful there. Nerissa would not boast of it, but he could boast for her.

A few days later, when most of the family and several callers were gathered in the drawing room for afternoon tea, Miles turned the talk to the amusements of London. "Have you decided yet what you wish to see," he asked Nerissa in an unnecessarily loud voice, "when you go to stay with the Haverfords in St. James's? Lady Haverford suggested several places, did she not?"

The visitors looked properly impressed and would no doubt spread word far and wide. Nerissa's answer was cut short as Euphemia turned purple and choked on a mouthful of currant bun.

Miss Sophie beat her vigorously on the back.

Miles grinned. That had taken the wind out of her sails!

"Invited to St. James's!" Euphemia gloomily addressed the family gathering she had summoned. "The neighbors will never snub someone who has an invitation to stay with a marchioness in St. James's. There is only one course left to us."

"Give in," said Sir Neville, still more gloomily. Sir Barnabas thought his brother looked even more fishlike than usual.

"Fiddlesticks! Don't be so poor-spirited, Neville, I beg. I shall bring you around yet. Matilda must seduce Miles . . ."

"Me?" Matilda croaked in alarm.

"Really, Euphemia," cried Jane, "you cannot expect my poor girl to sacrifice herself."

"Besides," Aubrey pointed out, "as you yourself once said, Cousin Euphemia, Miles is accustomed to the most beautiful of Paphians."

"But he has not seen any in five months."

Neville put his foot down. "Impossible. Should Matilda succeed, she would lower herself to Nerissa's level."

"Worse," said Sophie hotly. "Nerissa is no bit of muslin."

Everyone stared at her, and she blushed.

"Wherever did you learn such a vulgar phrase?" Effie inquired witheringly. "From Miles or Nerissa, no doubt."

"Cousin Sophronia meant no harm," said Raymond, to his dead uncle's astonishment. "And if you intend, Cousin Euphemia, to suggest next that I must seduce Nerissa, I take leave to tell you that it is out of the question. I was prepared to take part in legitimate efforts to defeat the interlopers, but I am, after all, a clergyman."

Effie glared at him. "I hope Neville will remember your uncooperative attitude when he inherits Addlescombe. It is all up to Aubrey, then."

"Not I," said Aubrey hurriedly. "You know I've never been in the petticoat line."

"What a parcel of milksops!" Euphemia exploded, practically tearing her hair. "I wash my hand of you. You will just have to marry them. Come, Sophie." She stormed out.

"Oh, dear," said Sophie, scurrying after her.

Sir Neville sighed. "She is right, it's the only solution. Aubrey, Matilda, you have a little over a month to persuade your cousins to the altar, or we shall all molder away in Bath, where baronets are two a penny, for the rest of our lives."

"I daresay you will not dislike it excessively," Jane said anxiously. "If Sophie is right, Aubrey, and Nerissa is not a doxy, then marrying her will not be a complete disgrace. You might even be able to continue to conceal her background and . . ."

"Come, Jane," said her husband, and tore her away before she drove her son from discouragement to despair.

Sir Barnabas regarded his three remaining relatives with amusement. Aubrey stared at himself in the mirror over the mantelpiece, smoothing his dyed hair, straightening his elaborate neckcloth, and turning his head this way and that to study his profile. Raymond hooked his thumbs into his lapels and started sermonizing on the subject of celibate clergy, apparently unable to make up his mind, now, whether he was in favor or against. Matilda sat sunk in an uncharacteristic apathetic dejection.

Raymond suddenly noticed her. He went to sit

beside her and gently took her hand. "Do you not wish to wed Miles, cousin?" he asked. "You need not, you know."

"I daresay I should like it well enough," she answered gruffly. "He's turned out to be a sporting chap after all, not afraid of a rasper. But he's not in the least interested in me and I'm damned—dashed—if I have the least notion how to go about flirting with him. Do you want to marry Nerissa?"

"I have come to believe her a virtuous young woman," he said with caution, "and she has the interests of my parishioners at heart. However, like you, I am aware that she has no interest in me and I find the prospect of a probably unsuccessful pursuit distasteful and most undignified."

"I shan't do it," said Aubrey loudly, still at the looking-glass. "Dash it, I *want* to live in Bath. It may not be as fashionable as London, but there are plenty of people there who appreciate a fellow's efforts to keep up with the mode. It's here among the undiscriminating yokels I'm moldering away."

"That is all very well for you," Matilda told him, "but it's a decent hunt I want and all my hunting friends are here."

Raymond took a deep breath. "Then marry me," he said.

Matilda gaped at him. Aubrey swung around, creaking, and gaped. Sir Barnabas gaped.

"It makes sense," Raymond defended himself, pink-cheeked. "Uncle Barnabas left you a dowry besides your hundred a year, so we could refurbish the vicarage and live more comfortably than I can on my own. And you would remain within reach of the Blackmoor Vale."

"Do you mean it?" Matilda asked, her voice husky, her leathery face as pink as his.

"I do. I expect we should go on well enough together."

"Then damned if I don't do it," she roared, and wrung his hand. "It's a deal."

Raymond winced but smiled bravely and even kissed her cheek.

Aubrey at last wiped the stunned expression off his face and felicitated them. "But don't tell anyone," he warned. "Not until April, or Cousin Euphemia will do her best to embarrass us again."

"True," Raymond said. "In fact, we had best all three at least try to make friends with Miles and Nerissa."

"I shan't mind," said Matilda. "On the whole they are both pretty good chaps."

And, exchanging a glance, Raymond and Aubrey agreed.

April first, April Fool's Day, Sir Barnabas thought with glee. He could not have managed it better if he had chosen when to die.

Once again Harwood had covered the library desk with papers, so the late baronet was forced to perch on the inkwell. He did not really mind. In fact, he could quite easily have hovered in midair. His substance had thinned and he was more tenuous now than on that day six months before.

The clock in the front hall chimed nine.

The tubby lawyer, his only close friend for so many years, glanced at the inkwell. "Are you there, Barnabas?"

"Yes." His voice was a whisper of stirring leaves. "You were right, William—most of the time."

Harwood beamed. "I'm glad you have been able to stay to get to know your granddaughter."

"And it's just as well she never got to know her crabby old grandsire." Dry as the rustle of dead leaves tossed by the wind. "Here they come. I am going to enjoy this."

Euphemia took the lead, even in defeat, her face sour with the taste of black bile. Neville and Jane followed, sullen, their titles no compensation for loss of the wealth they had always coveted. After living at Sir Barnabas's expense for thirty-five years, they had saved plenty on which to live in modest comfort in Bath.

Aubrey, at least, was anticipating Bath with pleasure. The delight his painted face was unable to express showed in his exuberant violet coat and primrose waistcoat. Very seasonal: A vase of violets and primroses picked by Nerissa stood on the far corner of the desk.

Matilda, on the other hand, had escaped the narrow restrictions of Bath society. She and Raymond came in together, looking well contented with each other. Silently their uncle wished them happy.

Sir Barnabas was less sanguine for poor Sophie. The prospect of life in a small cottage with Euphemia was enough to daunt the most resolute. Sophie's mouth drooped in her round, sweet face, usually so determinedly optimistic. Sir Barnabas cursed himself for not making better provision for her.

"Come and sit beside me, Sophie," commanded Euphemia.

Sophie turned back and whispered to Nerissa, "I am so very glad for you, dear." Reaching up, she kissed Nerissa's cheek, patted Miles's arm, and scuttled to join her sister.

Nerissa, a graceful, elegant figure in deep rose trimmed with white lace. Still the living image of

Anthea, yet how changed from the timid mouse of six months past, afraid of entering a room full of people. His granddaughter had metamorphosed into a gracious young lady quite capable of presiding over a house party of blue-blooded guests.

And Miles was largely responsible for the change. The care-for-nobody scapegrace had patiently taught her, built her confidence, protected her from plots and conspiracies, while at the same time learning to manage the estate. Given the chance to use his energies in a constructive manner, the boy had come through with flying colors. Sir Barnabas had no qualms now about entrusting his precious Addlescombe to his godson.

As he seated Nerissa in the back row of chairs, his irrepressible grin of triumph called forth a smile from Sir Barnabas. Yet a hint of puzzlement lurked in those blue eyes, an undefined dissatisfaction. Released from an impecunious life on the fringes of society, master of a fine estate, Miles was not entirely happy.

Nor was Nerissa. In fact, she looked downright unhappy, though she had won a fortune and was about to return to her beloved parents.

Her doting grandfather glared at Miles.

Nerissa glanced up as Mr. Harwood cleared his throat. The lawyer was another friend she was going to miss. Right from the first he had done his best to smooth her way insofar as his instructions permitted.

But she would willingly consign all her new friends to oblivion in exchange for the love of that dear, infuriating, crooked-nosed gentleman seated at her side. How was she to live without him?

"Ahem." Mr. Harwood settled his gold-rimmed spectacles on his nose and picked up a single sheet of parchment. He peered over his spectacles. "Are we ready? Then first let me inquire as to whether anyone present believes that either Miles Courtenay or Nerissa Wingate has failed to observe the terms of Sir Barnabas's will, as disclosed in this room six months since."

The only response was a snort of utter disgust and loathing from Cousin Euphemia.

"In that case," Mr. Harwood continued, "it gives me great pleasure to confirm that all the late baronet's 'worldly goods and chattels, including the manor and demesne of Addlescombe and all moneys whatsoever not hitherto accounted for,' shall be divided equally between Miss Wingate and Mr. Courtenay. I am further instructed to inform you that had both Miss Wingate and Mr. Courtenay failed to qualify for their inheritance, Sir Barnabas's entire fortune was to be bequeathed to the Society for the Suppression of Vice."

In the stunned silence that followed his announcement, a curious, rusty chuckle whispered around the room.

A babel of indignation arose, and Nerissa was sure she had imagined the strange sound. Miles leaned over and said in a low voice, "It's All Fools' Day! Anyone would think the old man had planned to die at the end of September."

She smiled wryly. "I would not put it past him. He has had us all dancing to his tune for half a year."

"But at last we are free. Can you be ready to leave for London tomorrow, or shall we wait till the day after?"

"Tomorrow will do." What a hurry he was in to see the last of her! He was free—free to return to his lightskirt actresses—but he held her heart captive.

He stood up and moved forward, hushing the uproar. "Nerissa and I shall leave for London tomorrow," he announced. "I shall return in a fortnight. I trust that is sufficient time for you all to remove to your new homes."

They all started arguing at once. Nerissa slipped away and went to talk to Mr. Harwood. In expectation of the outcome, he had already drawn up papers detailing the rent Miles would pay her for her share of Addlescombe and the division of the rest of their joint assets.

She must be practical, though she felt more like running away to hide in a corner and weep.

"Come, Sophie!" Cousin Euphemia's peremptory voice cut through Nerissa's heartache. "We shall not stay where we are not wanted."

Miss Sophie followed her sister toward the door, despondency in every line of her small, plump figure.

"Wait!" cried Nerissa. "Pray wait, Cousin Sophie."

"Come, Sophronia!" Effie marched on.

Miss Sophie paused, gazing after her, then turned and pattered back to Nerissa. "Yes, dear? Can I do something to help?"

"You can indeed, dear cousin. I know you are independent now with your two hundred a year, but I shall be so very glad if you will agree to come and live with me. Mama and Papa will always be so much occupied with the theater, I shall need your companionship. Do say you will consider it."

"Oh, my dear!" Tears of joy sparkled on Miss Sophie's lashes like raindrops after an April shower as she beamed up at Nerissa. "I need not consider it. If you truly want me, of course I shall come."

Nerissa hugged her. Miles, having ushered out the

last of the family, turned to see Mr. Harwood nodding benevolently.

"Miss Sophie is coming to York with me, Miles," Nerissa explained, her expression and her voice guarded. "If Lady Haverford does not wish for another guest, we shall stay at a hotel in London."

"Lady Haverford will not mind," he assured her.

London! At last he was at liberty to return to the pleasures of the city. The luscious redhead of his last night—what was her name?—would have found a protector by now, but with money to add to his personal charms, he might entice her away. If not, there were plenty of others. The theater greenrooms were full of deliciously flamboyant, voluptuous actresses looking for liaisons.

The gaming tables awaited him, too. He'd never risk losing Addlescombe, that went without saying, but he had money to spare now. Not that there would be much thrill in wagering if his livelihood did not depend on the turn of a card. He might as well bet imaginary palaces; mere guineas would be dull by comparison.

Still, he had every intention of spending a good deal of his time in London in the future, though Addlescombe would be his home. Setting up a mistress in the country was simply not the thing.

His gaze returned to Nerissa, talking soberly with Miss Sophie and Harwood, serious, even sad. In his memories she was more often cheerful, laughing, teasing, riding with him, indulging wild flights of fancy over the cards, warm in his arms. . . . She was tall, slim, elegant, gracious, as different as could be from the Cyprians he had always favored. Perhaps his tastes had changed and a different kind of mistress would suit him better now.

Desire stirred. Whoever he found, he'd keep the girl abed for a week after six months' abstinence!

Of course, he'd steer clear of both females and gambling hells as long as Nerissa was in town. Once he had seen her off to York . . .

A hollow, sinking feeling expanded within him. See her off? How could he let her go? Unthinkable to come back to an empty house, bereft of the constant delight of her presence! It wasn't merely a mistress he wanted, it was Nerissa. How thoroughly he had persuaded himself he regarded her as a little sister!

He wanted her desperately, and the only way to have and keep her was as his wife. What maggot had gotten into his head to make him swear he was not a marrying man?

"Nerissa, marry me!"

Three startled faces turned to him. Nerissa's lips parted, her glorious gray eyes shone, and she took a step toward him.

"Oh, Miles, I thought you'd never ask!"

Fiercely he clasped her in his arms. "Say you will. I cannot live without you."

She linked her hands behind his neck and said, half teasing, half fiercely earnest, "No more actresses?"

"I shall never so much as look at another one— except for my mama-in-law, of course." In her ear he whispered, " 'The first inter'gatory that my Nerissa shall be sworn on is, whether till the next night she had rather stay, or go to bed now . . .' "

Blushing delightfully, she said with proper severity, " 'By heaven, I will ne'er come in your bed until I see the ring.' "

Miles laughed. "Raymond shall read our banns with his own, unless you had rather be married in

York? Never mind that now." Over her shoulder he saw Miss Sophie and Mr. Harwood tactfully tiptoeing from the library. "Miss Sophie," he called, "don't you dare leave the house. We shall soon need you to play grandmother."

"Dear Miles!" A youthful spring in her step, Sophie followed Mr. Harwood out. As Miles pulled Nerissa even closer and their lips met, Sir Barnabas wiped a tear from his eye. "All's well that ends well," he murmured.

Miles broke off their kiss to say in a wondering tone, "I should never have found you if it were not for the old bastard's will."

"Sir!" said Nerissa saucily, putting her finger to his lips. "Pray mind your tongue."

He grinned. "Old dastard. Now, don't interrupt."

Drifting upward above the entwined couple, the old dastard chuckled as he silently faded away.

Author's Note

I have taken liberties with my use of the *Arabian Nights' Entertainments*. Translations available before Burton's (1885) were in fact heavily expurgated to be suitable for the polite drawing room.

ZEBRA'S REGENCY ROMANCES
DAZZLE AND DELIGHT

A BEGUILING INTRIGUE (4441, $3.9
by Olivia Sumner

Pretty as a picture Justine Riggs cared nothing for propriety. S
dressed as a boy, sat on her horse like a jockey, and pondered t
stars like a scientist. But when she tried to best the handso
Quenton Fletcher, Marquess of Devon, by proving that she w
the better equestrian, he would try to prove Justine's antics we
pure folly. The game he had in mind was seduction — never ima
ining that he might lose his heart in the process!

AN INCONVENIENT ENGAGEMENT (4442, $3.9
by Joy Reed

Rebecca Wentworth was furious when she saw her betroth
waltzing with another. So she decides to make him jealous
flirting with the handsomest man at the ball, John Collinwoo
Earl of Stanford. The "wicked" nobleman knew exactly what t
enticing miss was up to — and he was only too happy to pl
along. But as Rebecca gazed into his magnificent eyes, her erra
fiancé was soon utterly forgotten!

SCANDAL'S LADY (4472, $3.9
by Mary Kingsley

Cassandra was shocked to learn that the new Earl of Lynton w
her childhood friend, Nicholas St. John. After years at sea a
mixed feelings Nicholas had come home to take the family tit
And although Cassandra knew her place as a governess, s
could not help the thrill that went through her each time he w
near. Nicholas was pleased to find that his old friend Cassand
was his new next door neighbor, but after being near her, he wo
dered if mere friendship would be enough . . .

HIS LORDSHIP'S REWARD (4473, $3.9
by Carola Dunn

As the daughter of a seasoned soldier, Fanny Ingram was acc
tomed to the vagaries of military life and cared not a whit abo
matters of rank and social standing. So she certainly never fo
saw her *tendre* for handsome Viscount Roworth of Kent wi
whom she was forced to share lodgings, while he carried out l
clandestine activities on behalf of the British Army. And thou
good sense told Roworth to keep his distance, he couldn't st
from taking Fanny in his arms for a kiss that made all hea
equal!

*Available wherever paperbacks are sold, or order direct from t
Publisher. Send cover price plus 50¢ per copy for mailing a.
handling to Penguin USA, P.O. Box 999, c/o Dept. 1710
Bergenfield, NJ 07621. Residents of New York and Tenness
must include sales tax. DO NOT SEND CASH.*

ELEGANT LOVE STILL FLOURISHES —
Wrap yourself in a Zebra Regency Romance.

MATCHMAKER'S MATCH (3783, $3.50/$4.50)
Nina Porter

save herself from a loveless marriage, Lady Psyche Veringham pre-
nds to be a bluestocking. Resigned to spinsterhood at twenty-three,
yche sets her keen mind to snaring a husband for her young charge,
nanda. She sets her cap for long-time bachelor, Justin St. James. This
an of the world has had his fill of frothy-headed debutantes and turns
e tables on Psyche. Can a bluestocking and a man about town find true
ve?

RES IN THE SNOW (3809, $3.99/$4.99)
Janis Laden

cause of an unhappy occurrence, Diana Ruskin knew that a secure
arriage was not in her future. She was content to assist her physician
ther and follow in his footsteps . . . until now. After meeting Adam,
ke of Marchmaine, Diana's precise world is shattered. She would sim-
y have to avoid the temptation of his gentle touch and stunning phy-
que — and by doing so break her own heart!

RST SEASON (3810, $3.50/$4.50)
Anne Baldwin

hen country heiress Laetitia Biddle arrives in London for the Season,
e harbors dreams of triumph and applause. Instead, she becomes the
ughingstock of drawing rooms and ballrooms, alike. This headstrong
iss blames the rakish Lord Wakeford for her miserable debut, and she
ws to rise above her many faux pas. Vowing to become an Original,
tty proves that she's more than a match for this eligible, seasoned Lord.

N UNCOMMON INTRIGUE (3701, $3.99/$4.99)
Georgina Devon

iss Mary Elizabeth Sinclair was rather startled when the British Home
ffice employed her as a spy. Posing as "Tasha," an exotic fortune-teller,
e expected to encounter unforeseen dangers. However, nothing could
ve prepared her for Lord Eric Stewart, her dashing and infuriating part-
r. Giving her heart to this haughty rogue would be the most reckless
zard of all.

MADDENING MINX (3702, $3.50/$4.50)
Mary Kingsley

ter a curricle accident, Miss Sarah Chadwick is literally thrust into the
ms of Philip Thornton. While other women shy away from Thornton's
epatch and aloof exterior, Sarah finds herself drawn to discover why
is man is physically and emotionally scarred.

*vailable wherever paperbacks are sold, or order direct from the
ublisher. Send cover price plus 50¢ per copy for mailing and
ndling to Penguin USA, P.O. Box 999, c/o Dept. 17109,
ergenfield, NJ 07621. Residents of New York and Tennessee
ust include sales tax. DO NOT SEND CASH.*

WHAT'S LOVE GOT TO DO WITH IT?

Everything . . . Just ask Kathleen Drymon . . . and Zebra Books

CASTAWAY ANGEL	*(3569-1, $4.50/$5.50)*
GENTLE SAVAGE	*(3888-7, $4.50/$5.50)*
MIDNIGHT BRIDE	*(3265-X, $4.50/$5.50)*
VELVET SAVAGE	*(3886-0, $4.50/$5.50)*
TEXAS BLOSSOM	*(3887-9, $4.50/$5.50)*
WARRIOR OF THE SUN	*(3924-7, $4.99/$5.99)*

Available wherever paperbacks are sold, or order direct from the publisher. Send cover price plus 50¢ per copy for mailing and handling to Penguin USA, P.O. Box 999, c/o Dept. 17109, Bergenfield, NJ 07621. Residents of New York and Tennessee must include sales tax. DO NOT SEND CASH.

VICTORY'S WOMAN
by Gretchen Genet

(~~~~, $~.~~

Andrew—the carefree soldier who sought glory on the battlefield. and returned a shattered man . . . Niall—the legendary frontiersman and a former Shawnee captive, tormented by his past . . Roger—the troubled youth, who would rise up to claim a shocking legacy . . . and Clarice—the passionate beauty bound by one man, and hopelessly in love with another. Set against the back drop of the American revolution, three men fight for thei heritage—and one woman is destined to change all their lives for ever!

FORBIDDEN
(4488, $4.99
by Jo Beverley

While fleeing from her brothers, who are attempting to sell he into a loveless marriage, Serena Riverton accepts a carriage rid from a stranger—who is the handsomest man she has ever seer. Lord Middlethorpe, himself, is actually contemplating marriag to a dull daughter of the aristocracy, when he encounters th breathtaking Serena. She arouses him as no woman ever has. An after a night of thrilling intimacy—a forbidden liaison—Seren must choose between a lady's place and a woman's passion!

WINDS OF DESTINY
(4489, $4.9
by Victoria Thompson

Becky Tate is a half-breed outcast—branded by her Comanch heritage. Then she meets a rugged stranger who awakens he heart to the magic and mystery of passion. Hiding a despera past, Texas Ranger Clint Masterson has ridden into cattle count to bring peace to a divided land. But a greater battle rages insi him when he dares to desire the beautiful Becky!

WILDEST HEART
(4456, $4.9
by Virginia Brown

Maggie Malone had come to cattle country to forge her future a healer. Now she was faced by Devon Conrad, an outla wounded body and soul by his shadowy past . . . whose ey blazed with fury even as his burning caress sent her spiraling wi desire. They came together in a Texas town about to explode in s and scandal. Danger was their destiny—and there was nothi they wouldn't dare for love!